A CURSE OF MEMORIES

THE GREATEST SIN BOOK 5

Published by Tangled Sky Press
www.tangledskypress.com

First printing, July 2017

ISBN: 978-1-944334-20-8

A Curse of Memories is a work of fiction. Names, places, and incidents are either products of the authors' imaginations or used fictitiously.

Map and cover Copyright © 2017 by Alexandra Brandt
Feather Copyright © 2017 by Alyssa Brandt
Ring Copyright © Ekaterina Staats | Dreamstime.com

A CURSE OF MEMORIES

THE GREATEST SIN BOOK 5

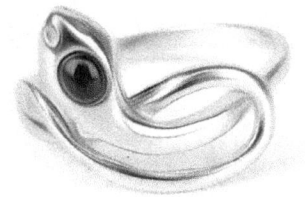

ERIK KORT
LEE FRENCH

TANGLED
SKY
PRESS

ACKNOWLEDGMENTS

ERIK KORT

I think that working on this book really demonstrated the love people in my life have for me. Which is a fancy way of saying that I was pretty miserable to be around for large chunks of time. So to my ever patient, ever understanding Alex, thanks. You not only made the book better by not strangling me before it was done, but you did a damn fine job in making it really shine when my part was done. And my thanks go to Bethany and Lesla, who prove that found family is important too. That's even a lesson Chavali can get behind—hopefully I'm easier to be around than she is, at least when I'm not under deadline.

LEE FRENCH

For my mom, who makes sure I eat while in the throes of mad typing and watches my kids while I work conventions. She's my Penny, but with less gray hair and more magic.

BOOKS BY THE AUTHORS

The Greatest Sin Series

epic fantasy

The Fallen

Harbinger

Moon Shades

Illusive Echoes

A Curse of Memories

ERIK KORT

(as Erik Marshall)

Wards of the Thicket

adventure fantasy

Children Without Faces

Children Without Voices (coming soon)

LEE FRENCH

In the Ilauris setting

standalone fantasy tales

Damsel In Distress

Al-Kabar

Maze Beset Trilogy

superheroes in denim

Dragons In Pieces

Dragons In Chains

Dragons In Flight

Spirit Knights
young adult urban fantasy
Girls Can't Be Knights

Backyard Dragons

Ethereal Entanglements

Ghost Is the New Normal

Darkside Seattle
gritty cyberpunk
(as L.E. French)

Street Doc

Fixer

Mechanic (coming Winter 2017)

Non-fiction
with Jeffrey Cook
Working the Table: An Indie Author's Guide to Conventions

Anthology Appearances
Into the Woods: a fantasy anthology

Merely This and Nothing More: Poe Goes Punk

Unnatural Dragons: a science fiction anthology

Missing Pieces VIII: short stories from GenCon's Authors Avenue

Artifact

What We've Unlearned: English Class Goes Punk

Bridges (as Editor)

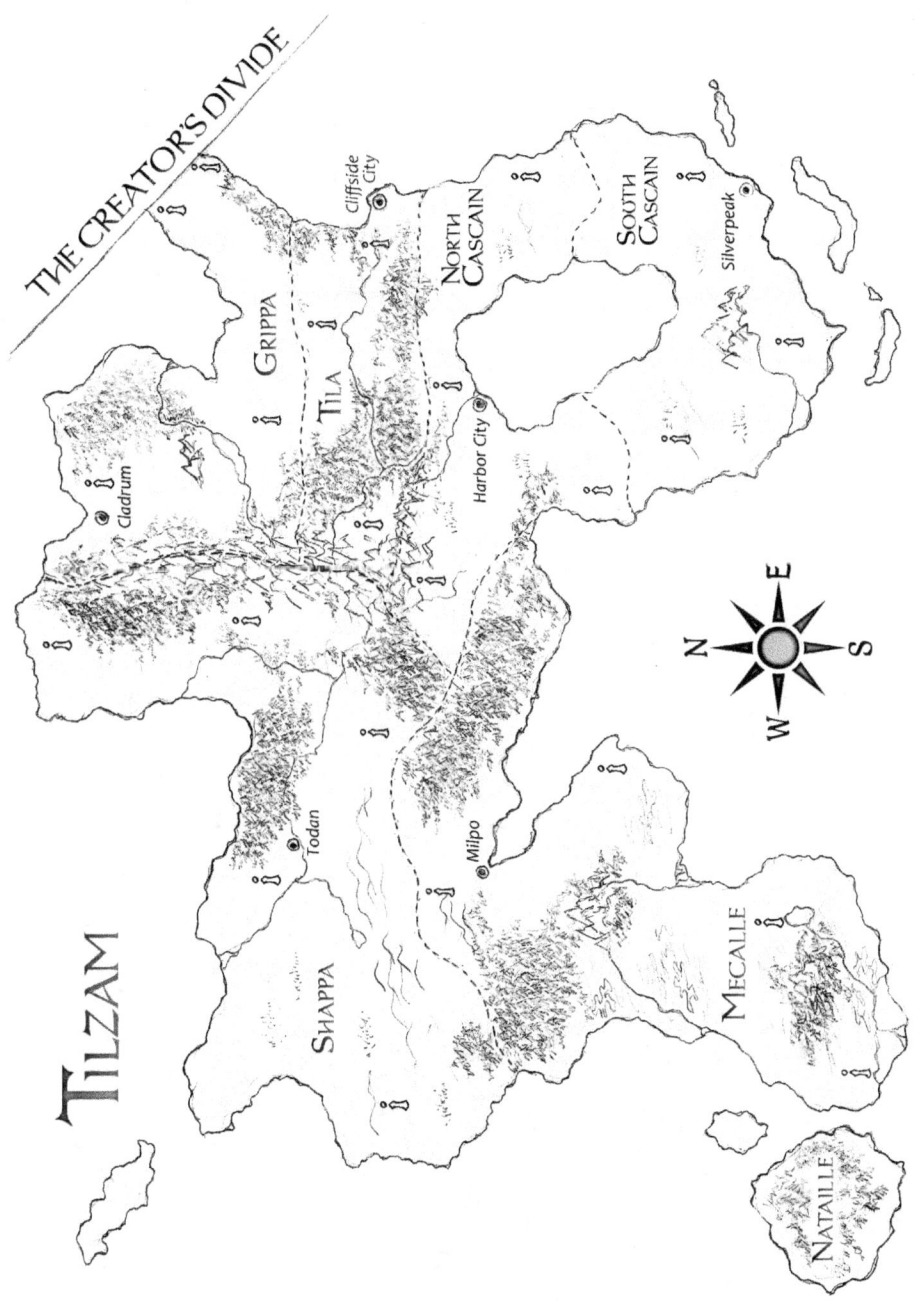

CHAPTER 1

Chavali pulled down her cloak's hood in the dim, fishy light of oil lamps, revealing thick, red-brown hair and the pink feather sprouted from her forehead. Not that she could see the colors for herself anymore. Over a decade ago, she'd lost the ability to perceive color when she assumed the mantle of Seer for the Blaukenev clan. The costs had, at the time, chafed, but she'd accepted her duty.

Grime crusted the tiny tavern's windows, inside and out, allowing through nothing more than a bare glimmer of weak morning sun. Behind the driftwood bar, an aged, emaciated woman festooned with an excessive number of metal ornaments flashed Chavali an empty smile with too few teeth.

Next door, Violet, the fellow Fallen agent tasked with this mission, wriggled her way into a locked shed. Chavali trusted her to do her part. The alternative meant trying to wedge her own hips through a gap too narrow for any normal person. Violet had claimed she could manage this feat. Her certainty had convinced Chavali to focus on her own part of this mission and not worry about the shed. Either it held the other part of their quarry or it didn't.

Four men occupied the small room, filling it enough to create the sense of crowding. Two had seen too many summers to ride the fishing boats anymore. The other two each lacked enough body parts to be useful in that trade without substantial accommodations. Thanks to a pack of rabid children roaming the paths between shacks, Chavali knew that more than half the village now sailed in the warm ocean waters to the west, hoping to catch enough migrating fish to replenish their stores after a long, lingering winter.

The man missing one eye and arm matched the description she'd been given for her contact here. Numerous scars puckered his tanned, leathery face and neck. Uneven stubble covered his chin and pate. He sat alone at a square table with his missing parts facing the wall, nursing a wooden cup of dark liquid.

"Can I get you anything, dearie?" the bartender asked. Her voice rasped and gurgled.

Chavali had no plans to touch anything inside this building, including its occupants. If she could have avoided the floor and door, she would have. Drinking whatever swill they favored appealed as much as slicing her own wrist open. "No, thank you."

She approached her contact, noting that the bartender's interest shifted to suspicion. The woman's hand reached below the bar, perhaps for a club or similar object.

Tension slithered through the room, as thick as the stench of rotting seaweed.

Keeping her hands inside her dark cloak, Chavali stopped beside the man she'd come to meet. "Are you Darrin?"

He craned his neck up and bared his teeth. "Who wants to know?"

"Someone in need of a boat." She tossed a small envelope onto the table. Coins inside it clinked. The package had been sealed already when Eldrack placed it in her hands, but she estimated it held enough to fill this man's cup with his usual foul drink for several months.

"Boat, hmm?" He slid his hand from his cup to the envelope. His fingers fondled the folded paper. "What kind?"

She raised an eyebrow and resisted the urge to touch him and let the spirits siphon his thoughts to her. The direction of his gaze told her enough about his interest in the money. "Are there options? Do you have one with places to hold snacks?"

Darrin barked a laugh as he scooped up the envelope and stood. "C'mon. You can have your pick."

Though the room relaxed, Chavali sensed something different from the bartender and men—anticipation. The room felt like a trap ready to spring.

Perhaps she shouldn't have left Violet alone after all. Her decision had been made in the interest of keeping this wretched excursion as short as possible. Eldrack hadn't thought they'd face anything more challenging than grumpy old fishermen.

Ready for an attack, she slid her hand behind her back to grip the hilt of the dagger sheathed on her belt. These people seemed incapable of causing much trouble or danger, but she knew better than to underestimate someone based upon appearances.

Darrin opened the door. Chavali followed him outside. Sunshine warmed Chavali's head and salt drifted on the air. As she stepped upon the front stoop, her boot grinding errant sand against the wood, someone tackled her from the side.

Her training carried her into a roll with her assailant. They fell into slushy sand together.

Chavali twisted her attacker's arm, forcing them to release her, and sprang to her feet with her cloak swirling and her dagger in hand.

"Eh," Darrin said. "She's not bringing trouble."

The bar patrons crowded the doorway, watching with gleeful grins.

"Not unless you make me," Chavali snapped, ready to fight.

The attacker shook out his arm and clambered to his feet. All gangly limbs and floppy hair, the teenage boy glared at her. "She talked to everybody in town. I saw her!"

"Is that criminal here?" She relaxed enough to present the suggestion she considered the boy no threat to her. Confidence, she knew, won many battles before they began. "A fine way to treat visitors."

The boy huffed and brushed wet sand from his tattered pants. "She's suspicious. And has a knife."

"She's a traveler. She'd be stupid to go unarmed." Darrin cuffed the boy and shooed him away. "Go do something useful, like mending nets or pestering children."

The boy scowled and stormed away, wrenching his shoulder as if to brush past her, but he avoided contact with her.

"Sorry about that," Darrin said with a light chuckle.

The men inside grumbled their discontent at being denied a show and shuffled out of sight.

Chavali sheathed her dagger and shook her skirt. "No harm done."

"Good. He's too old to be a child and too fluff-headed to go on the boats."

"I'm familiar with the type." Boys in her clan had tended to grow up without much prodding, but every group had its idiots. "In my experience, giving them responsibility either fixes the problem or creates a monumental disaster."

Darrin laughed, the rich, deep sound reminding her of Colby in his rare moments of levity. "Sounds about right."

He led them to one of a cluster of driftwood shacks sharing walls, each lacking a door and too small to do more than hold a sleeping person and a chest of valuables. Shells and polished stones decorated the walls in patterns Chavali suspected must involve color she couldn't see.

He chose one with carved wood pieces adorning shelves. These curios in the shapes of animals Chavali had never seen stared at her with eyes made from bits of broken shells. Rippling light bathed the room, created by a column of water-filled glass set into a hole in the roof.

Chavali waited on the sandy path between several six-shack clumps of wood while Darrin flipped his chest open. He rummaged through cloth and lumps of wood. When he straightened, he displayed four wooden boats, each small enough to hold in one hand. All four craft had different contours and shapes.

"Which would you like?"

"The blue one."

Darrin offered her a boat with a square space on top and a hole in each side. The interior could hold a few small stones. "Enjoy."

When Eldrack had sent her to pick up a blue boat, she had thought it would function as a code word to interact with an agent of the Fallen. Instead, she held a toy boat. "Thank you." Of all the idiotic assignments he could have sent her on, this one felt less valid than the one when she'd first collected Harris.

Shying away from thoughts of Harris, she tucked the boat into a pocket inside her cloak and left Darrin to find Violet. Though she needed to delve into the memories of Harris she'd tucked away, she needed to do it someplace safe. With what she knew already, the information locked inside her mind promised unpleasant revelations. Besides, she needed to be able to focus to prod through that.

Violet fell into step beside her before she reached the tavern again. The thin, sinuous woman's effortless grace meant no disruption in Chavali's pace. They angled toward the road and remained quiet until they'd left the sand behind and could no longer see the village.

"Did you encounter any trouble?" Chavali asked.

"No. I don't think anyone saw me, and I don't think anyone will notice this missing." Violet held up a striated spiral shell the size of two fingers. "I wasn't expecting it to be so...literal."

Chavali showed Violet the boat. "Nor was I."

Violet giggled. "I wish he'd just tell us when a mission is busywork. He made it sound like an important mission with serious repercussions."

"Indeed."

Every time Eldrack dispatched Chavali for something like this, he took her away from what remained of her clan and the people she'd come to find pleasant for conversation. That he wasted her talents on something so frivolous rankled. He could at least send her to argue with someone or to find information. But no—they came for a toy boat and a seashell.

"At least we're only a day's walk from home." Violet tucked the shell into her pocket. "I've been sent places where I had to walk three days to get there and back. The journey is nice compared to staying underground all time, but it gets tiresome when you can't stand the people you're traveling with."

"So true," Chavali grumbled, thinking of more than one occasion when she'd been stuck with a baffling lunatic, infuriating gossip, or appalling idiot. "Thank for not being such a person."

"You're welcome." Violet beamed. "And thank you for not living up to your reputation. We've only played cards before, so I knew you're an accomplished liar, but you're definitely not as much of a prickly pain in the ass as everyone claims."

Arching an eyebrow, Chavali tucked the boat back into a pocket. "You're welcome, I think." She knew gossip around the Fallen painted her in a somewhat unflattering light, as well it should, but she hadn't realized they'd taken it quite so far. Among her clan, they called her "difficult."

"Sean thinks you're misunderstood, and I agree with him."

Chavali offered no response. She'd spent far too much time with Sean, one of the Fallen's most prolific gossips. He'd seen her in the midst of an unexpected investigation into a werewolf murder, of all things. Thanks to that fiasco, the entirety of the Fallen believed a number of ridiculous things about her and the feather in her skull. At least he'd also spread around her inability to see color. Having people know that had simplified her life a tiny bit.

"We should have brought horses," Chavali said after a long pause. They walked through grasses at as swift a pace as she could manage.

"Oh really?" Violet batted her eyelashes. "Any random horse you wanted to ride, or a particular one?"

Chavali narrowed her eyes. "I'm not in a relationship with Colby. He's nothing more than a friend. His horse merely reminds me of the family I lost. Unlike the other beasts in the stable, I have permission to see him whenever I wish."

In truth, the horse kept her sanity intact, but Karias preferred for no one to understand his nature, not even his rider. She believed him to be a spirit of the dead trapped in a horse's body, or something similar. Her ability to sense thoughts through skin contact allowed him one precious avenue to communicate with more than a stamp of his foot or whinny.

Violet batted her eyelashes. "I didn't say a name."

Heaving a heavy sigh, Chavali shook her head. "I'm aware of the gossip around the tower, thank you. And again, there is no relationship."

"Sure. I believe you." Violet's disbelief oozed from every pore.

"He has been teaching me to read."

"I've never heard it called that before."

"Shut up." Chavali wished for a swift end to this day.

CHAPTER 2

The sun dipped below the horizon as the two women reached the expansive farming fields surrounding Cloverdale, the town clustered around the entrance to the Fallen's tower. In the deepening dark, Chavali saw nothing more than indistinct outlines of the wooden buildings surrounding the tavern and bright spots of light from their windows.

A chill breeze, the fading remnant of winter, tousled Chavali's cloak. She saw the glow of lamplight from the windows of Marcus and Penny's farmhouse on the fringes of town and stopped. Her small clan needed to see her often. It had been almost a week since she'd last had time to stop in. The squat, aging house, kept in good condition by Marcus's careful hands and Penny's subtle magics, beckoned.

"Go ahead without me."

Violet produced the shell. "I was going to stop in the tavern for a while. Do you mind handling the report before you turn in?"

Taking the shell, Chavali shooed her away. "I wish to speak with Eldrack anyway. I doubt a delay will be disastrous for this report anyway."

"You could probably leave it for a week without him noticing. See you around." Violet waved and hurried into town.

Chavali snorted and returned the wave. She skirted mud on the narrow wagon path flanked by flowers heavy with unopened buds. At the heavy wooden door, she knocked twice and entered without waiting. "It's only me," she called into the house. Warmth embraced her. She tugged off her cloak and hung it on a hook for the purpose. As she bent to untie her boots, a little girl with dark, flowing hair plowed into her leg. With a grunt, Chavali stumbled into the wall of the mudroom.

"Chavali!" The four-year-old wrapped her arms around Chavali's hips. "Almost missed Grandpa's birthday!"

She opened her mouth to protest, but stopped without speaking. Had she lost track of time? Last she knew, it had been another week before his birthday. Marcus had claimed he didn't want a fuss, but the children had demanded cake and a day without chores so they could play with their adoptive grandfather. Chavali was supposed to spend the day handling the chores in their stead.

Biholtz, her dark hair cut short since the last time Chavali had seen her, appeared in the doorway, her arms crossed and shoulders sagging with weariness. The thirteen-year-old had taken the extra chores on herself. Chavali knew this because she knew Biholtz. "We still have some cake."

Chavali picked up Haizea and settled the girl on her hip. "I'll make it up to you as soon as I can."

"Yes, Seer." Biholtz turned her back on Chavali with a sigh and shuffled to the kitchen.

Following in her wake, Chavali thought of all the promises she'd broken since she awoke from death as Fallen. Eldrack seemed to have an uncanny tendency to send her away when her clan needed her most.

Yes, she needed to speak to him.

The bright kitchen, warmed and lit by soft globes in the upper corners, smelled of honey and vanilla. Marcus sat at the table with Danel on his leg, waging a frosting battle. Each used as his weapon a finger smeared with creamed sugar in their tiny, messy duel. Marcus's laugh seemed more brittle than it had the last time she visited. Did his weathered face have more wrinkles and crags than before, or did the frosting daubed on his cheek make them stand out?

Penny's face crinkled with a smile as Chavali set Haizea down and handed her a plate with a piece of cake. Stray strands of the elder's white hair, escaped from her utilitarian bun, floated around her face. "We thought you weren't going to make it."

"I walked all day to be here." While true, the words tasted sour. Lying to clan always felt wrong. Forgetting her obligations to them, though, bothered her more.

"I'm glad you made it before we cleaned up the cake."

Biholtz stepped to the sink and plunged her hands into water, scrubbing plates without complaint.

"Grandpa built us a playhouse," Danel said.

Marcus chuckled. "That's a very generous description. It's a lean-to at best."

Chavali sat and smiled at Danel. "That was a nice thing for him to do. Did you thank him?"

Danel nodded, but he turned to Marcus and said, "*Eskerri ekako.* That means 'thank you.'"

Penny smirked. "Amazing how we haven't heard that one before."

"Scandalous. They've been using Shappan so much, they're forgetting their own language." Chavali tried a bite of the cake and found it sweeter than she preferred. She ate it anyway.

Haizea gasped and covered her mouth with her hands. "Never!"

Biholtz used the clan tongue. "They don't understand much yet."

Though the teen offered no sense of rebuke, Chavali took it as one. "I understand. I'll do what I can to minimize my absences, but I'm not in control of my own destiny here."

"We know," Biholtz said. "You were around for all of our birthdays, so that's something. Will you be able to come to the Spring Festival?"

"I have no idea, but if I can, I will." Chavali tousled Haizea's hair. "I can't stay long tonight. I have to see Eldrack before I sleep."

"I understood 'Eldrack,' " Penny said. She gripped Chavali's shoulder and squeezed. "He'll take all you have if you let him."

"Yes, I'm starting to notice that." Chavali sighed and kissed the top of Haizea's head. "I hope to return tomorrow for as much of the day as I can."

"Good," Marcus said, "because you look like you could use a day off."

"Chavali needs to play!" Haizea grabbed Chavali's fork, stabbed the cake, and rose on her tiptoes to shove the cake into Chavali's mouth. Frosting smeared across Chavali's face and cake went up her nose. "Start now."

With Haizea's joyous and dubious assistance, Chavali finished as much of the cake as she could stomach. She shouldered Biholtz aside to both wash cake from her face and finish the dishes. When she finished, she kissed everyone goodnight and trudged into town to return to the underground tower she had no choice but to call home.

If she abandoned the Fallen or refused to follow orders, she'd die again. Her first time had been unpleasant enough, and no one got a third chance at life.

She hurried down the endless stairs of the inverted tower, passing the tenth floor with her own room and continuing deeper. The people—Healers, Fallen agents, and servants—she passed on the wide, stone staircase nodded to her. After four months, she knew most of the Fallen on sight, though she still recognized precious few of the white-clad Healers. Their uniforms gave her reason to ignore their faces. Fallen, on the other hand, dressed as they pleased.

At the thirteenth floor, she shoved open the door for Eldrack's office. He sat alone at his desk, flipping through papers and taking notes on a piece of parchment. The regal dragon statue on a shelf behind him glinted in the soft light provided by a magical stone on his desk. Other knickknacks, sheafs of paper, potted plants, and books occupied the rest of his bookcases.

"Chavali." Eldrack looked up and rubbed his eyes with a finger and thumb. Like Marcus, he seemed older to her for some reason. Perhaps her own weariness weighed on her perception of others. Other than that, he looked like the middling bureaucrat she'd always seen him as, with a slight paunch and too little muscle on his limbs.

She retrieved both shell and boat to place them on his desk. "This mission meant nothing and we both know it. I'll make a report if you want, but it would be a waste of both our time, and mine has been wasted more than enough already."

"It wasn't meaningless." He leaned back in his chair and gestured for her to sit.

"Of course not," she grumbled. "It took me away from my clan. Which hardly means noth—"

"Chavali, close the door."

Eldrack cut her off less often than she divulged clan secrets. Normally, he waited patiently for her to wind down. Normally, his acute sense of sympathy filled his words with the thick, cloying stench of understanding. Normally, he wanted everyone to get along. Even when angry, he still avoided harsh words and stern tones.

Chavali stared at him long enough to be certain he meant it, then pulled the door shut. She sat in the wooden chair opposite him and raised her brow. Whatever he had to say, she wanted to hear it.

"I have a problem and I need your help."

"I trust this problem involves more weighty matters than fetching toys from fishermen."

"It's about Harris."

Chavali went still. She'd been tasked with crafting arguments to convince a healer to make whatever sacrifice resurrection required, and had yet to meet the woman. His memories, buried inside her mind, beckoned. Until she delved into them, she wouldn't know if he truly deserved to return to life after his murder. Of course, she thought he did, as he'd been a good agent.

"His memories have proven challenging to examine," she said.

Eldrack stared at her for a beat, then shook his head with a grim smile. "No, not that. I've been working on trying to narrow the suspect pool for those who might've leaked the information about his caravan and caused his death." He tapped the papers on his desk. "Knowing we have someone doing that, I've gone back through reports for missions that have gone sour for the past year. I'd hoped to find someone to question, or at least a common thread.

"Nothing." He rubbed his eyes. "Everything aside from Harris's mission can be explained by the missions themselves—bad weather, a murderer that was caught, foolish choices. Someone in the tower is working against us all, and I have no idea who they might be. You're one of a very few people I trust, and your skills are well-suited to ferreting out a traitor."

Chavali frowned, not sure how to pursue this. In the clan, no one ever thought to betray the Seer or the elders. It never happened. "Who else do you trust?"

"Railan and my healer."

After a few moments, Chavali realized he had no intention of adding names to that list. "What do you expect me to do?"

"Use your talents to conduct a murder investigation as quietly as possible. Colby already dealt with the person who killed Harris, but not the person who caused his death. Your suspect pool is three hundred eighty-seven people, minus the four of us."

She thought of Portia, who'd risked her life and done so much to help Chavali for nothing in return, but carried hints of a nefarious past. Colby had been compromised in Ket. Eliot had a weakness in Patrick, the man he loved. Sean would tell anyone anything if it amused him. Everyone carried secrets, darkness, and lies. Revealing theirs meant prodding in turn to reveal her own.

"I know many of these people. We all live here. It's not the same as dealing with strangers in a city you can leave."

Eldrack sighed and nodded, bleeding sympathy at her. "It won't be easy. Whoever's responsible is highly skilled and capable, and they won't want to be found. If I had your skills, I'd do it myself. If I trusted the others who have similar skills, I'd ask all of you to divide and conquer. But you're what I've got."

Despite wanting to tell him to shove his suspicions in unpleasant places, Chavali nodded. Harris deserved this, whether or not she could convince a healer to bring him back. And if someone she considered a friend had arranged for his murder, she wanted to know so she could do reprehensible things to them in return. Harris also deserved that.

"I'll keep you informed," she said as she stood.

"Thank you. Good luck."

Leaving his office, Chavali mused that at least she could count on Colby to fail at hiding something like this. He couldn't even keep himself from admitting he'd put the wrong kind of herb in her tea, thrown it out, and brewed her another cup. As a matter of procedure, though, she'd speak to him tomorrow anyway. One blunt question and she'd have one less suspect.

For now, she needed rest.

CHAPTER 3

At the landing for the tenth floor, Chavali heard her name. Her lip curled at the sound of her healer's voice. Kelly insisted upon hunting her down at the most inopportune moments, such as whenever Chavali least wanted to talk. The woman had, for unknown reasons, assumed responsibility for Chavali's mental health, as all healers did for their Fallen charges.

Ignoring her never worked. Chavali kept walking to her room, knowing Kelly would find her. As she reached her door, Kelly called out her name again. Chavali looked up and saw Kelly with two other women, all in white healer robes. One, she'd met briefly in Eldrack's office and knew her as his healer. The other, she didn't recognize. Kelly seemed as vibrant as ever, with her light hair piled atop her head in a messy bun.

Chavali waved to Kelly, inviting her and the other two inside her room. Beads hanging from her door clacked as she opened and shut it for the three women. Kelly upended the opaque vase holding her light stone to let it illuminate the room. The other two women sat in the two chairs at her small, round table while Kelly stepped across the room to lean against Chavali's dresser.

Though she had the option to sit at the foot of her wide bed,

Chavali chose instead to remain at the door. She crossed her arms and raised an eyebrow, waiting for an explanation for this invasion.

"I know you don't like being bothered here," Kelly said. One corner of her mouth quirked up. "Or anywhere else, for that matter. But I saw you from the stairs, and we were just talking about you. This is Jacqueline." She gestured to Eldrack's Healer, a middle-aged woman with gray streaks in her dark hair.

"We've met," Chavali said with a nod.

"Yes. Under unpleasant circumstances," Jacqueline said. "This is Alene. She's the one you need to convince to be Harris's healer."

Alene flashed Chavali a friendly smile. She seemed soft to Chavali, as if her life had never tested her. The rest of the healers all struck Chavali as women who'd made hard choices or suffered hardship. "Everyone says you knew him best." Even her voice sounded soft.

"Among the Fallen, I suspect so, yes. I brought him here and took responsibility for him."

All three women watched her. Silence—thick, heavy, and grating—hung in the room. Chavali, though, had never met a silence she couldn't endure. She waited for one of them to break it because she didn't know what they wanted. Perhaps they wanted her to argue on Harris's behalf now, but she thought it awkward do so at their first meeting.

"Chavali," Kelly said, her tone chiding, "you have to convince her Harris is worth bringing back."

She shrugged, not eager to examine the subject, especially while tired. "He's loyal and capable. I brought him here because I believed him a valuable and worthy asset. This hasn't changed."

"Can you be more specific?" Alene asked.

"Specific? About what? Is there something more critical than his competence and loyalty?"

Kelly sighed. "I thought I told you to prepare for this."

"Tell her what kind of man he was," Jacqueline said.

The words that came to mind—foolish, idiotic, pathetic—seemed unlikely to improve the situation. She remembered sitting with him in Ket, both wearing bathrobes while their clothes dried. Crackling fire had warmed them both. He'd been determined to pursue the implausible task of wooing her. She smirked. "Charming, in his peculiar way."

"And?" Kelly gestured for more. "I realize you're not the type to gush, but we need a complete picture."

Chavali waved to dismiss them. "Faced with his own death, he failed to betray Eldrack and the Fallen. Is this not enough?"

Though Alene seemed uncertain, Jacqueline stood and said, "No. It's not. Kelly said you carry at least some of his memories. Haven't you examined them yet? Alene needs to understand who he was before she'll commit."

Alene's presence suggested the girl had already committed to the Fallen. Chavali didn't understand why she needed an extra layer of connection to his life. "I was under the impression I had some level of confidentiality," she said to Kelly.

"You do. But this is about Harris, and what you requested isn't a frivolous matter. Alene is here because you spoke up for him and Eldrack thinks he'd continue to be a good agent. That's enough to bring her to you. It's not enough to get her to help raise him. Have you accessed those memories or not?"

Chavali curled her lip. "No." Anything else she had to say on the subject felt private.

Jacqueline tugged Alene's hand. "Then we'll leave you to deal with that. Let us know when you're ready." She opened the door, causing the beads to clack, and left the room with Alene.

Though Kelly took a step toward the door, Chavali shut it and stood in front of it with her arms crossed. "I've had a long day and I'm tired. Nevertheless, you're not leaving until you explain this to me. Why does Harris have a higher threshold than me? I know you had no one to question when they brought my body."

"That's not true. I questioned Teryk, Colby, and Eliot."

"They spent a few hours in my presence. Whatever they said, it couldn't have been much more than I've just given about Harris. And you had no way of knowing about the prophecies before making that sacrifice."

Kelly rubbed her arm and shook her head. "This is a very different situation. Railan described what happened to your clan and Eldrack asked me personally to sacrifice for you. He suspected something—maybe not the gift specifically, but something. Besides, he's...hard to turn down."

One day, when Chavali could read Shappan well enough to understand it, she'd go through all the prophecies she had spewed between resurrection and waking. For now, she knew where to find the records of them. Kelly had made those records. She'd sat beside Chavali's body and written down every word Chavali unknowingly spoke. Because she'd made some mysterious bargain with the Creator to restore Chavali's life.

"What is this wretched sacrifice you all speak of without naming?" She pointed to the door, letting her annoyance surface. "What am I asking that woman to do or give up for Harris? She's already wearing the white robes, so I know she's decided to stay with the Fallen. Is this about the connection to the Creator and the Wasting we all share? She has to subject herself to some stricter form of the oath she must have already taken?"

"Sometimes, I wish you weren't so perceptive." Kelly dropped her gaze to her hands as she covered her belly with both. "We give up the ability to bear children. Before we've had any."

Chavali snapped her mouth shut. She had no desire to bear children—the idea of sharing someone's thoughts during sex repulsed her almost as much as the prospect of enduring the unending thoughts of a developing child in her womb. For other women, though, she knew the desire to become a mother could burn with the ferocity of a bonfire.

"Ah." Eldrack had told her that children had no place inside the tower. His reasons had made sense, but he'd left out the angle of cruelty to the healers. She'd never realized speaking about Danel, Haizea, and Biholtz might cause Kelly pain. "Am I correct to suspect that women with no interest in childbearing are unsuitable healer candidates?"

Kelly nodded. "That wouldn't be much of a sacrifice, would it?"

"No, it wouldn't." Chavali shifted to the side so she no longer blocked the door. "I'll continue to make what effort I can on Harris's behalf. I considered him a friend and should do nothing less."

Wiping her cheeks though she'd shed no tears, Kelly nodded again. "That's all we're asking." She crossed the room to leave.

Chavali stopped her with a hand on her shoulder. "Thank you. For failing to turn down Eldrack. If you still wish to join the clan, I'll bring it up with them."

"That might be the nicest thing you've ever said to me."

"I don't doubt it."

Kelly smiled. "I would've told you sooner, but since you adjusted to waking up?" She shook her head. "There always seems to be something else going on with you."

"This is, I think, how life works as Fallen and clan."

CHAPTER 4

As much as Chavali wanted to sleep, she forced herself to try delving into Harris's memories. She lay on her bed and closed her eyes to focus. In her mind, Harris's memories had been translated into a locked chest. Every time she'd tried to open it before, Keino's spirit had interrupted. With Keino finally receded into the background after what had happened in Harbor City, she expected no resistance.

Blaming Keino for her reticence after that mission seemed right and proper. In life, the ass had been more annoying than fifteen wandering goats and twice as frustrating. Meeting him as a spirit had let her say goodbye, but it had also meant watching him die again. She hated him. She loved him. She missed him.

Her opinions on Harris, best described as "muddled," had also stopped her. She considered him a valuable asset, an ally, and a person she trusted as far as she could throw him. Perhaps she trusted him farther than that. As she'd once told him, she had no romantic interest in him. The ache in her chest from his death suggested otherwise, but she ignored it. Her heart made stupid choices, like with Keino.

At this rate, she suspected she'd fall asleep before accomplishing anything. Renewing her focus on the chest holding his memories, she forced herself through the meditative exercises Railan had taught her. The more-experienced telepath had been a great help, except Chavali had still gained no control over her irritating gift.

Again, her thoughts had strayed. She pictured the chest. Heavy wood formed a rectangular box with a thick lock secured through a steel loop. A person of her size could fit inside it with room to spare. When she'd first encountered it inside a vision of a clan wagon, it had seemed out of place.

She stood inside the wagon again, half-expecting Keino to burst through the door and stop her. As in life, the wagon appeared without color. The large bed occupied one end. Six baskets held clothing for six people. Soon, they would've added a seventh for her brother's baby. At that point, Luken would've asked for his own wagon to hold his own family. With their father among the elders and Chavali as the Seer, one would have been built as soon as he made the request.

Turning away from what might have been, Chavali crouched in front of the chest and ran her fingers over the surface. Scarred, pitted metal formed the edges and covered the seams in the wood. Harris had been that kind of man. Between the steel strips, smooth, sanded wood hinted at what he might have once been or, perhaps, might have become.

The keyhole in the lock had a smooth, round shape. Ignoring the potential implications, she stuck her finger into the hole and twisted her hand until she found a small bar inside. Flicking it made the lock click open and fall apart. Now, nothing stood between her and the memories.

Knowing she had no physical presence here, she took a deep breath and pushed up the lid. The hinges creaked. Pure, golden light spilled out, bathing the colorless room with a gentle, yellow glow. Chavali stared into the chest, wishing it held things she could remove and inspect.

As she lifted her foot to climb in, tendrils of bright red and orange flame shot out and wrapped around her body.

Her flesh burned. She screamed in shock and pain.

The fiery ropes yanked her into the chest and threw her at a solid wall of packed earth. Struggling against the fire, she rolled over the dirt until the flames died.

Rising to her hands and knees, she saw burning walls surrounding her with no way out. Beside her, a small brown book puffed with black smoke.

Dark green shrubs with a leaf shape she recognized from visits to Mecalle lined the walls, not interacting with the fire. Emerald grasses lined the path Chavali had landed on. Five arrows with different colors of fletching stuck in the earth.

This scene made no sense.

The walls reminded her of Colby's memory of his death, but she'd never seen a path with arrows like this in his memories. If she hadn't seen it, she couldn't summon it here. The arrows likewise reminded her of nothing that had happened in her own past. That left Harris's memory.

Railan had warned her not to touch things without knowing they needed fixing, but she couldn't affect either Colby or Harris here. She reached out and wrapped her fingers around the nearest arrow, one with red fletching.

An image of several scruffy men in ill-fitting leathers appeared. Chavali recognized this unkempt band as the men who, with Harris, had attacked her and Algie. They'd met Harris because of it, but this moment had nothing to do with that ambush.

The leader of that band kicked her gut. Instead of pain, empty force told her where the blow connected.

The archer Chavali had killed held her legs. Another man laughed as he sorted through items pulled from her pockets. The fourth taunted her with her bow and dagger, waggling both out of reach. The rest of the men, none of whom Chavali recognized, watched the road in both directions.

Chavali released the arrow. Harris had been that person on the ground.

Why he had joined with a group that beat him, she had no idea. For now, it mattered that Harris had stored his memories in arrows, which made sense. His city-based memories probably came in dagger form.

Colby's memories mingling with Harris's puzzled her. Had she been so careless in her own mind? Or had she connected them in some subtle, underlying fashion she hadn't yet noticed in her daily life?

This needed fixing.

She stood and stepped between the arrows and the book. Each served as an anchor, so separating them seemed appropriate.

Loathe to touch the arrows again, she picked up the book. Never in Colby's mind had she opened one of his memory books, making this one safe to handle.

Keeping an eye on the arrows, she tossed the book through the doorway filled with flames. Something hit her from behind, hard enough to knock her to the ground. She tasted blood and greed.

With a groan, she patted her back and found...the book. Something had linked these two memories, and they didn't want to become unlinked.

If these memories wanted to fight, she could fight.

She could always go back to Colby and sample his memories again, so all his artifacts were expendable. Harris's required more care.

Gripping the dagger at the small of her back, she sat on her feet with a groan. Though Railan hadn't taught her anything about using a weapon in these bizarre quasi-dreamscapes, she picked up the book and stabbed it.

Her blade plunged through the cover and out the other side. Burning blood gushed through the lower hole, drenching her dress and puddling on the path.

Chavali watched the liquid ooze toward the arrows, thinking she should stop it. Somehow.

Careful not to throw the book too far, she flung it aside and lunged forward to make a dam with her arms.

The blood pooled against her arms, setting her sleeves on fire. Flames tickled and licked at her neck and upper chest.

The bare flesh at the base of her neck surprised her, and she noticed her clothing had shifted into her old fortune teller costume. Bunched and ruffled dark fabric hung off her shoulders, baring more skin than she ever showed any other time. Her Seer's pendant, a precious heirloom she now kept safe in her room, hung from its gold chain around her neck.

As the fire crisped her flesh, the pendant heated. When she could no longer stand the growing agony of scorching metal pressing into her skin, she let go.

The flames fled from her body while the blood surged forward. She scrambled to the arrows on her hands and knees, avoiding the blood.

Before it reached the first arrow, she gripped two at once and yanked them free.

At once, she saw two visions overlaid on the same stretch of path. One depicted an ambush about to spring on two figures approaching the bandits' hiding spot. Chavali recognized herself and Algie. From Harris's perspective, they appeared as nothing more than a lightly-armed, bickering husband and wife. He considered Algie the main threat. In fairness, he had been—and remained—more deadly than she.

The other memory showed a different ambush already sprung. Two corpses feathered with arrows lay on the ground beside a pair of wagons. Nine other people, one with an arrow lodged in his arm, had surrendered. One man negotiated with the bandit leader. Harris watched a young woman weeping in the shelter of the negotiator with a queasy feeling in his belly.

Both memories together ensnared her. Harris avoided hitting Chavali on purpose when he fired his arrows. He purposely shot to kill the two wagon men.

Where he watched Chavali with a healthy dose of lust, he wanted to protect the girl.

One Harris gulped as Algie and Chavali argued about how to handle the situation. The other Harris blanched as his leader grabbed a fistful of the girl's hair and dragged her away from her family.

Two different versions of Harris warred for dominance.

"I'm sure there's nothing to read in the fact that your version of the First Blaukenev looks like your bodyguard." Pasha, Chavali's younger sister, sat on a chunk of wood inside Chavali's fortune teller tent. Flames crept along the edges of the waterproof fabric.

"Shut up," Chavali snapped. She scowled and clawed a hand through an illusion she'd crafted of Keino.

"Quit screaming," the bandit leader snarled as he hauled the girl into a ditch.

"You can't just stand there and discuss—" The bandit leader growled his frustration. "Tactics! You're talking about tactics for fighting us right in front of us!"

Colby fell to his knees with a limp girl in his arms, gasping for breath. He'd stopped sweating, and noticed her chest no longer rose and fell. Other children screamed in another room. Karias couldn't reach him. He'd failed, and had no strength left to save himself. Overhead, support beams cracked as they crackled.

Chavali screamed, overwhelmed by too many memories hitting her at once.

Someone covered her eyes from behind, wiping all the visions away. She remembered how to release the arrows, cutting off Harris's memories.

No peeking! Pasha's voice giggled inside her head.

"Hurry up already." Chavali waited with her hands on her hips, knowing everyone had planned something for her birthday and eager to get it over with.

Once she'd become the Seer, the clan had an unfortunate tendency to do far too much for it. Seer Marika had endured her own birthday celebrations with grace and aplomb, and Chavali strove to emulate her.

Excitement rendered Pasha's thoughts fidgety. She removed her hands, leaving Chavali standing on the path again, flames dancing on the surface of a wide pool of blood that had engulfed the remaining three arrows.

The book continued to pump out more blood. Fire had infected the shrubs beside the walls, shriveling their leaves.

Chavali clucked her tongue in annoyance at the mess. Railan had taught her a great deal about fixing memories, but nothing she'd encountered in Colby's head had been so entangled as this. "I need more sleep," she grumbled. Nothing else explained how this happened.

Wrapping a ragged sleeve around her hand, she picked up the two discarded arrows and set them aside. When this didn't force the memories on her, she knew what to do.

CHAPTER 5

Chavali woke to a knock on her door. She groaned and ignored it. Whoever wanted to share breakfast with her would take the hint and go away. Light in the room confused her after the muddle of memories she'd slogged through last night.

She'd never gotten up and covered her light stone, which meant she must have fallen asleep without waking from her trance. Considering the mess it had been, she might have fallen asleep in the middle and only dreamed of continuing to sort them.

She tried to pull the covers over her head, but her body remained atop them. Once she realized this, and that she still wore yesterday's clothes, she had woken too much to fall back asleep. Sitting up, she noticed she still wore her indoor shoes. She thought she remembered taking off her boots and not putting on these shoes before lying down.

Considering how tired and harried she'd been lately, it seemed plausible she'd think of something so trivial and not do it, or do it and forget.

Running a hand through her hair to tame it, she shuffled out of her room. She and Marjeline, her neighbor, waved to each other. The thin, delicate woman seemed in good spirits, of course. As she passed other

Fallen who lived on her floor, everyone seemed in good spirits, as if they smiled to spite her.

She returned the smiles anyway, eager to avoid discussions and rumors about her mood.

The stairs seemed more daunting than usual. Keeping one hand on the outside wall, she took her time descending to the dining hall on the nineteenth floor. At the landing for the sixteenth floor, she paused to rest. More Fallen waved to her, which she assumed meant she'd succeeded in fooling them all.

A woman in dark armor on her way up saw Chavali and stormed toward her. The woman's expression hardened with fury as she marched.

As Chavali had never introduced herself to this Fallen agent, she had no idea what had happened to infuriate her.

She opened her mouth to ask what the woman needed...and reeled as her cheek exploded with pain. A sharp slap knocked her to the floor. In that moment of contact, the spirits pulled the woman's outraged sense of violation.

Others on the stairs stopped and gasped.

"Never, ever do that again," the woman growled. She lifted her chin and hurried up the stairs.

Chavali rubbed her cheek and blinked. "What?" Her question came too late to reach her assailant.

Those around her averted their eyes and continued on their way. Perhaps Sean could explain this. He'd undoubtedly hear about it within a few hours.

She stood with the help of the wall and hoped tea would chase away the headache creeping in. At the nineteenth floor, she entered the dining room to the usual buzz of chatter. With over two dozen round tables, the hall had plenty of space to fill with busybodies.

Furtive glances in her direction happened every time she appeared, this time included. Rumors always swirled here, and she seemed to inspire more than most.

According to tower gossip, she drank demon blood, sacrificed babies under the full moon, pursued a torrid romance with Colby, pursued a different torrid romance with Eliot, had an affair with Sean behind his wife's back, infused her tea with hallucinogenic leaves, had been given the feather in her skull by the Creator, used Eldrack like a puppet, and spoke the language of the dead.

Only the last came close to the truth, as the clan's tongue had only four native speakers left, and could be considered dead.

No one bothered her as she selected her breakfast from the long buffet left out and maintained by servants at all hours. When she had a chance, she'd ask Sean about the mysterious slap.

Until then, she had a traitor to find.

She needed a tactic. Reading everyone's thoughts would work, but she hated doing it. Touching everyone to do it required explanation or subterfuge. In addition, Railan had warned her she would encounter others with telepathic ability in the tower. She could accidentally trigger a mental duel, even with someone possessing a minor gift.

This task required someone with experience. Or, at least, she needed someone to help her with ideas.

As before, Colby sprang to mind. She trusted him, and he might have dealt with spies before. That trust, however, didn't extend to him keeping his mouth shut. Once he knew about her task, his inability to lie would reveal too much. Eldrack had asked for her discretion.

His horse, on the other hand, had good sense, had witnessed a great deal, and understood more about people than his master. Best of all, even if he wanted to betray her trust, he couldn't. Only telepaths could speak to him, and she had a strong suspicion no other telepath had ever tried.

Set on a course, she picked up two extra apples and faced the challenge of nineteen flights of stairs. Frequent pauses and a stop for her boots and cloak finally brought her to the tavern at the surface. Brilliant mid-morning sunshine streamed through the windows. Few patrons filled the room at this hour. Chains of paper flowers had been hung across the rafters in preparation for the upcoming Spring Festival. Chavali passed through with a wave for the spindly bartender who never seemed to leave his post.

Behind the tavern, a large stable held the mounts belonging to Fallen agents as well as those available for agent use. She hauled the high, wide wooden door open and shut it. Horses inside huffed at her. One, a gray beast she'd once used to haul packages, stuck his head over the partial door preventing his escape and whinnied for her attention.

Her two apples had been intended for Karias, but she chuckled as she passed his stall to reach the gray. "Yes, I'm sure everyone ignores you, especially the stablehands. They're never around, are they? No, they're not. Muck the stalls and goof off, that's all they do. You poor, neglected baby." She offered him a green apple and pet his nose as he took it from her. The creature's simple thoughts expressed affection unfettered by human problems.

Hooves scraping on wood and shifting straw came from the first stall. Karias stuck his head over his own partial door and watched her. Like his master, Karias stood taller than any other of his kind she'd ever seen, and carried his significant muscle with grace.

"I'll see you again soon," she told the gray in front of her. With one last pat, she tore herself away from the allure of his uncomplicated innocence. Her clan's horses had shared the same devotion to her. After all, anytime they had a problem, she soothed them and fixed it. The goats, on the other hand, had all been annoying brats.

She left the gray behind and tossed her other apple at Karias. The white horse caught it in his teeth and whuffed at her. With his mouth full, he couldn't let her in, so she tugged the string to release the latch on his stall door herself and stepped inside.

Of all the mounts, only Karias had the ability to come and go as he pleased. According to Colby, he'd waged a quiet battle with the stablehands for weeks to assure this accommodation.

To pass the time while they talked, Chavali chose a currycomb and applied it to his coat. Her hand followed the comb, staying in contact with him to keep their conversation smooth.

I'm also a poor, neglected baby.

Chavali laughed, pleased with herself for choosing to visit him. Along with Karias's other benefits, he had a strong sense of humor. In her experience, many Fallen lacked this. "Yes, you are. Colby spends far too little time pampering you."

I agree. You should point that out. Tell him I'm languishing and the mangy curs in the back get more attention than me.

"I suspect he might point out how many times you stood with him in the rain or mud, or perhaps snow or high winds. Being allowed to laze about in a warm stable may qualify as enough pampering to last forever."

Lazing about is driving me mad. I'd rather stand in a blizzard, watching hapless recruits struggle to put up tents against the wind and snow. It's more entertaining.

"No doubt."

Obviously, you're here to lavish me with attention, but is there any other reason I'm graced with your presence and not Colby's? You don't often come to see me outside of missions.

"I require confidential counsel, and you've provided it ably in the past."

I see. Should we take a walk to avoid being overheard? Not that I want you to stop brushing, but if you need it kept quiet, this may not be the best place to talk. The stablehands and other Fallen come and go at unpredictable times.

"I suppose so. A ride, perhaps? Around the town?"

Yes, please. I promise not to throw you.

Chavali put away the comb. Between a box and Karias lowering himself, she clambered onto his back. He yanked on the latch release with his teeth and kicked the stall door shut after using it. At the main door, he hooked a leg around a thick peg installed for the purpose and dragged it open. Once his head fit in the gap, he shoved his way through. Outside, he kicked it shut with his hind hooves.

Karias took her away from the center of town. The villagers had begun preparations for the Spring Festival outdoors. Pots of flowers, real and fake, sat in clusters, waiting for distribution around town. Life-size wooden sunflowers, intended for planting in various locations, leaned against a house in a stack. Portia had told her the townsfolk already had gallons of sweetened tea steeping in the sun, and half of it would have alcohol added to make it "a real party."

Tell me the situation.

"Eldrack wishes me to find whoever betrayed Harris without revealing this as my task. He has nothing to help narrow the possibilities beyond everyone living in the tower except himself, Railan, his healer, and me. I'm confident Colby lacks the guile to keep this kind of secret from me, so I also trust him. And, by extension, you."

Ah. A weighty task. And one outside your expertise, I'm guessing. Within mine, though. The Fallen as a group is similar to a royal court in many ways. Spies flourish in courts because those outside the court want one or both of two things—information and influence. Considering the Fallen and what you do, I expect information is the more critical point. If someone wanted influence over the Fallen, it would make more sense and require less resources to approach it from the angle of the Shappan Royal Court.

Karias's chosen path took them to the town's vast farming fields. With winter recently lifted, men and women toiled at planting enough grains to feed all of Cloverdale and the tower. He skirted the edges, keeping them from passing close by anyone. Under the warm sunshine, Chavali's dark cloak warmed her back and shoulders enough to counter the breeze caused by Karias's trotting gait.

"How do you mean less resources? Wouldn't influencing a king be more challenging than getting agents killed?"

Not at all. All these courts have had spies for centuries. It's a known, expected part of the whole royalty thing. They can't have wars because of the Creator's Towers, so they all spy on each other. The challenge at that level is to make their influence subtle and deft so it goes unnoticed. *With the Fallen, placing or cultivating a spy is the challenge. Placing a spy requires either defeating a rigorous vetting process or being killed and resurrected, neither of which is a reasonable prospect. Cultivating an agent takes time, and you only have five years in service. After that, your access—and therefore your utility as a spy—is minimal.*

This means anyone who wants to cultivate an informant among the Fallen first has to know about the group's existence, then encounter the right kind of agent, and finally coax them into seeking out the right kind of information and passing it on before their term of service expires. This is no simple feat.

Chavali frowned. "So I'm likely looking for someone nearer to the end of their service than the beginning."

Yes. I'd discount anyone who's been in service less than two full years. Three or four is more likely.

Every Fallen Chavali knew, except for Colby, had been in service at least two years. Eldrack hadn't sent her out with anyone less experienced than herself, and her floor seemed full of those in the middle of their terms. "This doesn't narrow the field much. Is there anything else I can discount?"

People like Colby make lousy spies. No one with half a brain would ever approach him. Unfortunately, until you get to know someone, it's hard to tell if they're actually honest, loyal, and noble or just playing at it.

"So true." She mulled over everything Karias had said. Nothing gave her good ideas. "Do you have any suggestions for how to begin?"

The majority of spies are caught because they make a mistake, get greedy, or devolve into paranoia. These things typically happen when pressure is applied, such as an announcement or rumor you know there's an informant. Eldrack is a smart man, and he's very good at his job, but I disagree with his interest in discretion. He is, however, in charge. I am not.

They'd looped around town to the north end, where the clan lived. As they neared the farm, Chavali caught sight of a sizable group of riders galloping down the road from the nearby Creator's Tower and into town. Karias stopped to watch them without getting in their way.

I imagine you can't see the red-on-blue design on their livery. Those horses belong to the King. Him sending people here means something is afoot that you should stick your nose into. Because I want you to tell me about it later.

CHAPTER 6

By the time Karias reached the tavern, soldiers stood near the door with horses. A quick count told Chavali at least three riders had gone inside already. She jumped off Karias's back, aware of the soldiers watching her. They seemed uncertain, as if no one knew how long they'd stay and they weren't sure of their level of authority regarding the tavern.

She breezed past them and stepped inside the tavern, making an effort not to seem hurried. Three soldiers stood at the bar, each holding a helmet tucked under an arm. The woman in the middle, her hair wrapped in a tight, severe bun atop her head, spoke to the bartender while the other two acted like bodyguards.

"Let me rephrase," the woman said. "I want to see Eldrack *now*."

Chavali slipped around, pretending to ignore them, and did her best to melt into the thin crowd. Of those she recognized, half lived in Cloverdale and the other half were Fallen. Tension hung in the room, thick and heavy.

The bartender leaned on the bar and looked through Chavali as if she didn't exist. He gave the impression of taking the woman into a confidence, but his low voice slithered through the room. "Then let me rephrase. You can't go downstairs."

The woman retrieved something from a pocket and slapped it on the bar with a clunk. "You can't stop me."

"Maybe, maybe not." The contours of the bartender's face shifted, making him seem thinner and less human.

Chavali resisted the urge to squirm as the spirits buzzed in her ears. They saw something unpleasant in the bartender. She didn't blame them. The air cooled enough to notice, and she wanted to look anywhere but at the confrontation at the bar. Around her, people shrugged their clothing tighter and turned away. Chavali slipped a hand to her dagger.

"The fact remains you can't go downstairs." The bartender smiled without showing his teeth.

Though the woman rolled her shoulders in discomfort, she scowled at him. "Knock it off. I'm not afraid of you."

"Changes nothing. If I don't want you downstairs, you don't go downstairs."

"Someday, someone is going to—"

The cellar door creaking open interrupted the conversation. Eldrack stepped through, panting. "It's fine, Walt. Thank you." He offered the woman a shallow bow. "Excuse me, Your Highness. No one sent word of your visit."

The bartender nodded and straightened, his face and the room returning to normal. He moved away from the woman and attacked a spot on the bar with his rag as if nothing had happened.

Chavali let go of her dagger, thankful for her cloak concealing it. Had they noticed her overt threat, the two guards probably would've done something about her.

"This is something of an emergency." The woman scooped her possession off the bar and tucked it into a pocket without Chavali seeing it. She imagined it somehow declared or proved the woman's identity. "Would you like to discuss it here, or shall we retire to your office?"

Eldrack caught his breath and stood aside, gesturing for the woman to join him. "Chavali, come with us, please."

The woman's gaze snapped to Chavali. She took in the feather and Chavali's own mild surprise at being asked. "I think this should be a private meeting."

"I think you should listen to me." Eldrack beckoned Chavali forward.

Her loyalty on Eldrack's side, Chavali strode forward and through the door. A bolstered wooden staircase in excellent repair took her to the floor of the tavern's supply cellar, filled with barrels and shelves holding liquor and other provisions.

"Fine," the woman said with an air of conciliatory gravitas. "You can have this one, but Railan will *not* be at this meeting."

Eldrack shut the door as Chavali reached the shelves concealing the tunnel to the tower. He sighed and followed his guest down the stairs. "You can trust her. She has scruples."

"As far as you know."

Chavali wrenched a lever in the wall to slide the shelving unit up. She waited for the pair, amused by the argument between them. "May I suggest suspending this charming bickering until we reach the privacy of his office?"

Eldrack coughed and covered his mouth. The woman regarded her with a cool, unamused stare.

Both breezed past her. Chavali followed and shut the door. They marched down a narrow spiral stair, perfect for creating a chokepoint in a battle, and through the winding maze and wide expanse of the two defensive levels at the top of the tower, then down the wide spiral stair that ran to the bottom of the tower. Chavali guessed the woman had been here before, because without prompting, she stopped at the thirteenth floor and tossed open the door to Eldrack's office.

When Chavali closed the door, Eldrack gestured to the woman. "Chavali, this is Princess Aislynn, the daughter of Martef, King of Shappa."

Aislynn sat in the chair normally reserved for Railan. "I thought she was supposed to be eerily perceptive about people."

Chavali stood behind the other chair and shrugged. She already disliked Aislynn enough to poke her. "I've never paid much attention to the identities of royalty. They've never mattered. That you were part of the Royal family of Shappa, however, was obvious before I stepped inside the tavern."

Flashing Chavali a warning glance, Eldrack sat in his chair. He clasped his hands on the desk and leaned on his arms. Tension bunched his shoulders and deepened the tiny lines around his eyes. "To what do we owe the honor of your presence?"

"Your incompetence."

Because she wanted to slap Aislynn, Chavali crossed her arms and remained standing. Better to keep herself out of arm's reach than to tempt fate. Eldrack frowned on fighting in his office.

Eldrack nodded like he'd expected this. "I see. Is there something in particular, or have I inspired a rather general sense of disappointment?"

"Don't get cute. You know as well as I do that the Fallen are compromised. That caravan attack was just the latest screw-up, and you should've known someone would get killed eventually."

Chavali raised an eyebrow at Eldrack. He'd told her, to her face, that he didn't believe any other operations had been compromised. "Are you certain other missions have been affected?" she asked.

Aislynn narrowed her eyes. "I have no reason to trust you with anything. For all I know, you're the informant."

"From the way you reacted to her, I thought you knew who she was."

"I know exactly who she is—the one who spews the prophecies. That doesn't exempt her from suspicion."

"However," Chavali said, biting back a growl, "she *is* standing in the room, and she was close to the man who was killed."

"Oh really?" Aislynn's brow lifted. "Close enough to—"

"Ladies, please." Eldrack sighed and shook his head. "Your Highness, I trust Chavali. She's one of my most capable agents, she has no connections to the outside world, and she hasn't been here long enough to get wrapped up in the politics of anything. Besides, she is, as you pointed out, the source of the prophecies. The Creator sent her to us, to hasten our efforts. That is our mission, after all—seeking Reunion."

"You're soft and sentimental, Eldrack."

Chavali regarded him. Hearing his opinion of her, even if he'd tempered it for her ears, provided another tidbit of insight into the man. And another reason to appreciate having him in his position. "I agree with you," she told Aislynn, "but he's managed to turn that into an advantage somehow. It's a curious, vexing ability."

Aislynn stared at her for a heartbeat, then she laughed. "Fine. You trust her. But that doesn't matter much. People are calling for your head, Eldrack. The nobility is against you. My father backs you, and I think you've done an admirable job herding all these people. But make no mistake, I'm here because there's a problem. If removing you is the best way to solve it, you'll be removed."

"If I may," Chavali said, "I don't understand. Why is the nobility against him? I thought this was all rather secretive?"

"Our purpose and methods aren't well known." Eldrack met Chavali's gaze, something she no longer believed meant he spoke honestly.

Once upon a time, he'd promised never to lie to her.

He'd never promised to tell her the truth.

He continued. "But our existence is. Something this size can't stay a complete secret. Cloverdale produces far too much food and never trades it. We use the Creator's Towers for free. And more. People know the King has a group of operatives who handle delicate situations on his behalf. They don't however, know details about what we do or how we do it." He tapped a finger on the table, drawing Chavali's attention to it. "*Your* identity isn't known to anyone outside of the Princess and the King."

"And we're keeping it that way." Aislynn waved dismissively. "Because this isn't about prophecies of negotiable value, it's about a traitor among your people and the threat that represents to Shappa. My job is to find this person and report on your suitability to continue as administrator. You are, after all, ultimately responsible for who becomes a Fallen agent, and for making sure the terms of this venture are maintained. The existence of a traitor is your direct failure."

The princess placing low value on the prophecies seemed beneficial in Chavali's mind. The less Aislynn thought of them, the better.

Shifting the focus of the conversation away from Eldrack also seemed prudent. "How do you intend to discover this person?"

"Internal investigation," Aislynn said. This seemed inadequate to Chavali, but the princess said nothing else.

Eldrack tapped a finger on his desk, the only sign of his impatience. "The Fallen has a handful of highly capable investigators. Chavali is arguably the best. She's certainly the most consistent in terms of results. If you're unwilling to utilize her talents, you might as well arrest us all and disband the organization. It would be simpler. I promise you want her working with you, not against you."

"I'd consider anyone working against me to be aiding this traitor."

Chavali snorted. "Because there are only two options in any situation. He means that if you choose to treat me like a suspect, I'll behave like one. And while you focus on me and how suspicious I seem, the true traitor will continue to operate. That is your choice. I will pursue this on my own, whether you approve or not, because I care about the people who pay the price for this person's actions. Whether you and I work together, separately, or in opposition makes no difference to me."

Aislynn smiled at her, syrupy sweetness not quite covering venom. "And why would you seem suspicious?"

"I always seem suspicious." Chavali smirked. "Ask anyone. They'll tell you any number of interesting rumors about how suspicious I am."

"I believe it." Aislynn's gaze flicked over Chavali from head to toe and back. "I don't see any value in applying the usual Court techniques here. They'd take too long. Call everyone to a meeting. We're going to sequester all the Fallen to prevent further information escape. Patrols will run in the town to keep anyone from leaving, in a group big enough to stop any single person or pair. Two plus two soldiers should be satisfactory. Five or six patrols at a time so they can also keep an eye on each other."

"I'm not sure that's the best option," Eldrack said. "It may solve the problem, but it also prevents anyone from doing their job."

Though Chavali did want to stay in Cloverdale for a few weeks, to spend time with her clan, the idea of enforced confinement chafed. All her life, she'd lived in a moving wagon. Every day had brought different scenery. They rushed to evade the snow in the north and the tropical rains in the south. New places held new secrets and delights.

She managed without that now because she knew she could wander for a day if she wanted.

"Many will..." Chavali paused, groping for the right words. "I suspect the mood will degrade rather fast."

"We can speed this up by using telepaths to interrogate everyone. Fallen, staff, Healers, and Cloverdale residents."

"No," Eldrack and Chavali said at the same time, both with vehemence.

Chavali bared her teeth, imagining Aislynn rifling through her mind. Her clan numbered only six, but their secrets remained valuable and Chavali's pledge to protect them remained her primary concern.

Worse, the children had been subjected to psychic assaults before, and she would murder to prevent it happening again. Colby needed protection from this as well, and strangers would foist paranoid questioning on Karias over her dead body.

"That would be a gross violation of privacy," Eldrack said. "Any telepaths willing to perform it aren't telepaths I'd trust."

With Eldrack on her side, Chavali tamped down her anger.

Rational thought appealed to this woman, not barking and snarling. "I will never comply with an order to allow such a trespass. Neither will I stand by and allow it to happen to others."

Aislynn scowled at Eldrack. "You're both impeding an investigation."

"There are many ways to pursue one," Chavali said, looking down her nose at the princess. "Destroying trust among your loyal agents is the least effective in the long term. Which, as someone presumably trained in the art of managing morale, you should already know."

Raising her hands in exasperation, Aislynn stood. "I see why you like her," she grumbled at Eldrack. "Call a meeting. No telepaths, but everyone will still be interviewed with a Truthfinder present. No one leaves Cloverdale until the interviews are complete. This isn't negotiable. If you can't handle that, you're my number one suspect."

"My presence is no longer needed here." Chavali resisted the urge to stomp or slam the door as she left. Once outside, she stormed to the stairs, her earlier weariness lost under a tide of indignation. This woman swept into the tower, staked her claim, and issued demands. Royalty galled Chavali. The whole idea needed abolishing. People with too much self-importance caused too many problems.

Intent on her seething, Chavali walked into a wall of muscle on the stairs. Colby caught her as she bounced off him and her foot slipped. His hands under her arms, he lifted her and set her on the landing for the eleventh level.

Someone cooed as they passed them on the stairs.

Chavali shifted away from him with a growl. Yet another rumor had been added to the pile.

He urged her through the archway and toward his room. Because she didn't hate him, she let him do it for the sake of escaping sight.

Leaning closer, he kept his voice low as he said, "What's going on?"

"Nothing," she snapped.

"You just left a meeting between Eldrack and the Princess of Shappa with a snarly scowl so deep it would make puppies flinch, and you expect me to believe nothing is going on?"

"Oh. That." She stopped and pushed his hand off her back. Someone else would see them and jump to ever more wrong conclusions.

Colby snatched his hand away and frowned at her. "Have you been sleeping?"

"Of course I have." Chavali crossed her arms and glared at his chest. She had to crane her neck if she wanted to look him in the face, and he deserved none of her wrath. For now.

"Enough?"

She rolled her eyes, though she had to wonder what she must look like to make him ask. "I'm fine."

"Your version of fine and mine are about the same, so I know something's wrong. Is it something with the kids?"

The clan needed to understand what Aislynn intended to do as soon as possible. Before the meeting seemed important.

Chavali's anger disappeared into the background. "Yes. I need to go." She dashed away before he could stop her.

CHAPTER 7

Marcus handed Chavali a mug of tea as he sat beside her at the kitchen table. Haizea sat on her lap, drawing flowers on paper with a piece of charcoal. Several previous flower attempts littered the round table and floor. One rough drawing of a wagon had been tacked to the wall alongside a paper covered with letters in Danel's shaky hand. Penny had stepped outside to fetch Biholtz and Danel, both busy digging holes for Spring Festival decorations.

"Are you sure this is a subject fit for young ears?" Marcus held his own mug in both hands. Streaks of dried mud stained his pants.

Chavali arched an eyebrow. "Of course it is. Children don't become sensible by magic. They should be shielded from nothing but the most basic dangers. If a child is too brainless to heed her parents, she deserves to fall off a cliff and tumble to her painful death. Likewise, if her parents are too brainless to point out that falling off cliffs is deadly, they deserve to suffer the loss."

"That's...well, that's something. I guess I was raised a little different than you."

"Falling off a cliff is bad," Haizea said. "Iparre fell off a cliff once."

"Yes, she did." Chavali tousled the girl's hair. "Iparre is one of the

51

goats from our stories," she told Marcus as a reminder. He and Penny hadn't heard the tales of the clan's four goats from birth as the children had. "Because she didn't listen to Ekia. And it was terrible, wasn't it?"

Haizea nodded. "Stuck with broken legs for lots of days. Crows pecked out her eyes."

Marcus blanched. The back door opened with a creak, letting in Danel and Biholtz, both covered in dirt. Penny followed them inside and shut the door. She seemed amused by the look on her husband's face before he smiled at her.

"Grandma says we shouldn't bother to clean up," Biholtz said, making it half statement and half question.

"I agree. This won't take long. I haven't told you that one of my friends was killed a few weeks ago. Not Eliot. His name was Harris. Someone inside the Fallen betrayed him, and the Princess of Shappa is here to figure out who it was. She or her soldiers may come to ask questions. It's critical that we all understand how to answer. They care about this informant and nothing else, but may ask questions that tread on our oaths to clan."

"Why would they ask us questions?" Biholtz asked. "We're not part of any of this, we just live here."

"Because for once," Penny said, her gaze on the far wall, "Chavali is wrong. Not about the clan. I doubt they care about that, but they definitely care about more than this informant. It's the Crown. They always have five visible reasons for doing something and ten more you have to guess about it. How exactly is she conducting this questioning?"

"With a Truthfinder." Chavali curled her lip. "Eldrack and I convinced her not to bring in telepaths to creep inside everyone's minds."

Penny and Marcus both seemed surprised. "Penny's right," Marcus said. "This isn't about an informant. If that was her opening offer, she came intending to do it. I'd wager my dinner she has a telepath or two with her in that group of soldiers waiting for her."

"And if she came to snoop in everyone's heads," Penny said, "she wants to do it for a reason. Watch out for her, Chavali. She has an agenda, and it's probably not to your benefit."

Chavali agreed. Despite Aislynn's protests to the contrary, she suspected the princess wanted more information about the prophecies. Until she knew more about Aislynn's motives, Chavali had no intention of trusting her.

"Worse, there are other factions to consider." Penny poured her own tea. "We've been out of most loops for a while now, so I can't say who's ascendant now, but you shouldn't assume it's all about the Crown. I'll see what I can find out for you about who might be pulling strings here, but I'm not sure how many of my contacts are still around. At the least, you should be aware of the Great Spire, the Continental Trade Syndicate, and the Security Guild. They've all been important in Shappan politics since before my time."

The Continental Trade Syndicate had already earned Chavali's ire after their behavior in Eagle Falls. Any group mentioned in the same breath couldn't be good. "The Great Spire is mages, yes? They do research?"

"Yes. The Guild is Shappa's army that's not an army."

No country could raise a true army without earning the notice of the Creator's Towers. Even Chavali knew that each nation had devised a way to avoid this. Colby had been a member of Grippa's version. The sprawling networks tended to include spies and assassins, not that anyone admitted to such.

"Thank you," Chavali said. "That's helpful. This mess is murky, and Aislynn made it clear that there are multiple factions arrayed against Eldrack. She threatened to remove him from his position."

"How interesting," Penny said.

"Eldrack is a snake," Biholtz hissed. "A vile, worthless snake."

Chavali chuckled. "I imagine he is from your perspective, yes. Don't forget that your view is only one of many."

"Hegoa always makes dumb mistakes when he forgets he doesn't see things the same as the other goats," Danel said.

"Just so." Chavali smiled at him, and the boy beamed his pride.

"Those are some amazing goats," Marcus said.

Chavali nodded. "Goats are important for the clan."

Marcus scratched at the sparse white stubble decorating his cheek. "I suppose we could look into getting some now that winter is over. We might have to convince the chickens they don't mind sharing the property."

Penny chuckled. "We'll see what we can find. In the meantime, you said we'll be questioned. Marcus and I have both handled that before, plenty of times. We know how to say things without saying anything, and we're loyal to Eldrack and the clan. What do you want the kids to do?"

"They're outsiders, so we don't speak the clan tongue in front of them." To Chavali's satisfaction, all three children nodded solemnly. They hadn't forgotten the important lessons. "Refuse to answer questions without me present. You may tell them I'm your aunt, and you may refer to Marcus and Penny as your grandparents. If they persist and demand answers before I arrive, you have my permission to say rude things to them, so long as you do so in Shappan."

Marcus laughed. "I don't imagine they'll expect that."

"The Blaukenev clan excels at confounding expectations." As much as Chavali wanted to stay and enjoy her family, she knew the meeting would start soon. Her absence might go unnoticed, but she wanted to hear what Aislynn told the assembled Fallen. "I need to return to the tower, but with all of us restricted to the town, I'll be back soon."

Danel and Biholtz waved as they tromped outside to finish their digging. Marcus squeezed Chavali's shoulder and followed the two children out. Chavali kissed the top of Haizea's head and reminded her to do her chores before smiling at Penny and leaving.

Walking back, she saw the guards had dispersed and found somewhere to leave their horses. Few patrons sat inside the tavern, all of them locals. She suspected most Fallen had heard about the Princess's visit and wanted to know why she came. Attempts to discover that would have taken them all downstairs.

She plunged into the tower and had reached the cavernous third floor when she heard a deep bell tone that resonated in her chest. The sound battered her ears. Stopping to let the sensation pass, she wondered what it meant. No one had ever mentioned such a thing to her, let alone explained it. Silence after the gong faded seemed unnatural.

Crossing the enormous room, she noticed the buzz of conversation growing in the distance. When she neared the stairs down, several people came into view climbing up. She recognized Kiron, the elder smith from the fourth floor, speaking to women who worked on the fifth floor. He'd once promised to provide her with a dagger, but she'd forgotten and never visited to learn more about his offer.

Kiron saw her and smiled. White hair tied in a tail lined his aged, weathered face. He wore loose clothing plastered to his body with dampness and carried leather gloves tucked under one arm. Dark stains Chavali suspected to be soot or a similar substance decorated his sturdy leather boots.

"I remember you," he said, his voice warm and deep. "But not your name."

"That's Chavali," one of the women said.

"Oh, right. The one who's seeing Colby. That boy takes more metal to outfit than anyone I've ever met before."

Chavali narrowed her eyes. "I am not seeing Colby." She remembered why she'd never returned to discuss weaponry with him.

As they spoke, others emerged from the stairwell in a steady stream.

"Sure, sure. Do you need a weapon yet?" He stretched out an arm as if to wrap it around her waist.

"I have one, thank you." She failed to facilitate his unwanted embrace.

He let his arm fall and didn't seem upset by it. "Really? Can't be much good, since it didn't come from me. Let's see it."

Rather than stand and argue with him, she drew the dagger and held it for him. The straight, plain blade tapered to a point at six inches of length with a dark, leather-wrapped handle and a narrow, pointed guard.

Kiron held out his hands, and Chavali deposited the knife on his open palms. He grimaced. "You call this a weapon? This is an overglorified meat knife."

"It performs its function."

"Cutting roasts?"

"Slitting throats." The memory of murdering a man for the sake of mercy turned her stomach. He'd thanked her with his dying thoughts. For killing him.

His brow raised, Kiron offered her the knife. "I can make you something better for that job. Come see me after the gathering and we'll figure out what'll work best for you."

"Gathering?" She returned the blade to its sheath.

Kiron snorted. "I'm not surprised that nobody ever mentioned it. The bell. It's for a gathering. When it rings once, everyone is supposed to drop whatever you're doing and come up here. This is the only place big enough to hold us all without going outside. If it rings three times, it means the tower is under attack."

"Ah. Of course. This is the obvious answer."

He grinned. "Exactly."

Chavali watched people pour into the room from below. Eldrack arrived with Aislynn and both stopped by the wide archway at the head of the stairs. Uninterested in others knowing of her full complicity in this, Chavali moved deeper into the room. She recognized many people, but stopped when she saw Rennet, a woman she'd met in Eagle Falls.

Rennet, who stood shorter than Chavali, wore fur-lined slippers with her plain linens. Her dark hair stuck out at odd angles, and she yawned. Someone still half-asleep had little chance of saying anything to fray Chavali's already strained temper.

She flashed Rennet a friendly smile and opened her mouth to greet the woman. Before a sound escaped her, Eldrack's voice filled the room. Chatter across the room ceased.

"Thank you all for assembling with haste. Princess Aislynn is here with us, and she wishes to address you on an urgent matter."

Chavali noticed a murmur rippling through the room. She thought it interesting Eldrack would lay this at Aislynn's feet instead of making the announcement himself.

Aislynn's voice boomed across the room. "As I'm sure most of you are aware, a Fallen agent was murdered a few weeks ago. His death came as a direct result of someone in this room passing information about his route and mission to unknown parties."

The room heaved a collective gasp that seemed torn between shock and disgust. Not wanting to tip her hand about knowing this already, Chavali pretended to find this distressing. This fabrication took little effort.

"Until such time as this person's identity is revealed and confirmed, all Fallen agents, healers, and other personnel are hereby sequestered inside Cloverdale and will be subject to individual interviews. No one is allowed to venture beyond the outer ring of buildings except with special permission from me, which will only be granted to those wishing to assist the farmers working in their fields. Fallen agents will patrol the perimeter with assistance from members of my guard retinue to ensure compliance with this order."

Defiant shouts bounced off the walls, drowning out Aislynn's attempt to continue her announcement. Rennet sighed and rubbed her face. Chavali felt the same.

"SILENCE!" Eldrack's one-word shout quieted the room. "This is not a forum for grievances, and we serve at the King's pleasure."

Aislynn continued. "Should the individual responsible wish to come forward, know that I do not suspect you passed this information with malicious intent, and the crime is minor. As such, if you turn yourself in by dusk, punishment will not be severe. There's no need to fear trial, imprisonment, or worse. Likewise, if you think you may have inadvertently assisted, come see me without fear of judgment. Let's resolve this swiftly together so everyone can resume their routines and the Spring Festival can happen as scheduled. Those on the first patrol shift will be notified shortly. Thank you."

Thick, seething anger filled the space. Chavali vibrated with it. Harris's true murderer would go unpunished. That fact filled her with so much unwavering, unyielding rage she could barely see.

She didn't believe for one moment the informant had cared whether anyone died or not, or that they'd given the information without realizing it could happen. That person deserved worse than death. They deserved the slow, agonizing bleed Harris had suffered with grace and an astonishing amount of integrity.

If she discovered the traitor before Aislynn or Eldrack...

She needed that new dagger.

CHAPTER 8

Chavali retreated to the privacy of her room. Pacing from one side to the other of the small space, she waited for her thoughts to settle. More than anything, she needed rest. Between the tasks of convincing Alene to sacrifice for Harris and discovering who'd betrayed him, she couldn't decide which should take priority. Each demanded all her time and effort. She doubted she could do both at once.

Of course, Harris's corpse couldn't cause more trouble, unlike the traitor.

According to Karias, this situation should cause them to panic or make a mistake. If they tried to leave, Chavali had no doubt the patrols would catch them. Likewise, she suspected Aislynn would have the archives monitored.

If she wanted to discover the traitor before Aislynn had a chance to whisk them away in a swirl of forgiveness, she needed to move fast.

She pictured Harris as he'd appeared in the eyes of his murderer. He lay on the ground, surrounded by trees and errant grasses. A single, bright yellow flower shone in a thin ray of sunshine beside him. His chest rose and fell with the rapid breaths of pain and impending death. Far too much dark, wet blood covered everything.

The man who had tortured him for lying had approached his grim task with amusement and enjoyment.

Harris's final breath had rattled out as a groan that sounded like the word "vengeance" with him staring at his killer.

Chavali wondered if he'd known she would see it later.

Something in his brown eyes reached for her, accusing her of not coming to help him. While he'd endured pain beyond her comprehension, she'd been playing games with the children.

Then Harris fled, leaving behind an empty, still shell. The killer had lamented the severity of Harris's initial injuries, because there hadn't been enough time to torture him properly.

Chavali covered her face and rubbed her eyes, though that did nothing to banish his haunting stare. No wonder she couldn't sleep.

Harris lay on a slab in the deepest depths of the tower, waiting for her to find words to express this gaping hole he'd left, when she didn't know the boundaries of it.

How long did she have? Would they give up waiting for her and bury him? She wanted to see him, though she knew already that she didn't. His killer hadn't had time to put out Harris's eyes, but he'd done more than enough. If she failed to convince Alene, would they let her have a finger bone to add to her collection?

With that thought, she realized she had no relics of her own clan beyond a few aged bones in her bauble pouch, yet she wished for one from this near-stranger. Finding bones of her clan meant going back to the site of the attack. She doubted anyone had made the effort to collect bodies and bury them. More likely, the nearby town had left the site to the elements.

She opened a drawer and retrieved a wad of smooth, dark cloth.

Within it, she kept her Seer's pendant, the only true piece of her clan she possessed. Clan Seers had decorated it with tiny carvings for hundreds of years until no space remained for additions. Rubbing her thumb over the aged metal, she remembered Seer Marika.

Above all, nothing is more important than clan. Her predecessor had repeated that mantra hundreds of times during Chavali's five years of apprenticeship. Everyone knew this, but the Seer embodied it.

If only she could convince someone to bring back more of her clan...but they had no bodies. And she could imagine Papá's horrified reaction when he learned of the sacrifice made on his behalf. No one would appreciate the binding to the Fallen.

Still, the idea appealed to her. She missed Pasha. Her feelings toward Keino carried far more complexity, but she'd rather have him than not.

Covering the pendant again, she pushed the thoughts away. Clan came first, but the living came before the dead, and the Seer needed rest to tend the living members of her clan. All five of them.

She sighed and sat on the edge of her bed. No one she'd yet encountered and considered worthy of inviting into the clan could or would bear children.

Penny and Marcus had left childbearing behind many years ago. Eliot and Patrick might adopt a child, but they'd never bear their own. Even if one or both fathered children, the mother's blood mattered, not the father's. The same applied to Colby. Whatever sort of idiot woman he attracted would obviously never earn Chavali's approval. Kelly had already revealed she couldn't bear children long before explaining why.

She sipped water from a glass on her nightstand and thought she needed to spend more time with women like Portia, Violet, and Rennet. Any of them would bring valuable skills and an infusion of interesting talents. When Harris recovered from his death, she thought she'd consider asking him.

This matter needed to lie for a while, much like Chavali. She set her glass down and lay on the bed. Closing her eyes, she thought she'd leave the matter of Harris's memories for later.

Between one breath and another, she opened her eyes with her hand on the knob of a sturdy, brown wooden door. Light rain fell, pattering on the thin, gray overhang protecting her. Behind her lay a swirling, muddy road lined with small houses crammed together with only a gray stone step separating each from the water sluicing down the sides of the street.

She opened the door to a drab, dingy house filled with too-large furniture in drab, dingy colors. A shadowy pall clung to the corners and a damp chill huddled on her shoulders. Stepping inside, she heard the distant buzz of arguing adults and the faint cry of a child in distress.

Two boys, one man, and one woman sat on the couch as if posing for a portrait. None smiled. They shared a minimal amount of touch.

They wore the coarse clothing of the working poor. The woman kept her dark hair under a drab kerchief. She seemed tired, harried, and miserable. Beside her, lines etched the man's face and weariness pushed his broad shoulders down, suggesting a life of outdoor labor.

On his lap, the older boy sat up straight and tall. A bright aura of strength and resilience surrounded him, and he held up a fist with a determined frown. The younger boy sat on his mother's lap with his face buried in his hands and his shoulders hunched.

With their tanned skin, dark hair, and brown eyes, she noted the similarities of their features and guessed at the identity of the young boy—Harris.

This depiction suggested he thought of his childhood as unhappy, though she thought he seemed the same age as Danel. Earlier years might have been happier.

Though she doubted interacting with the memory would accomplish anything positive, she reached for Harris. The moment her pink-painted fingernails touched his soft hair, the image spun. She stood in the center of a whirlwind. All four of them shifted around her as if she traveled through time too fast to stop and focus on any one event.

The disconnect faded in a brighter, cheerier version of the room, though the scenery still drifted beyond the primary focal point of Harris, a year or two younger, snuggling with his mother on the couch. She struggled to help him read a book beyond her own meager skill. They sounded out the letters together, taking their time with each word. As soon as he grasped a word, she kissed his cheek.

They disappeared, replaced with the father and his sons. While the boys played with sticks and colored rocks on the floor, the father sat and watched, too tired to participate. He offered encouragement between sips from a wooden cup.

Again, the scene shifted, the light dimmer. While the mother sliced bread for dinner, she tried to help the boys practice simple math at the table. Her skills couldn't match the older boy's, so he helped Harris and worked through his own by talking it out with his mother.

Another scene change displayed the father berating his sons for throwing a ball inside the house and breaking an oil lamp. The older boy shielded Harris, standing in front of him and taking the blame despite Harris's culpability. While Harris watched, his father took his older brother by the scruff of his neck for punishment outside.

More moments flashed past, showing both parents gradually growing more distant and Harris relying more and more on his older brother. Through all of them, the scenery remained a blur...until it all stopped in a different room.

Two beds stacked one atop the other occupied a dark room. Ragged curtains hung over a small window in one wall. Harris huddled under the blankets of the lower bed. His parents shouted on the other side of the door, about things he didn't understand. White flashed in the room. Harris's father suddenly stood in the room, bathed in morning sunshine from the open window and dragging Harris to his knees by the front of his shirt.

Harris cringed and cowered. "It was an accident, Papa, I swear!"

His father flung a handful of coins hard enough to hurt. "You call this an accident?" His voice slurred and his breath stank of alcohol. "This is stealing, boy. You know what they do to thieves?"

"I didn't mean to," Harris wailed. "Another boy—"

"Don't you blame someone else!" His father slapped him. "You always let someone else take the blame! Not this time." He kicked Harris in the gut and kept attacking, reminding Chavali of the beating Harris had taken at the hands of his gang.

Another white flash burst in the room and the father disappeared. The light shifted to the gloom of a rainy afternoon. Harris rummaged through drawers in a dresser, looking for a second clean sock to match the one in his hand. He jumped at the sound of crashing glass or pottery through the open window. No, he knew it was pottery. Mom's only vase had shattered into hundreds of shards. Harris did it.

The door flew open and his brother ran inside, holding his shoulder and dragging one foot as fast as he could. Blood drenched him, from head to toe.

"Go!" His brother glanced behind himself and pointed to the window. "Run while you can! I'm right behind you!"

Harris panicked. His brother shoved him toward the window. With a gulp, Harris dove through the window, smashing it. Chavali jumped after him to land in the kitchen. The family sat for a plentiful dinner, smiling in the glow of the oil lamp.

The brother beamed at Harris, his mouth full of roast potato. With food stuffed into his cheek, he said, "He got all the answers right on the spelling test today."

"Don't talk with your mouth full," the father said with an indulgent smile.

"I'm very proud of you. You're a smart boy." The mother patted Harris's hand.

In the distance, Chavali heard a strange, high-pitched noise. None of the people in the memory noticed it, so she didn't know what to think.

As the family continued to act like an ideal of warmth and loving, the noise grew in volume until it sounded like the shriek made by scraping metal across a stone, except with unending breath behind it.

Chavali covered her ears to no effect. A black puppy jumped to get Harris's attention. He laughed and set his plate on the floor for the dog. The creature blinked at Chavali as if to tell her it heard the screaming, and liked it.

CHAPTER 9

The sound faded as Chavali opened her eyes to see the stone ceiling of her room. She'd left her light stone out again. Sitting up, she noticed aches and pains all over her body. Her throat felt raw. Perhaps that screaming had been her own voice.

She reached for her glass of water and grasped empty air. When she leaned to check for it, she found a spray of broken glass on the floor.

She'd never thrashed in her sleep before.

Harris's memories seemed to affect her like Keino's spirit had. That experience had taught her to get help when these things went wrong. Meeting with Railan now, though, seemed problematic.

They'd do things Aislynn's people might detect or otherwise notice. This topic ranked second after clan on the list of things she preferred not to discuss with inquisitors of any sort.

Sliding off the bed on the other side, she cringed at her unhappy muscles. That wretched dream must have had her clenched and tense for her entire nap, however long it had lasted. She snatched her robe and padded to the bathroom. A hot bath helped soothe her body, though it did nothing for her mind.

She shuddered with a deep, sudden ache for Harris. So far, she'd kept busy enough to evade mourning. In the solitude of hot water and steam, she stared at the wall and thought of his clumsy attempts to woo her. As she remembered him waggling his eyebrows at her, another crushing wave of grief overcame her.

Tears rolled down her cheeks. He'd been such a pain in the ass.

Something between a laugh and a sob, both and neither, choked out of her as she felt a third heavy pang of loss. She remembered him pretending to stumble across her by accident. Exhausted from a round of intense combat training with Eliot, she'd waved him off and said nothing.

Once again, a torrent of grief rolled over her. She considered, not for the first time, slipping under the surface of her bath and refusing to save herself. But that was as stupid an idea now as it had been every other time she thought it. Harris hadn't been the sum of her world, and feeling this much for his loss seemed...odd.

To stem the flow of thoughts about Harris, his death, and his childhood, she focused on combing her wet hair without catching the feather.

When she returned to her room, she kept herself moving. She re-strung the beads on a lock of her hair. She braided the second feather, which she rarely wore here, into a different lock. She used her one book to sweep up the glass shards. Using a sleep shirt as a makeshift bag, she carried the glass to the door to dispose of it into a bathroom trash can.

On the other side of her door stood a tower servant, interrupted in the act of raising her fist to knock. Both paused and stared at each other. Chavali broke the strange, awkward silence.

"What does Eldrack want?"

"I don't know. I was sent to ask you to come to meeting room five."

Eldrack wouldn't send her on a mission now unless the traitor had confessed already. Even then, she'd been clear about wanting to stay here for a while. If he thought she'd willingly leave for another idiotic mission to keep her busy, he was wrong. She could talk him into sending someone else.

"What time is it? And can you take care of this for me?" She held up the shirt-pouch. "I broke a glass. But I want the shirt back."

"Yes, of course. It's six in the morning." The woman took the bundle and hurried down the hall.

Chavali blinked in surprise. She'd slept for most of a day and night, and still felt tired. Perhaps she'd slept too long for some reason, though that didn't explain her body aching. She could've been locked in the memories without realizing it. The experience had felt like a nightmare, not a memory. Except she'd acted in some parts and only observed in others.

Stepping into the hall and closing her door, she frowned. After wrangling with Eldrack, she'd seek out Railan. She needed guidance from an experienced telepath. Whatever Eldrack wanted, he'd be persuaded by her issues with the memories, especially if she admitted how long she'd slept.

Few people roamed the halls or stairs at this hour. Chavali passed no one she knew on her way to the thirteenth floor. Meeting room five had two occupants when she arrived. She didn't recognize either man sitting in two of the eight chairs around the polished wood table. Expecting they must be Fallen, despite the folder in one man's hand, Chavali ignored them and sat to wait for Eldrack.

"Charuly Blookeen?"

She raised an eyebrow at the man with the folder and gave him a closer look. Though his clothing seemed casual on first glance, the shirt, tunic, and pants fit him well, with a flattering cut for the muscle underneath. His rough hands managed the folder well, but without the smooth ease of a bureaucrat. Combined with his middling age and the shortness of the sword belted at his waist, she guessed he must be a guard who'd moved into a less active position within the past few years, and didn't like it.

The second man also dressed well, in a shirt, vest, and pants. The pockets and buttons of his vest all bore the same symbol, a stylized mountain peak with an arc slashed across it. The Order of the High Path, people who centered their Greatest Sin beliefs around the distribution and protection of knowledge, used that symbol.

The Truthfinders came from that order. Chavali's one previous encounter with such a person had left the other woman in tears.

This meeting meant the traitor remained at large, and Aislynn had chosen to have Chavali interrogated early by a former guardsman and an idiot obsessed with truth.

Which made Aislynn a petty brat.

Chavali offered the first man a smile so fake a child could see through it. "Chastity. And you?"

He frowned and opened his folder. "I'm Dowal. This is Truthfinder Andres. That's not the name listed here, and that's clearly not your name."

"If you say so."

Andres furrowed his brow and stared at her. She ignored him.

Running his finger down the paper in his folder, Dowal chewed on his lip. "There can't be anyone else with a feather like that. How do you pronounce your name?"

"Is this some kind of inquest relating to my accent?" She chose to let slide her usual attention to soften the clan accent, instead allowing it to thicken. For good measure, she stopped making an effort to remember to use contractions in her speech. "This is quite rude. I have no more control over it than you do over your receding hairline."

Dowal snapped his head up and narrowed his eyes at her. "I beg your pardon?"

"I appreciate begging, but I doubt it will gain you anything. I am quite particular about what kinds of appeals I accept."

Andres huffed. "That, at least, was true."

"This is an interview ordered by Princess Aislynn," Dowal snapped. "Do you understand?"

"Perhaps."

"Please answer yes or no," Andres said.

"Yes or no." Watching the two men grow irritated with her refusal to cooperate filled Chavali with a warm glow of satisfaction. She rested her chin in her hand, her elbow on the table.

Dowal growled. "Look, missy. I've dealt with people like you before."

"I doubt that."

"You think you're so smart." Dowal huffed. "Fine. When was the last time you saw Harris?"

"This morning."

"That's impossible," Andres said. He turned to Dowal. "That can't be true. He's dead."

Dowal jabbed a finger at her. "Did you sneak past the guards to go see his body?"

Chavali had to stop herself from laughing. The corner of her mouth twitched despite her best efforts. "Do you frequently visit corpses? Is that something the Princess and her people consider normal? Consorting with death is unclean."

"When was the last time you saw Harris while he was still alive?" Dowal asked through gritted teeth. "I don't care if you were alive then or not."

"Ah," Chavali said, as if this phrasing meant she would behave for them. "That was yesterday. Today, I have only seen him dead."

"This is pointless," Andres said with a huff. "She's still telling the truth. Which makes no sense. I can't get any control over her."

She bared her teeth. "This is a common problem among men. Ask anyone here. They will agree."

Dowal snapped his folder shut. "We'll see how funny you are when Princess Aislynn interviews you herself. Get out."

Chavali stood and turned with a swirl of her skirt.

Yes, Princess Aislynn would see what happened when she faced the Seer of the Blaukenev clan, in a war over secrets and lies.

CHAPTER 10

"You look terrible," Kelly said as she sat beside Chavali in the dining hall. "And also smug." Her tray held a muffin, a bowl of cereal, and a large glass of milk.

Chavali shrugged. She had a cup of tea and nothing else yet. "Aislynn has no idea what she has unleashed here."

"Your accent is thick this morning. Are you getting enough sleep?"

"Perhaps not."

"Hm. Cagey too. I take it the interviews have begun, and you've already irritated one of her minions."

Chavali snorted. "Am I so predictable?"

"Only for certain things. Do you want to come to my office to talk about why you're not sleeping? Or are you ready to speak with Alene?"

"I believe I require Railan's expertise." She wanted to face Alene, but knew she needed to sort out all the memories first. "Have you seen her? I have not in several days."

"No, but that's not uncommon. I understand she leaves on errands from time to time. At this point, I don't know if they'd let her back in."

"Not without interrogation, certainly. Speaking with you may assist, but I believe the problem is more of a..." Chavali groped for the right word and found none.

"Telepath thing?"

"Yes."

Kelly nodded and ate her cereal. They sat in silence for several minutes. When Kelly pushed her bowl aside, she leaned close and murmured, "Are you sure you don't want to talk about Harris?"

His last gasp filled her mind. That desperate stare and those glassy eyes sent a shiver down her spine. She winced as it woke the aches she'd eased in the tub. "Perhaps. But not now. I promised my time to the children. I have not seen them enough lately."

"I understand. They do you a lot of good anyway, so I can hardly complain."

Chavali nodded, agreeing with the sentiment. Seeing her clan usually did improve her mood. "I have given more consideration to your interest in joining the clan, and believe I will bring it up. If you still wish this, of course. If you have changed your mind…?"

"No." Kelly smiled. "I'd like to be part of something full of that much joy. And I'd be delighted to help raise those children, as well as any others who come along. I always wanted…" She sighed. "If I can't have my own, someone else's will suffice."

Amused by the idea of becoming responsible for the well-being of the woman whose duty revolved around responsibility for Chavali's well-being, Chavali nodded. "Then I will speak to Marcus and Penny. They will likely want to meet you first, and perhaps get to know you before agreeing."

"Thank you for explaining."

At least one thing had settled. Chavali stood. "I believe I am ready to eat now."

By the time she returned with food, Kelly had gone. Chavali ate in peace, surrounded by the hum of conversation at other tables. She planned to spend her day with the children, hoping to avoid most people. On the way up the stairs to her room, she evaded Sean and his healer wife by ducking behind people between them. Her escape from the tower otherwise proved uneventful.

In the tavern, Walt caught her eye and flicked his gaze to a man sitting at the bar. The gentleman in question, someone she considered plain and ordinary, lifted his head to see her. Chavali noted his gaze traveling to her feather, then he scribbled in the book lying open in front of him. Though she would have spotted him as out of place on her own, she appreciated Walt drawing attention to him. Aislynn had men trying to blend in.

For the next few days, Chavali tried to adhere to a routine in visiting the clan. Every night, she faced more strange memory-dream-nightmares and woke less rested than the day before.

Three days in, Sean cornered her on the way out of his interview, all smiles and glowing, wanting to compare notes.

"Chavali!" Eliot bellowed from behind her, offering an avenue of escape. "Where's your dagger? How many times have I told you to never walk around unarmed?" He grabbed her arm before she had a chance to thank him and hauled her down the nearest hallway. "Sloppy. Foolish. You're supposed to hate fools!"

She yanked her arm without dislodging his steely grip. "If I carry my dagger at a time like this, I'll stab someone. Like you, for example."

He thumped her against the wall and stuck his finger in her face.

"You'd never have the chance," he growled. The muscles on his wiry frame held her in place with little effort. They stood near the same height, making it easy for him to glare into her eyes. "Because you don't practice enough. We're going to fix that."

Guessing he'd also just come out of his interview, Chavali let him vent. The Seer took care of her clan, even if they hadn't been inducted yet.

He hustled her into a practice room and moved so fast he might as well have been made of lightning. Before she had a chance to react, he held his knife at her throat from behind.

She'd been in this position before. Then, Keino had rescued her. Now, she had to rescue herself from her teacher.

Of all his lessons, she'd been most appreciative of the one most useful in this situation, and had convinced Colby to let her practice against him for added challenge.

Colby wore protective gear for those practice sessions. Eliot had no such luxury. Chavali jabbed her elbow into his gut. With Colby, because he stood so much taller than her, the elbow strike had proved effective on its own.

Despite that, she'd practiced a foot stomp and punch to the privates for use against lesser men. Such as Eliot.

Eliot dropped his dagger and groaned. Chavali twisted away, kicked his knee, and scooped the blade off the floor.

While she bounced out of his reach, he fell to the floor in a crumpled heap.

Aware of his skills with faking distress, she stayed on guard. "I believe that I do, in fact, practice enough."

"You win," Eliot said, his voice a strangled croak.

Chavali remained out of reach as she sat on the sanded wood floor. She dropped the dagger and noticed her hands shaking. Though she hadn't feared he would kill her, he'd been enraged enough for her to believe he might hurt her and regret it later.

"What did they ask about?" She gripped her knees to stop the shaking.

"Patrick. Eagle Falls."

Chavali knew every mission concluded with a report. She'd assisted with composing them on multiple occasions. Aislynn couldn't have gone through every report...but she could have elected to review all of Chavali's mission reports because of her interview performance.

If so, Chavali's situation could have put all the werewolves of Eagle Falls in a precarious position.

"Are they in danger from the Crown?"

"I don't know." He covered his face and laid flat on his back. "They think Patrick is a security risk. And I was supposed to go see him for a few days, but the tower lockdown stopped that. I can't even get a message to him to let him know why I didn't show up."

"Should he attempt to find out, the guard patrols will likely explain it."

"And that'll go so well."

Chavali smirked. "I apologize for using such a base attack on you to get free. But I have been practicing."

Eliot sat up with a wince. "I can tell. It was my fault for attacking with a knife. I'm just going to sit here for a while. You can go."

"As soon as I leave, someone else will attack me. It's inevitable." She shifted closer and leaned her back against his. "I'll hide here for a while, thank you."

He chuckled, then he sighed. "I broke a chair."

"I broke a Truthfinder. Mine is, perhaps, the worse crime. I feel no remorse, though. The next one I meet won't fare any better. They may, in fact, suffer more."

Two more people stepped into the room and stopped. Portia blinked and stared at Chavali and Eliot, her eyes crackling with too-long-unspent mage energy. Aside from her South Cascain coloring, she reminded Chavali of Chavali's little sister, Pasha. Behind her, Teryk's broad shoulders filled the doorway. His gaze went to the dagger.

"Are either of you hurt?" Portia asked.

"No." Chavali grinned. "I beat up my teacher. His ego requires recovery time."

Eliot laughed until he fell onto his side and curled into a ball.

"We may yet be here for a while," Chavali said. "Perhaps finding a different training room would be prudent."

Portia nodded and pushed Teryk out as she left the room.

"I hate being surprised by who chooses to bed whom," Chavali said as soon as she felt confident neither Portia nor Teryk would overhear. "Mecalle nobility doesn't seem her type. I thought she'd be attracted to someone more like you, except interested in women."

Eliot subsided and sat up to lean against her again. "Are you gossiping at me?"

"Of course not. I don't gossip. I make observations."

"Of course. You know, you and Colby train together."

"And? You and I also train together."

"That's all Portia and Teryk were here to do."

"Yes, that's why he put a hand on her shoulder and let her do all the talking." She shook her head and pointed at the door even though Eliot couldn't see it. "Teryk is a leader. He can't help it. He takes charge and gets things done. When that kind of person lets someone else do all the talking, they're smitten."

"Uh huh. Maybe you didn't notice, but Colby is a leader. He led a military unit. As far as I understand, he was good at it. If he hadn't died, he probably would've ended up high in the chain of command. You've trained him pretty well to keep his mouth shut."

Chavali's mood slipped as she wondered why everyone insisted upon pairing her with such an insufferable man. "Your attempts at humor fall flat today."

"Sure. Just making an observation."

Changing the subject seemed prudent. Chavali sighed and rubbed her eyes. "I'd like to know if you and Patrick might have interest in joining the clan."

After a long pause, Eliot said, "Patrick can't leave Eagle Falls."

"I am aware of this, yes. I doubt anything about your location situation would change, though induction into the clan might give him more control over his shapeshifting while away from the flowers. Not that I wish to give you false hope. It's merely a possibility. Exposure to the clan's binding could as easily make this worse."

He leaned away from her, and when she turned, she saw him watching her with a serious frown. "Are you sure you want to offer that?"

"Yes. I believe you both would be a great benefit to the clan, even though you would never provide children. The others may disagree, but I'm certain I can convince them."

Looking away from her, he furrowed his brow. She appreciated him taking the moment to consider it and come up with questions. "Do you think the clan will go back to traveling when your term is up?"

Chavali shook her head. "Those of us left have little skill with wagon-making or upkeep, and there aren't enough of us to handle all the chores yet. It seems unlikely, at least at first. The children are learning farming skills anyway." She shrugged. "Much can change in five years."

"That's true. I'll talk it over with Patrick. Whenever I can see him, I mean." He held out his hand.

She clasped his forearm, using their sleeves to avoid skin contact. "Take your time. It's no less weighty than being Fallen, in some ways. If he has questions, I can visit him to discuss it."

They helped each other stand, then he hugged her. "Thank you. I know what this means to you. I'm honored by the offer."

CHAPTER 11

Five days into Aislynn's quarantine, Chavali's temper had frayed too much to spend time in the tower anymore. If she had found Railan, she thought she'd stay, but the woman failed to appear. Eldrack had no time to even answer whether or not Railan was in the tower. Chavali gathered enough clothing to stay at the farmhouse with her clan for a few days and set out in the afternoon.

On her way to the house, she saw a mounted patrol of two Fallen with two soldier escorts riding toward her. Teryk rode the lead horse, but Chavali didn't know the other Fallen by name, or either soldier.

"Chavali! Stop where you are!" Teryk called out. On horseback, he looked like a smaller, less insufferable version of Colby.

She considered ignoring him, but had no reason to do so other than pique. Under some circumstances, that provided enough incentive, but not today. The fresh air and subtle scent of blooming flowers had already brushed away the annoyance of encountering bickering Fallen and healers wherever she went. Both unfortunately also provided reminders of the indefinite delay the Spring Festival had suffered.

Four horses surrounded her. Chavali knew enough about the creatures to understand the danger of her position. To defuse it, she held her hand out for Teryk's horse to sniff and scratched under its chin. The creature's simple thoughts spoke of concern for loud noises and an itch under its saddle.

"Sorry to bother you, Chavali. Just following orders." Teryk nodded to the two soldiers.

She rubbed the horse's nose. "Sunshine, flowers, crickets, and inquisition. Perfect for a picnic. No wonder so many are out today to enjoy the fine weather."

The others chuckled. Teryk smirked at her, though he seemed unamused. "Where are you going?"

Batting her eyelashes and smiling, she said, "I thought I might stroll up the road to use the Creator's Tower for a visit to Mecalle."

"Don't be cute."

"Then don't treat your colleagues like idiots. I'm staying inside the town. Beyond that is none of your business."

"Why are you carrying a pack?"

"Training purposes."

Teryk tried to stare her down. She ignored him and murmured to the horse.

"Why do you look so...gaunt?" he asked. "You don't usually have circles under your eyes. Guilt keeping you up all night?"

"Obviously, that's the only possible reason. Look, you've caught me. I'm the traitor because I can't sleep lately."

He narrowed his eyes and pursed his lips.

"C'mon, Teryk," the other Fallen said with a huff and a roll of her eyes. "We should get back to the perimeter."

Nodding, he led the group away. Chavali waited for the horses to trot a good distance away before resuming her walk. When she reached Marcus and Penny's house, she walked inside without knocking.

"You're a stupid pile of maggots," Danel snapped.

Haizea added, "And goat poop!"

"You listen to me," a man said. "I can have you removed from this village if you don't answer our questions."

Ignoring the mud on her boots, Chavali stormed into the living room and filled the doorway with her rage. Dowal and his pet Truthfinder Andres stood in the center of the room while the two young children huddled together on the couch. Papers with rudimentary drawings and lettering lay scattered on the floor with abandoned pieces of charcoal.

"Try it and see what happens," Chavali snarled.

Dowal glared at her. "Maybe I will."

"Does Aislynn know you're here, threatening children?"

"She sent us."

Though Dowal twitched as if Aislynn might not have phrased her orders that way, Chavali didn't care. Aislynn had sent these men, making her responsible for their behavior. If she thought storming underground to confront the princess would solve anything, she would've done it. But she'd come for her clan, and would stay with them.

"Get out," she snapped.

Dowal crossed his arms. "You can't throw us out."

"I can kill you, which is close enough."

Andres gulped. "She means that."

"Of course I mean that. Threatening my family makes you my enemy. I don't care who you work for. The Creator herself can't save you from my wrath, let alone the King or his daughter."

"We should go," Andres whispered.

Dowal's lip curled in half a sneer. "The Princess will hear about this."

"Yes. She will." Chavali pointed to the door.

Andres slunk past her like a dog with his tail between his legs. Dowal, on the other hand, swaggered as if he'd decided to leave of his own accord.

Whether Aislynn apologized for this or not, Dowal had earned Chavali's hate.

The moment the door shut, she swooped in and wrapped her arms around both children. They clung to her. To soothe them, she used the clan tongue. "They're gone. You're safe. Where is everyone else?"

"Penny and Biholtz went to the market to get flour," Danel reported. "Marcus is outside. Those men wouldn't let us get him, and they said we'd be in trouble if we shouted for him."

"We called them names," Haizea said.

"Yes, you did. I'm proud of you for being so brave and following your Seer's instructions so well."

Both children beamed under her praise. The back door opened and Marcus hurried inside.

"Danel? Haizea? Are you here?"

"Yes, they're fine," Chavali called to him. She saw him hurry into view.

Relief smoothed his wrinkles. "I saw two men leaving and thought they might've carted the kids off. I only stepped outside for a few minutes. Thank the Creator you happened by. What did they want?"

Chavali bared her teeth. "To fire a salvo in a war against the clan.

They will get more than they bargained for."

She spent the rest of the day helping Danel and Haizea practice better insults, cleaning up the mud she'd tracked in, and strategizing with Marcus and Penny.

At night, though Chavali slept better in a pile with the children, her Harris-themed nightmares continued unabated. Moments from his life flitted past in disjointed streams, showing her pieces of his life as a street kid, a pickpocket, a smuggler, and a bandit.

In the morning, Chavali sat in the kitchen with Danel on her lap and surrounded by clan for breakfast, when someone knocked on the door. Biholtz jumped to her feet and answered it. Everyone heard her greet the visitor with warm welcome.

"I can't stay," Colby said. The door shut. "I just need to talk to Chavali."

Danel slid to the floor, letting her go. Chavali stood and stepped into the hall. She smiled at the sight of Colby ducking his head to keep from hitting it on the ceiling. He wore his armor, though, and his smile in return seemed strained.

"Good morning," she said. "Are you on a mission?"

"No. I just finished a patrol. A servant asked me to deliver a message so she didn't have to slog all the way out here. You've been summoned for an interview in Eldrack's office. I can give you a ride in."

"Ah. You haven't slept yet."

"You don't look like fresh sunshine either."

She waved him off. "No one does lately. I'll be a minute."

"I'll wait outside."

Chavali knew everyone had heard. She said goodbye and took a jam-slathered biscuit for Colby. By the time she stepped outside, he waited on Karias's back. She handed him the biscuit first, then stepped on his foot and took his help to climb behind him. One hand on Colby kept her in place. The other on the horse's back let her hear Karias.

These patrols are awful. Everyone hates doing it, and the soldiers are real bores. If you can make it stop by spewing venom at people, do it.

"I'm surprised they didn't interview you sooner," Colby said as they trotted through town.

"They did."

"Ah. I'm glad you've been able to spend some time with the clan. I was worried when I couldn't find you anywhere for the past few days, but I should've realized you'd come up here."

She arched an eyebrow. "Why were you looking for me?"

"You didn't show up for your reading lesson."

And you haven't come to visit me with treats again. You didn't even bring me a treat this morning, which I take a personal insult.

"Oh. I forgot about it. I'm sorry."

"I don't blame you. Even I'm having trouble keeping my temper in check. Stupid fights keep breaking out in the dining hall and stairwell. No wonder Eldrack likes to send us all out on stupid little missions. We're terrible all trapped in one place."

They reached the tavern. Karias stopped and Chavali took Colby's help to climb to the ground. She patted Karias's flank.

Venom, Chavali. Toxic, noxious venom. Be horrible. Do it for the clan.

She stifled a grin and waved to Colby. "I'll see you later."

"Let's take a quick run before heading inside, Karias. I need some real air."

Chavali watched the horse launch into a gallop, wishing she could join them for the ride. With a sigh, she entered the tavern and waved to Walt. He nodded to her with a keen look as if to wish her luck. He'd probably overheard the servant asking for Colby's help, or maybe he'd heard rumors.

She plunged into the tower, readying herself to duel with Aislynn. The woman had done more than enough to earn Chavali's worst, and she'd get it.

Each level Chavali passed sank her mood deeper into the colorful flavors of anger. Though she encountered no arguments on the stairwell, the entire column felt charged with annoyance, as if the stones reflected it.

By the time she reached Eldrack's office, she had to stop outside the door to smooth her expression away. Inside, the enemy wanted knowledge she refused to give them. She would not be bent or broken.

With one final deep breath, she stepped inside the office, interrupting a conversation between Eldrack, Aislynn, and a Truthfinder. Though she didn't recognize the Truthfinder, she didn't care. He, like all his kind, shared the same stupid ideas.

"Chavali, please come in." Eldrack pointed to the chair she usually took with an air of grave concern.

She stepped behind the chair. "I'll stand."

"No." Aislynn gave her a mildly annoyed glare. "Sit."

"No, thank you."

"If she wants to stand," Eldrack said, "that's fine. We don't need to begin this with a pointless, petty argument."

"Yes," Chavali said, "let's move straight to the pointless, petty interrogation."

Aislynn huffed and shot a heated glare at Eldrack. "Fine." With a wave at the Truthfinder, she said, "Orlin, ask your control questions."

"State your full name, please." Orlin had a pleasant, melodious voice.

"Chavali. I have no family name. "

Orlin blinked at her. "You're supposed to answer these questions honestly."

Aislynn picked up a thick folder and waved it at Chavali. "There's a family name in your file."

"Ah, but is it my family name? Perhaps I made it up for Eldrack's benefit so he'd have something to put in that space in the file. Or, perhaps, my family used it as a name even though it's not our name to make everyone else comfortable. There really are many possibilities, aren't there?"

She saw Eldrack's mouth twitch a tiny amount.

Aislynn rolled her eyes. "Stop playing games and answer the control questions." She gestured for Orlin to continue.

"How old are you?"

"Twenty."

"That's not true either," Orlin said with a huff.

"Or is it? Such hubris."

"Your file claims you're twenty-six," Aislynn said.

Chavali narrowed her eyes. "Does my file indicate the ages of the two children your men came to interrogate and threaten without an adult present? I can assist if it does not. They are four and six. Would you not consider such persons too young for such treatment?"

"Of course they are," Aislynn said, "but that's not what happened."

"It is nice to know that men searching for liars can find them by looking in a mirror." Chavali noticed her temper flaring and knew she needed to keep it under control. If she let it rule her, she'd say things she didn't mean in ways she'd regret.

"Please," Orlin said. "I just need a few honest answers from you. Can you give me that?"

"Yes, of course."

Orlin rubbed his face. "I think I understand why Andres is so upset."

Eldrack rubbed his forehead, hiding a half-smothered grin from both Aislynn and Orlin, but not Chavali.

"Fine," Aislynn snapped. "Never mind him. Are you loyal to the Fallen?"

"Yes."

"What's wrong with you?" Orlin moaned.

"So your loyalty is questionable," Aislynn said, her eyes narrowed. "I see. What's the price? How much did you sell out Harris for?"

Once again, Chavali restrained the urge to slap Princess Aislynn. "I do not have a price," she growled. "Do not make the mistake of thinking you understand me. My loyalty lies with my clan first and the Fallen second. You do not place on that list."

"The clan." Aislynn's eyes glittered like she'd uncovered a precious gem where she expected garbage. She flipped open the folder and pointed to a piece of paper Chavali recognized as a mission report. "In direct defiance of Fallen procedures, you brought three children into the Fallen tower without permission, and refused to give them up."

"As you have my file, I can only imagine this question is intended to create a circumstance under which I wish to murder you so you can then take my attempt as a sign of traitorous guilt."

Orlin gasped. "Are you armed?"

Chavali snatched her knife and pointed it at Orlin's nose faster than she'd thought she could. Anger usually made her sloppy, not swift and precise. The tiny gap between weapon and man made him gulp. "Do you think me stupid? Of course I am armed. There is a traitor running around the tower."

"Chavali," Eldrack said, sounding mildly amused, "please put away the knife."

Because Eldrack asked, she sheathed the blade.

"You're coddling her," Aislynn said with a huff. "Why did you bring those kids here in clear violation of the strictures on the Fallen? Eldrack did explain them to you, didn't he?"

Unwilling to take the bait about Eldrack, Chavali arched an eyebrow. "Should I have abandoned the last of my kin so the man who murdered everyone they'd ever known could keep them and do as he pleased? Were they your nieces and nephew, who had suffered psychic assaults at the hands of telepaths after watching their parents, brothers, sisters, grandparents, aunts, and uncles killed, would you have left them in the hands of strangers?"

Aislynn checked the folder again. "I'm not a monster. Of course not."

Orlin stared at her, his mouth hanging open. "Creator's sacred breath, that's horrible."

Chavali raised her brow. "Is this really the most horrible thing you've ever heard?"

"No, but it's still awful. I'm so sorry you and your family went through that."

These people didn't deserve to see her pain. Chavali nodded her acceptance of his sympathy and said nothing.

"The people watching your children above ground," Aislynn said, reading a page in the folder. "Marcus and Penny Whitefield, former Fallen agents. Their terms ended some time ago. Why are they watching the children?"

"This is none of your business."

Aislynn looked up, her expression mild and unamused. "You said your first loyalty is to your clan. As such, your clan is entirely my business."

The anger simmering below the surface threatened to overflow. Chavali paused to breathe before answering. "No."

"Excuse me?"

"No." She lifted her chin. "There is no excuse for this. It is not excusable, and I will not tolerate it."

"Should we move to arrest, then? Is that what it takes to make you talk?"

Chavali understood why Eliot had broken a chair during his interview. This chair, however, belonged to Eldrack. Its destruction had no effect on Aislynn.

Chavali flicked her gaze to Eldrack and saw a man who knew Aislynn had pressed beyond the point of no return. All traces of amusement had fled, and he now stood as a bystander unwilling to participate. At least he chose not to get in the way.

"Perhaps my file is incomplete. I will, for you, fill in the gap that apparently exists. My clan is dead because a man, a telepath who chose to forsake the ethical limitations of his order, felt he deserved to possess me and all the information I hold. Rather than grant his wish, I killed myself." She held up her wrist and revealed the thin, white scar from a knife she no longer possessed. "You may do whatever you wish to me, Aislynn, but in the end, I will always choose death over betraying my clan. Always. Be clear that death need not be my own."

"Believe her," Orlin whispered.

Aislynn's gaze flicked from the scar to Chavali's eyes. "Was Harris a member of your clan? Are the Whitefields? How many members of the Fallen do you claim?"

"I am sure you would like to know." Chavali spun and stormed out, ready to do violence.

Behind her, Eldrack finally spoke. "Let her go." He shut the door.

CHAPTER 12

"Chavali!" Sean's bright, chirpy voice, full of excitement, grated on Chavali's spine.

She gripped the hilt of her dagger and ground her teeth to avoid drawing the blade on him. "What do you want?" she asked as she stalked past him, climbing the stairs to reach the solitude of her room.

Sean fell in beside her as they walked around the thick center column. "I think—" He stopped himself and lowered his voice. "I think I have some leads on who the traitor might be. I have reason to believe—"

She put a hand on his face and pushed him away. While watching to make sure he didn't fall and break his neck, she walked into something. Once again, she bounced off Colby.

"We have to stop meeting like this," Colby said with a chuckle as he caught her from falling.

"You're so adorable together," Sean gushed from two steps down.

"Shut up," Chavali snapped. Her hands formed claws in the air as she sought to prevent herself from murdering anyone. Her muscles tensed, and she wanted to scream. "Stop spewing idiotic, incompetent, foolish, deme—mmph!"

Colby covered her mouth and pulled her close. *Don't hate me for managing you.* "Hold that thought, Sean." He picked her up and carried her.

Chavali wriggled and squirmed, struggling to escape despite knowing she couldn't free herself. At the same time as she'd been practising to deal with such situations, he'd been practicing holding on despite her efforts.

Besides, she had no desire to hurt him. Sean, she wanted to hurt, but not Colby.

You seem about ready to kill someone. I'm only trying to prevent that. I'm taking you to your room. Please stop trying to escape.

She gave up. He set her feet on the floor and took his hand off her mouth. They walked to her room and he followed her inside.

"I am not going to thank you for doing that." Chavali paced between her dresser and table, full of too much anger to sit.

"It would surprise me if you did." Colby leaned against the closed door with his arms crossed.

"Aislynn is evil."

"I haven't met her."

"Of course not." Chavali snorted. The idea of him saying anything in the initial interview to rouse suspicion was laughable.

Colby let her pace in silence for a short time. "Do you want to talk about the new nightmares?"

"What?" She stopped and stared at him. "What makes you think my nightmares are new?"

He opened and shut his mouth, then sighed. "I stopped by on my way up for a patrol the other night, wanting to check on you, and heard your voice through the door. It sounded like the kind of mumbling you sometimes do before the screaming, but not quite the same."

She'd shared rooms and camped with him on missions. She trusted him to know what she sounded like in her sleep. "No, I don't want to talk about them."

"Do you need some space to scream at your walls?"

She hated to send him away for no reason, but in here, she threatened no one. Sean had set her off, and she doubted she could avoid someone else doing the same. "Yes."

He nodded and didn't seem hurt. "Talk to Kelly if you need to. Remember that's her job." Before she could say anything else, he left.

For several long moments, Chavali stood in the empty room, staring at the empty space where Colby had been. He'd understood and acted. Eliot could have done the same, though not with raw strength. No one else would have intervened unless the situation had come to blows.

She picked up a chunk of a broken pot, one she'd bought in Harbor City. The design had appealed to her then, and still did now. Running her fingers over the glazed swirls, she thought about the woman who owned the ceramic shop that had been devastated by a nearby explosion. She'd surveyed the destruction and begun cleaning up to make new pottery and fill her shelves again.

Chavali breathed in and out, wishing she could stop losing people to death, just for a few years. Or decades. This duty probably meant she'd see more and more, over and over. They had a dangerous job, one that brought them all into conflict with hate, betrayal, and desperation.

She leaned against the wall and slid to the floor. Another foray into Harris's memories might distract her from thinking so much. Walking in the fresh air might prove better. Playing games with the children outside sounded ideal, especially if those games were silly. Had she seen Harris playing a game similar to one from the clan? Children all thought the same, it seemed.

A knock on her door startled her. She hadn't realized she'd sunk so deep into her thoughts. Though she said and did nothing, the door opened and someone slipped inside.

Eldrack shut the door without rattling the beads hanging on the outside. He turned around and saw her sitting on the floor. "I thought I might find you here."

Chavali rubbed her thumb over the swirls on her pottery piece. "Did she send you to chastise me?"

"No." He crouched beside her, reminding her of the moment after he had bound her to the Fallen. "I'm sorry she put you through that." He lowered his voice. "She ordered me to keep quiet or I would've interfered more."

"Is that all you came for? To assuage your guilt?"

"No." The corner of his mouth twitched. "Do you remember the announcement a week ago?"

"Of course." Chavali scowled. How could she forget Aislynn's deranged promise. "As if mercy is the right answer."

Eldrack nodded and oozed sympathy. "I understand how you feel. But that's not what I wanted to discuss." He rocked on his feet and winced. "Can we stand or move to the table? I'm getting too old for this. I have chairs in my office for a reason."

His admission pushed away her anger. Chavali nodded and stood, then offered him a hand. He clasped her forearm, avoiding skin contact, and let her help him up with a groan. They moved to the chairs at her table.

Eldrack scooted his chair close and kept his voice quiet. "The first morning after Aisylnn sequestered everyone, you felt something strange, didn't you? Not anger. Something strong and out of place."

"No." The moment the word slipped out of her mouth as an automatic response, Chavali remembered her excessively dramatic reaction to thinking about Harris's death in the bathtub. At the time, she'd brushed it aside as the product of meeting Alene and learning about the sacrifice. "Yes."

He nodded. "Four Fallen were killed while on a mission at that time. I don't know how you know when they die, but you do. Maybe it's the same reason you react strangely to healing."

"What? I thought I was mourning Harris excessively."

"That makes sense, in a way. The next time you feel it, I want you to come see me right away. But more importantly, Aislynn won't let me send anyone to retrieve their bodies. She thinks it's a ploy to expose more Fallen, or to let the traitor out to meet their handler."

Murdering Fallen to attract more Fallen seemed foolish. No one knew how Eldrack selected people for missions, which meant the traitor had no way to ensure his inclusion. In addition, the force sent out would be more wary of attack or ambush. "Why are you telling me this?"

"Because I need someone I trust to get them and bring them home. They're in a town called Meckit to the south of here. If you're fast, you can get there in a day on horseback. Don't use the Creator's Tower."

Chavali furrowed her brow and stared at him. "You want me to sneak past the patrols with a horse, be gone for two days without anyone noticing, fetch four bodies, and sneak back in with them?"

"Yes. You're resourceful and clever. You can figure out a way, and since you visit the clan so much, no one will care that you're not down here. You can't take any other Fallen with you, though. If anyone is noticed missing, Aislynn will push even harder."

"I can't carry one body, let alone four. How do you expect me get them here?"

"Do whatever you have to." Eldrack paused and raised a finger. "Within reason, of course. But the less I know about your plan, the better. Can I count on you, Chavali?"

His earnest question made her sigh and rub her face. Of course she could find a way. Chavali worked miracles, everyone knew that. No one drank demon blood for fun, after all. Or whatever nefarious thing the rumor mill thought she did this week.

"Good." Eldrack patted her shoulder. "Thank you. In case anyone noticed me coming to visit you, don't leave immediately. But don't wait long either."

She nodded. He left.

Leaning back in her chair, she tried to imagine how to accomplish this impossible task. First, she needed a horse or two. The gray one in the stable would do anything for her, but she doubted that poor creature could haul four bodies, no matter how she trussed them. She'd need another to help him.

She knew one other horse quite well. Karias did often complain about boredom, and he'd also whined about the patrolling. If she convinced him to leave, Colby would notice when he went for a patrol and found no horse. Even if he earned a reprieve for a few days, he might notice anyway through his empathic bond with the horse.

Whatever she did to overcome that obstacle led to the next. Traveling alone was stupid. Karias might be worth two soldiers, but appearances mattered. By herself on a horse, she'd attract anyone with the slightest thought toward banditry. Not to mention having to do all the lifting and securing herself.

Outside of the Fallen, she had her clan and the people of Eagle Falls. Given she'd saved their lives, the villagers would help her. But the village lay in the wrong direction and she couldn't afford the time for that long a detour. Which left her clan. A traveling family roused no suspicion. Though the children might hinder her, Marcus, Biholtz, and Penny would be invaluable assets.

To take so many, plus dead bodies, they'd need a wagon. Sneaking out of town with a wagon sounded harder than everything else so far. Acquiring one on the road meant someone had to walk until they reached it, which would slow them down too much.

Borrowing one from a farm on the south end of Cloverdale, on the other hand, had potential. Penny and Marcus knew the Kemper family and had loaned tools to them in the past.

Then she had to consider evading the patrols. Penny might have ideas. She'd need to get the mages willing to patrol tangled up in something. Sean could help her. If she told him it meant helping solve the crime, he'd eat out of her hand. Maybe she could even use the damnable rumors swirling around the tower to her benefit.

She jumped to her feet despite weariness, energized by a cascade of plans to tend to before nightfall.

CHAPTER 13

*T*his is an odd time to deliver gifts. Karias crunched the apple Chavali had offered him in the darkness.

"I'm stealing you," she whispered.

Three hours ago, Chavali had openly accompanied the clan to a shared dinner with the Kemper family on the south end of town. When they left, they'd borrowed a wagon hitched to the gray horse with the stated intent of using it for a few days to remove some fallen logs on the Whitefield property. They'd refused help, saying the children needed the experience and exercise.

Penny had used magic to enable them to circle around, evade patrols, and slip out of town. Chavali had gone back to the tavern on her own for a patrol to see. Instead of going inside, she'd slipped around back to the stable. So far, everything had gone well.

Really? He gave the impression of chuckling. *I've never been stolen before. I should probably resist.*

"I have four carrots in my pocket and an adventure to carry out."

Karias bent so she could climb onto his back. *Look at me, I'm resisting so much you accidentally fell onto my back. When you report on my conduct to Colby, you'll naturally include that scuffle we just had. I defied you admirably. In the end, I couldn't overcome my baser horse instincts enough to turn away from your bewitching treats. Sorcery. Tell him you used sorcery to befuddle my loyalties.*

Chavali snorted as he took tentative steps out of his stall. "Assuming he notices," she muttered. As expected, no stablehands came to see who took a horse. She'd convinced the two young men to sneak into the tavern pantry and play cards with two bored Fallen who needed something to do.

He might notice when he comes for patrol in a few hours, or will we be back by then?

"We will not. He doesn't have patrol tonight. Someone else is stepping in to give him a few days off. Now hush. We need to sneak out of town on the south end."

Amused by everything, the horse ceased directing coherent thoughts at her and concentrated on evading notice. For a bright white creature of his size, he moved with remarkable stealth. Chavali had noticed his skill before, but had never ridden while he used it.

Karias placed his hooves with care to avoid making noise. He flitted from one building to another like a moth following a wisp lure. He evaded pools of light and people with equal deftness. They waited in the shelter of a firewood lean-to while a patrol bearing magical lights passed and headed to the next house toward the edge of town.

"Can you make that?" Chavali whispered, pointing at a pine grove where the clan waited. Between them and the trees, empty farming fields offered nothing to hide behind.

It would be much easier in the fall, when the crops are high enough to slink through. There's no cover to use. Can you craft an illusion to hide us, like you did in Harbor City?

"Not while we're moving. Penny created a diversion to get everyone else there."

Wait. I get to meet Penny? He had to stifle a whinny of delight. *You should steal me more often.*

"I'll keep that in mind."

The area we have to cross is visible at three different points of the patrol path on this side of town. One is obviously here, where the patrol will pause on the other side of that house. Yes, they're doing that now. Hm. They don't have any mages with this team, which is lucky.

Chavali smirked. "It's not luck."

My goodness, you've been busy. The next time they'll see the area is on the next road over. I can probably get us between the two points if I go as fast as I can. If we wait until they leave that road, we'll have about the same amount of time before the next patrol reaches the third point the area is visible from. Colby, Teryk, and two of Aislynn's soldiers designed the patrol paths to minimize the time any one point is out of sight.

"If you weren't white, this would be easier."

There's always a problem with any plan.

Chavali saw the firewood and thought of soot. They didn't have time for that, even if the ground here had enough to cover a giant horse. She remembered concealing herself and the Lady of Ket inside an illusory cloud once. That hadn't relied on blending with the scenery, only creating a blanket of black.

"I can cover us with darkness."

Why am I not surprised that's in your skillset? And why didn't you mention that sooner? Do it already. That should give us enough time to get far enough.

The patrol returned, so she said nothing about how the cloud blocked her sight as well. In this situation, she could set it up without blocking sight in front of them.

Karias's muscles tensed. Chavali twined her fingers through the spirits and summoned a sheet of billowing darkness. The patrol paused a few horse-lengths past their hiding spot.

"Did you hear something?" one of the patrollers asked.

Horses stamped and snorted.

Dammit. We don't have time for this.

"I heard you," another member of the squad said.

"Come on," someone else snapped. "This is annoying enough without jumping at shadows."

The team moved on. Karias waited an eternity before giving her a moment's notice and lurching to his feet. He focused on running with every fiber of his being. Chavali kept her concentration on the veil. She glanced back and saw nothing but bubbling blackness. Crossing the distance took far too long.

They reached the grove without hearing shouts. As soon as they'd passed several trees, Chavali dropped the darkness. On the edge of town, she saw light receding from a point where the patrol would've seen them. Without the darkness, they hadn't stood a chance.

Returning should be interesting.

"Yes." Chavali patted his neck and pointed him deeper into the wood. "I have nothing arranged for that. We're going to Meckit, as fast as we can manage."

Through the trees, Chavali saw the small light Penny had promised to set up to guide her to them.

Karias turned toward the beacon. *And what illicit errand sends us there?*

"Tending the dead." She slid off his back and greeted the clan.

While Chavali fed Karias his carrot bribe, Marcus hitched him to the open-top wagon. Penny drove the wagon, and Marcus rode the gray horse. Chavali settled in the back of the wagon with the children and watched the stars as Karias pulled them onto the road and away from Cloverdale.

Haizea and Danel fell asleep within minutes. Chavali drifted off and dreamed of Harris holding his bow on a family. Two elders traveled with their daughter and three grandchildren, moving from one town to another with all their possessions. He'd balked at shooting the old man, instead hitting the wagon. They'd stopped anyway. The nag pulling their cart had no chance of outrunning arrows and men in good shape.

"Please," Marcus begged, "this is everything we own."

Rybor snorted and pawed through the back of their wagon while Penny cowered with the children. Kervin held his sword on them. Dar's fist in Chavali's hair kept her head cranked back and her neck exposed for his knife.

"Don't any of you have a heart? Our son died in a fire that burned our house to the ground. We're just trying to start over. These kids need everything we can give them."

Harris saw no reason to doubt the old man's sincerity. He didn't like this part of the job. Sure, it put food in his belly, but he'd never robbed anyone like this when he'd run with a city gang. They'd lifted a coin here and a sellable bit there, and sifted through trash. The smuggling hadn't hurt anyone but fat merchants and government stooges.

"Maybe we should just let them go."

Rybor's head snapped up with a glare for Harris. "You getting soft, kid?"

As Harris lowered his bow, Rybor's eyes widened at something behind him. Harris turned to look and saw a squad of guardsmen bearing down on them. Colby, riding Karias, led the charge.

Chavali woke with a sharp intake of breath. Sunrise over the mountains washed away the stars in the east. The wagon still bumped down the road. All three children remained asleep, and Penny seemed to be nodding off. Taking care not to wake the children, Chavali sat up and saw Marcus drooping in his saddle. Karias seemed fine, clopping along with his head high and a springy gait.

Not wanting to waste time, Chavali woke Biholtz. She sent Marcus and Penny both to rest while she rode the gray horse and Biholtz drove the wagon.

Though Karias seemed to invite her to share in his thoughts more than once, she avoided moving the gray close enough. She knew how to behave around horses, but her experience riding one was limited. Nothing she had to say to Karias justified exposing the gray to possible injury.

Later, she'd chat with Karias. Perhaps much later.

CHAPTER 14

The mountains drew Chavali's attention over and over again. Between two tall peaks, a slash in the impenetrable wall marked the pass between Tila and Shappa that her clan had used many times. This wall of mountains had only a few passes, and the alternative, the Creator's Towers, had required too much coinage to move so many wagons through.

On that summer day when she had killed herself to protect everything she held dear, they'd gone through that pass only a few days earlier. Which meant her clan had died nearby.

She thought back to that day. For her, it had been four months ago, but nine had passed for the rest of the world. They'd stopped and set up a carnival for a small village.

Had they crossed this road? No, she didn't think so. They'd been heading west, though, on a road. The elders had wanted to get specialized metal parts for the wagons from a town in central Shappa before taking a slow, ponderous route to Mecalle's southern beaches for the winter.

She remembered the road had a peculiar kind of flower along the edge. Pasha had said they were bright pink. Amets had picked some for Pasha, and she'd tucked them into Chavali's hair because they matched the feather.

The cut flowers had wilted swiftly, not lasting until the next morning. Then the clan had died one sunset later.

Near mid-morning, she saw a side road with a spray of those flowers. Three pale petals formed a ruffled triangle with dark, fringed leaves for a backdrop.

In the distance, the mountain pass seemed in the right place to connect to this road.

Chavali used the reins to turn the gray horse and clucked at Karias. With Biholtz listening, she said nothing to him. He'd been clear about keeping his nature a secret, even from Colby.

"Biholtz, this way."

Karias whinnied his disagreement.

Instead of expecting the teenager to be able to control the large horse, she nudged the gray closer and slipped a hand under a leather strap of Karias's bridle. She tugged it to the side.

That's not the way to Meckit.

"I know," she murmured. "I wish to take a detour. It's important to me. Please."

Do you have more carrots?

"I'll get more in Meckit."

Deal. He turned the wagon down the road.

Less than an hour passed before she spotted the ruin.

Blackened, broken wood lay in heaps forming a rough circle. Dark, bare earth, devoid of life, covered the area within the wagon remnants. Tiny shoots of new plants poked through the dirt on the outer edge of the scarred land.

Chavali climbed off her horse and led it closer, then let it graze on the grasses surrounding the spot.

She stopped at the edge of the burned area, uncertain how to feel. Biholtz joined her first, slipping an arm around her waist and leaning her head against Chavali's shoulder. The rest of the clan crowded them.

"I didn't realize it happened so close," Penny whispered.

Chavali shook her head. "Neither did I."

Haizea pushed her face against Chavali's skirt. "I don't want to see them."

"They aren't here." Chavali touched the girl's hair. "Only our memories are here."

"You can wait in the wagon with me if you want," said Penny. "We won't stay long, will we?"

"No, not long," Chavali said.

She watched Penny collect Haizea and offer the same to Danel. He shook his head and shuffled toward the remains. The boy's intrusion in the space spurred Chavali to follow. Biholtz came with her.

"There." Bholtz pointed to a spot across the empty expanse, then she hugged herself. "He was going to kill me, but he stopped. He held me by the hair. I didn't have a weapon. He had a sword. But he stopped."

Chavali draped an arm around Biholtz's shoulder. "He thought you might also have the prophecy gift."

"Why me?"

"I don't know. Desperation, perhaps. Failure does strange things to people."

She scowled. "I wish he'd killed me."

"Having been dead, I must say that I prefer life. It's much more interesting." Chavali knew what Biholtz meant. She sometimes wished she'd rejected Eldrack's second chance. Death didn't hurt.

"Looks like someone cleaned up a bit," Marcus said.

Chavali nodded. "There's a village nearby. They probably buried any bodies left by the fire." The odious practice most people used to dispose of their dead made her curl her lip. The clan deserved the freedom of ash scattered across the continent. She had no way to give it to them. "And looted, I expect."

"We could visit. See if they'll trade for some of it."

Though Marcus's idea had merit, Chavali shook her head. "These ways are gone. Anything they took has become something different. Artifacts in their homes belong to them now, and can't be reclaimed. I wanted to come here...to see it, I suppose. To know in my heart what I already know in my mind."

Danel squatted beside a wagon and touched the charred wood. Biholtz drifted to the spot she'd pointed at.

"I understand." He patted Chavali's shoulder. "I'll wait with Penny and Haizea. Yell if you need anything."

Chavali saw tents. Ribbons fluttered from the ropes. Men stood guard, watching the gawking strangers. Pasha danced with other young women, twirling gauzy scarves in a hypnotic pattern. Luken and his friends thumped drums for the dancers. The scent of sticky, sugary treats hung in the air. Mamá and her friends sold goat wool scarves and blankets. Others offered dolls, play swords, simple jewelry, and trinkets.

The clan would never do any of this again. Not in Chavali's lifetime. They might travel or not, but these festivities belonged to the past. She would find another way for her clan to grow, learn, change, and survive.

"Stagnation is death," she said to no one.

"Look what I found," Danel said, holding up a small, light-colored rock.

Chavali crossed the circle of death to crouch beside him and take the rock. Holding it up, she shook her head. "This is bone." She traced the contours with a fingertip and found no cracks or other sign of violence. "From a toe, I think. Do you want it? We can carve and paint it, if you like."

He nodded and took the bone. "Do you think it came from my mother?" Stuffing it into his pocket, he pointed to the broken board he'd moved to locate it. Though soot covered it and the ends had burned to charcoal, she saw the design marking it as belonging to his family.

Anyone could have lost a toe here. The board could have been tossed or thrown aside. The bare bone offered no hint of its owner. Danel wanted a lie. She gave it to him. "I think so, yes."

"Good." He returned to his examinations of the dirt, perhaps hoping to find some other artifact of his family.

Chavali pictured the wagons on that day and walked around the circle to where her family's had been parked. Like every other spot, broken boards lay in a charred heap. She saw how people had gone through everything and perhaps taken wood they considered usable. Had they left these piles as a memorial for the colorful strangers who'd provided them with a day of entertainment for a few coins?

She found no sign of her family's mark, but lifted a board anyway, knowing she had the right place. The wood shifted with her effort, revealing a scrap of fabric. Chavali pushed more wood aside and found fabric with a pattern she recognized. She reached into a small cave of precariously perched wood and pinched the cloth between two fingers.

The fabric proved better entrenched than she expected. With a few mighty yanks, she fell backward clutching the corner of a sleeve still holding the bones of an arm.

Sitting on the ground, she stared at the bones and cloth on her lap.

Danel hurried to her side. "That looks like Pasha's dancing dress. Is it? It's her color. Is there more?" He stuck his head and arms into the hole.

Chavali picked up the arm and noted the sleeve and bones had been sheared off at the shoulder. Someone had severed Pasha's arm.

Biholtz scurried past them, gaining speed with every step. She ran to the wagon, throwing herself into Penny's arms and sobbing.

Though Chavali knew she should follow and offer Biholtz what comfort she could, the arm held her transfixed.

Then Danel wriggled out of the wood pile. The heap collapsed as he cleared it.

"I found more bones." He dumped a pile into Chavali's lap, showing no sign of concern for his near miss with burial.

"Thank you." She wondered if he had concrete memories of the day all this had happened. He might refuse to remember, or the telepaths could have smoothed it over for him. Poking it...she didn't know how it would affect him. Kelly would have insight on the subject.

"We should go, I think." Chavali twisted her skirt to hold the bones and held Danel's hand to return to the wagon. She dumped the pile of bones in and helped Danel climb up.

Biholtz wept into Penny's shoulder. For the moment, Penny provided the comfort Biholtz needed.

Chavali considered stepping in, but they didn't have forever to reach Meckit and return. Anyone might notice their absences at any time. The less time they spent on this trip, the better.

CHAPTER 15

"Why did you take us there?" Biholtz demanded. Chavali stood, rubbing a knuckle bone with her thumb, while the horses rested and drank from a cool spring near the road. Afternoon sunshine warmed her back. Gentle breezes ruffled her hair and cloak as well as the grasses around them. In the distance, the tiny dots of Meckit's buildings lay in a shallow valley, surrounded by farmland.

She glanced aside to see anguished rage painting Biholtz's face. "I died first." The simple statement felt weighty and flippant at the same time.

Biholtz growled in the back of her throat. "You abandoned us."

"Yes."

Covering her face, Biholtz shook her head. "Why? They attacked, and then we all lost our Seer. Everyone reeled from it because the mantle didn't pass. If you'd lived, they might still be alive."

Chavali sighed, feeling the sting of a rebuke she deserved. "We don't always have as many choices as we'd like."

"That's a crappy answer."

"Yes. Come." Chavali draped an arm around Biholtz's shoulders and guided her to the wagon, where Penny and Marcus kept Danel and Haizea occupied with sticks, rocks, and Haizea's doll.

She steered Biholtz to sit with them and faced all five of them.

The mantle of storyteller seemed more distant now than it ever had before. Once, she had draped it over her shoulders as easily as a cloak. Today, it seemed heavier than Karias. Her own grief mingled with her weariness and the unsettling effect of Harris's memories roaming freely in her head.

"One day, Ekia, Mendeba, Hegoa, and Iparre waited for the blooming of a flower they loved." She summoned the spirits to provide her with an illusion of a plant bearing five large buds and twice as many wide leaves. "Once a month during the spring and summer, the plant offered five flowers. If they ate all five flowers and all ten leaves, the plant would die. So, even though the flowers and leaves were delicious, they restrained themselves to one flower and two leaves per goat. This way, the plant lived and they enjoyed the beauty of the remaining flower until it faded and the new ones bloomed.

"They waited and watched as each petal unfurled, waiting for it to grow to its greatest glory." She tried to make the flowers a bright, arresting red, but had no idea if she succeeded. "When that moment came, each goat ate one stem, leaving the fifth to survive. The flavor filled them with joy, like a fine cake with thick frosting and jam in the center. They each knew what came next and separated while their bellies churned the petals and leaves. Within an hour, noxious fumes filled the space around each goat as the unfortunate byproduct of eating something so sublime.

"When the spell passed, the goats returned and stared at the remaining flower. This filled them with more pleasure, for they knew another five blooms would greet them in another few weeks. They nodded off to sleep and dreamed of their next chance to eat the flowers.

"They woke to discover the grass around them had been trampled. Though the goats hadn't been harmed, the single flower and its stem were gone. Ekia scrambled to his hooves first and inspected the site. 'A creature came and ate the last flower,' he said. Iparre pawed at the plant. 'It's dead,' she lamented.

"Mendeba threw herself to the ground and wailed her grief at the loss of something so precious. Hegoa huffed with impatience. 'It's gone,' he snapped. 'Crying won't solve anything.' Ekia shrugged. 'It wasn't that great anyway. Every time we ate it, the stench drove us apart.' Iparre sighed. 'The world has lost something beautiful, but it wasn't our fault. So long as we remember that, everything will be fine.'

"Though Hegoa wanted to turn his back on the dead plant and walk away, Mendeba wouldn't stop weeping for the loss. Ekia and Iparre bickered over her, each trying to convince her to look at it their way. Finally, Mendeba subsided. She stood and batted the remains of the plant with one hoof.

"Hegoa said, 'Finally. Can we go now and forget about this plant?'

"Mendeba shook her head. 'We lost something, and we all mourn it. When we go, we'll only have the memories of the beautiful flowers that brought us so much joy. We'll also have the smell. Both are part of these memories, and we should remember them. Maybe we'll find other flowers that aren't as pretty or sweet, but without the smell. Or maybe we'll find something better or worse. But we shouldn't forget something just because it's not with us anymore.' "

The story had another minute or two to go, but Chavali stopped.

She looked at the bone in her hand and didn't have the will to continue with the tale. When she'd first heard the story, Seer Marika had told it to help ease the passing of an elder member of the clan. Using it to help the children mourn the loss of the entire clan seemed disingenuous.

"I'm sorry I caused you so much pain." She sighed and turned away, not sure what else to say. The Seers had always borne this curse, but none of her predecessors had ever attracted someone as destructive to the clan. Before, when the spirits forced a prophecy on her for outsiders, they had always thought it a dramatic performance for the paying customer. The clan's slaughter had been her fault.

Haizea hugged her around the waist. "Don't leave us again."

Danel hugged them both. "Never again."

Chavali bent to hold them close. She couldn't promise what they wanted to hear, and they wouldn't thank her for it if she did. "We're making a new clan. They aren't the same as the old clan, but no matter who comes or goes, you won't be alone. None of us will."

Biholtz wrapped her arms around Chavali. "I miss them."

"I miss them too." Chavali sighed, grateful to Eldrack for having found these children, and for letting her go to rescue them. "We can talk more in the wagon, though. I think the horses have rested long enough, and if we reach the town before dark, we can get home sooner."

Marcus rode the gray again and Penny drove while Chavali sat with the children and told them stories about their parents and siblings.

She remembered Haizea being born, Biholtz punching Keino in the privates, Danel's mother dancing for his father, and many more moments. They laughed about Biholtz's father and Chavali's brother repairing a wagon wheel in the mud.

The wagon trundled on, taking them further from the ruin. Haizea's giggles eased the ache in Chavali's chest more than distance could. Until the moment she'd seen the burned, broken wagons, she'd somehow nursed a tiny flicker of hope for more of her clan to have escaped and survived.

Whether it made sense had never mattered. The door had stood open a crack.

That circle of scorched earth pushed it shut.

In the summer, once all this spy madness had ended, she thought she'd bring the children back to see the spot. They could speak to the villagers and hear their stories about the attack. A few more souvenirs might seem palatable once more time had passed. If she'd added more members to the clan by then, they'd also come.

In time, she'd craft the story of that day to pass along to her successor. Haizea would gain enough distance to tell it to future children. Life would roll on.

CHAPTER 16

As the sun sank lower in the sky and the wagon drew closer to the town, Chavali tucked the bones and sleeve out of sight. She wondered how she'd let Eldrack talk her into this mission without getting the names of the dead. He'd told her nothing other than their number. Four bodies, dead for a week already, needed collecting. Without knowing who she collected, she had no way to know if she could credibly claim kinship with them.

The wagon creaked and bounced over a small bridge, carrying them past farmland much less vast than Cloverdale's sprawling fields. Tiny leaves, not yet fully grown, decorated trees lining the packed earth road. Flowers clustered in front of the wooden houses. This town looked the same as dozens Chavali had passed through before. The clan probably had stopped to offer a carnival to Meckit before. If not, they'd stopped in many places like it.

As they drew closer and closer to the tavern at the center of town, Chavali fretted. She had no plan. This mission needed none of her skills, so far as she could tell.

Colby could ask about bodies without saying why, and townsfolk would respond to the air of authority on his shoulders. Harris would skulk around town until he found fresh graves and dig them up without asking for permission.

"I don't think this is a task for children," Marcus said as he dismounted and stretched his legs. "Penny, why don't you take the kids to get us two rooms at the inn while we check with the mayor to see if they're even aware of the deaths."

Chavali frowned. The town had a sizable inn, at least, and it seemed in good repair. The three-story building stood across the road from the tavern and stables. "Do we wish to stay the night?"

"I think we don't want to travel all night again. It's bad for the horses. Besides, I think I'd rather return home after dark tomorrow instead of during twilight. Can you handle this brute on your own?" Marcus nodded to Karias.

Conceding the point, Chavali smirked as she glanced at Karias. "Yes. He's no trouble at all."

While Penny collected Danel and Haizea, Biholtz helped Chavali remove Karias's hitch and bridle. Chavali avoided touching him until Biholtz shifted to fussing over the wagon. She laid a hand on his nose and walked with him to the stable.

We have a lot to talk about.

"I agree. But not now."

Of course. For now, if you could convince Biholtz to ease up on the reins, I'd appreciate that. She's holding on too tight. Which is probably true of a number of other things as well. I believe you should make the time to have a serious conversation with Eldrack about spending more time with your clan. They really do need you.

Chavali nodded and, with an apology, locked him into a stall too small for a horse of his size. She tipped the teenage stablehand to provide both horses with carrots or apples, whichever he could find first.

Outside, she found Biholtz arguing with Marcus.

"I'm not a child." Biholtz stomped her foot.

Marcus sighed. "This is about corpses. You don't need to see corpses."

"I've seen more than you!"

"I doubt that, young lady."

"Stop it," Chavali said, stepping between them. "Biholtz, it's rude to argue with an elder. You know better. Apologize. Marcus, Biholtz is old enough to deal with these things. She's never been sheltered before and won't be now."

She didn't wait to see the resolution. Breezing past them, she headed to the tavern attached to the stable. Inside the small establishment, she found bright light, laughter, and the smell of herbed, roasted chicken. If she hadn't eaten Penny's packed sandwiches on the ride, she would've indulged in the source of that enchanting aroma.

As she slipped around the tables full of people unwinding after a long day, habit turned her attention to the conversations taking place. No one spoke about deaths or strangers. The gossip covered an episode with a runaway cow and a shouting match between a married couple. As she reached the bar to speak to the bartender, Marcus let Biholtz inside.

"Excuse me," Chavali said. She took care to smooth her accent as much as possible. "I'm looking for four strangers who might have come through here. They're overdue at home."

The bartender, a portly man with an easy smile, foisted sympathy on her. "You'll want to talk to the mayor." He pointed to a middle-aged woman dining with a man of similar age and two more men about Chavali's age.

The woman noticed and raised a hand to acknowledge Chavali. She seemed to grasp the subject, or perhaps noticed the level of noise, because she pointed to the door and stood. Chavali hurried to meet her outside, along with Marcus and Biholtz.

Standing in the glow of the tavern's windows, Chavali gave the woman a friendly smile. "We're looking for four people, who would have been armed. They should have traveled from the north, passing through here about a week ago. They're a few days overdue, so we came looking for them. I didn't think this would be the place, but my father suggested we check anyway since we're stopped for the night."

"Oh, I'm so sorry." The mayor patted her chest. "They were here, but—it was awful. Jeddy found— I'm sorry, but they—" She sighed and shook her head. "Jeddy found the bodies in a field on the south side of town."

Chavali feigned shock and slipped into a persona. "How? One is my sister's husband." The odds Eldrack had sent an all-woman team of four seemed low enough to risk at least one being male and of an appropriate age.

"How awful!" The mayor patted Chavali's shoulder. "As far as we could tell, they were ambushed by people using swords, but no one here in town had anything to do with that. I checked up on everyone. We don't want some deranged killer loose in town. Best I can guess, they left after spending the night in town, then ran across bandits, though there haven't been any other attacks around here in some time. It's kind of puzzling, really. Not to put down the tragedy, I just don't know where those bandits might've come from or gone to, or why they targeted that group."

Chavali had a guess for the last question. "The bodies...?"

"Oh, of course. If you know them, please take them." The mayor gestured for the trio to follow her and led them past the nearby houses. "We did the best we could for strangers and buried them in the village plot. They didn't seem the type to have family come looking, and they definitely weren't part of the Guard. Not that I mean any disrespect. I can get a few boys to help you dig them up, if you like. Make the work go faster."

Chavali nodded. "That would be helpful. Did you discover anything that might help us report their murderers to the Guard?"

"They came to town, from the north like you said. Met with a traveling merchant, according to Dix. She said they chatted for a good ten minutes while she was checking her chickens. She's got a bunch of eggs about to hatch, you know. Anyway, seemed like both were passing through in the opposite direction. I didn't get the merchant's name, but he sold fabric too rich for our taste. Soft and shiny stuff. Pretty. Not real practical."

She stopped in front of a dark space at the end of a row of houses. Late-blooming trees with new buds stood in a cluster, barely visible in nearby lantern light as dark, jagged fingers reaching for the sky. "They're under that one. I had the boys wrap them up on the outside chance somebody came for them. So they shouldn't be much worse off than when they went in. Not so bad for transport, either. No disrespect to your sister, of course."

"Of course." Chavali found the woman charming and wanted to spend more time with her. She'd set herself up to play a part, though, so she played that part. "I don't suppose you remember anything about the merchant's wagon? The color or a mark?"

"No, sorry. We all looked at him, saw someone too expensive to deal here, and left him alone."

"That's a shame. But at least we can give my sister and the other families some closure. Thank you for your help."

"I'm sorry for your loss, all of you. Handful of young men'll be around with plenty of shovels in just a bit. We'll get you sorted as fast as we can."

"Thank you." Chavali watched the woman walk away. "A merchant, and possible bandits. I hope there's more to learn from the bodies."

Biholtz nodded and pulled her jacket tighter against a chilly gust of wind.

Marcus stared at Chavali. "Is that how you usually operate?"

"More or less."

He gave a low whistle. "No wonder Eldrack thinks so highly of you. All that just rolled right off your tongue. If I didn't know better, I would've believed you."

Boots scuffing on the ground and the chatter of men kept Chavali from answering. She thought Eldrack appreciated her results more than her methods. After all, he never came on missions with her. He might have taken her measure, but he'd never seen her work. Aside from the interrogation in Aislynn's office, of course.

Three young men approached with six shovels. They said nothing more than needed to coordinate digging. When they'd removed enough dirt to reach the first body, two men lifted it out and carried it away, saying they'd deposit it in the wagon. Marcus helped the next man carry the second body. Chavali and Biholtz carried the third. By the time they reached the wagon with it, the first two men caught up with the fourth body.

With the bodies in the wagon, Marcus thanked the three men and gave each a few coins for their help. As soon as they left, he said, "Should we take a look at the injuries?"

Chavali covered a yawn with her hand. "In the morning. More light, and we can do it away from the town."

Marcus and Biholtz both nodded. The trio trudged across the road to the inn. The innkeeper directed them to two rooms upstairs. Penny had taken both keys. Not sure which room she would wait inside, Marcus knocked on one door then the other. No one answered at either. Chavali tried knocking and calling names.

Four Fallen had been killed in this town. Despite her experience and magic, Penny had less skill than four agents. The children couldn't challenge such a person or group.

She imagined Penny lying dead on the floor with her throat slit and shadowy figures dragging Haizea and Danel to nightmarish torture. She thumped her shoulder into the door, thinking she should've found a way to bring Colby. He could break down doors.

Marcus laid a hand on her shoulder. "Chavali. Calm down."

"I'm calm," she snapped, cranking the doorknob as if it would magically unlock to satisfy her.

Biholtz pressed her ear to the other door. "There's no one inside this one. I'm sure of it."

"I'm sure they're fine," Marcus said. "Give me a minute and I can find Penny."

Chavali doubted the old man's abilities, but said nothing. He'd lived much longer than her, and clan respected their elders. She watched him close his eyes and take a deep breath.

Biholtz shoved Chavali aside and pressed her ear to that door. "No one here either. Maybe they went to...er...I don't know. Food? It did smell good in that tavern."

"That way." Marcus pointed at the door Chavali had tried to open. "But a good distance away. Probably a few blocks over." He hurried down the stairs and headed in a different direction than the cemetery.

Following in his wake, Chavali wished again for Colby. He excelled at rescuing people, and using those skills lifted his spirits. She remembered him coming to her rescue in Harbor City, though she hadn't needed it as much as he'd thought. Picking her up and carrying her through a half-ruined, burning building had given him a kind of grim satisfaction.

In fairness, she'd rescued him a few times prior to that, and that particular situation probably had felt somewhat like redemption for his death.

"There she is." Biholtz pointed at two figures chatting, one holding a lantern. They stood outside a small house with a covered porch.

Penny seemed at ease, though Chavali saw no sign of the children. Marcus reached her first. Chavali held her tongue and scanned the deep shadows puddled around the nearby buildings.

"This is Dix," Penny said, introducing her companion. "We were just talking about chickens. Hers are at least as troublesome as ours. I think it's just how chickens are."

"Where are the children?" Chavali asked, making an effort not to shout or grab Penny and shake her.

"They're fine." Penny waved off the concern. She shook hands with Hetta. "It was nice meeting you, Dix."

Dix smiled at everyone and stepped inside. Penny pulled Chavali away with an arm around her shoulders and lowered her voice. "We went for a short walk. Danel was restless. I noticed a rough-and-tumble sort of woman who seemed a bit out place and we followed her here. I'd bet our entire flock of chickens she's a mercenary of some sort.

"Before I could stop them, the kids scooted to the building and did who knows what. I might've followed the woman when she left, but for the kids. I struck up a conversation with Dix to make myself less suspicious. Seems that building is a message center. I didn't know they had one here."

Chavali frowned, unfamiliar with the term. "What's a message center?"

"It's a hub for messages. I don't recall ever seeing one outside of Shappa, and not every town has one. Cloverdale doesn't. People leave sealed written messages and pay a fee based upon where they want it to go. Merchants and other travelers looking to pad their purses pick up the messages and take them to a center in the destination town. You can also leave one for someone to pick up in the same location."

Danel emerged from the shadows around the building, Haizea's hand clasped in his. They ran to her and Penny, breathless and covered in dirt. Both children beamed at them.

"The lady told a man inside she was 'a Shadowhawk,' and the man gave her something."

Haizea nodded her agreement. "She had a bird."

"Not a real bird," Danel said. "It was gold and hung on her sword belt."

"Tiny." Haizea held up her thumb and forefinger, making a circle.

Chavali hugged both children, annoyed they'd made her worry, but proud of their initiative. "Good work," she told them. She checked the building and saw light still glowing from the windows. "I'll be right back." Leaving everyone else behind, she hauled the door open and stepped inside a warm, welcoming room.

The center had been designed in a similar fashion as a smith's shop or bakery, with a small area in front and a counter restricting access deeper inside. Signs hanging on the walls had too many words for her to waste time puzzling over. A nondescript man on a stool looked up from a book to smile at her.

"Can I help you?"

"Yes." Chavali flashed him a pained smile as she elected to wear the same persona she'd used on the mayor. "Or, rather, I hope you can. My sister's husband was among those slain a week ago, and someone told me that he and his companions may have stopped here on their way out of town. You may be the last person who saw them alive."

"Oh dear." The man frowned with distress. "I'm so sorry for your loss. But I don't think I was the last. They left one message that was picked up already. The second, they wanted it to go someplace in North Cascain, but I told them I couldn't guarantee it'd get there anytime soon and suggested they talk with a merchant passing through who'd picked up some other messages going south. So, that merchant would probably be the last person who saw them."

"I see." Chavali sighed and shook her head. "Did they seem...in good spirits, at least?"

His sympathetic smile faltered. "Yes, they were all in a good mood and not at all worried."

Chavali chose to accept the lie, thinking he'd offered it for a grieving relative with no other motive. This man had nothing nefarious about him, and had only done his job. "That's good. Thank you." She left, wondering what had bothered those four Fallen enough for that man to notice, but not enough to leave town or be on their guard.

Outside, she accompanied her clan back to the inn to get some rest, carrying more questions than answers.

CHAPTER 17

After a lousy night's sleep, the children rode on the front bench with Penny while Chavali and Biholtz sat with the bodies and Marcus rode the gray horse. They trundled in quiet under clear skies until midday, when they stopped to let the horses rest and eat in a clearing on the side of the road. Haizea and Danel dug up bugs and small rocks from the grass in Karias's shadow.

Chavali and Marcus unwrapped the first body until Chavali froze at the sight of the dead woman's face.

"What's the matter?" Marcus asked. He kept unrolling the wide, coarse linen, revealing the cause of her death—a gaping hole across her gut.

Chavali flashed on the moment when this woman had slapped her for no apparent reason, claiming Chavali had done something violating to her. Not quite a day later, someone had filleted her like a fish. "I recognize her."

"Of course you do," Marcus said. "She was Fallen."

She stared at the woman. "I don't know why I didn't expect to be acquainted with her."

"Because you didn't want to be. And you knew all your friends are fine."

For no reason, his mention of her friends made her worry about Colby, Eliot, and Portia. If this woman she'd barely known could die, if Harris could die from betrayal, any of them could.

She shook her head and peered at the enormous gash surrounded by bloody cloth. The woman hadn't been wearing her armor when she died. No other signs of violence marred her. Perhaps they'd been surprised in their sleep. "This wound is too big for a dagger."

"I'd guess a sword, combined with some serious anger. And I don't see anything else here." Marcus rewrapped the body. "Are you sure you want to see the others? We can leave it for Eldrack, or I can take a look while you ride."

"I'll ride, yes." She took over the gray.

Biholtz assisted Marcus as he checked the remaining three bodies. Chavali rode alongside, keeping her gaze on the road but her ears on the conversation. Marcus took care to treat the bodies well, which made switching from one to the next a time-consuming prospect.

"You see this, Biholtz? He took a hit to the face before he died."

"That slash looks like it happened in battle," Biholtz said.

"I agree. This other wound killed him. I'd say these also came from a sword."

They rewrapped the second body and moved on to the third. Marcus and Biholtz both made small noises of confusion for several minutes. Chavali resisted the urge to look.

"Ah, here it is," Marcus said. "Stabbed in the back. Again with a sword."

"Without it going through to the front?" Chavali asked. "How odd."

"It's kind of a slashy stab," Biholtz said. "I wonder if they managed to hurt the attackers? None of these people has any weapons."

"The townsfolk probably appropriated them to pay for burial," Marcus said, "or something like that. If we'd thought to ask, they probably would've handed everything over. I doubt we'll find coins, or much of anything else." He lifted a limp hand flecked with dirt. "At least they didn't take the Fallen rings."

Chavali glanced aside and saw the metal ring glint in the sunlight. Hers hung on a leather cord around her neck. She worried about someone noticing the design and either recognizing it or linking her to other agents because of it. Showing it to the mayor might have removed the need to lie, but would have opened the door for other questions.

She mulled over Marcus's findings while he finished with the third body and moved to the fourth. Two had been surprised, one hadn't. The woman with the bird pendant had carried a sword, making her the potential killer. On the other hand, after murdering four strangers, someone else who didn't fit into the town seemed the natural, obvious suspect. In Chavali's experience, those who caught Fallen agents off-guard rarely turned out to be the obvious option.

"If I had to guess," Marcus said, "I think this man died first. His throat is slit so deep it couldn't have happened in a fight. He must've been silenced to keep the other three from noticing. Then this one in the back. The one with the gut wound comes running and gets it from the front. The last one standing is able to fight back, but maybe he's distracted by the other deaths. He might've been having a relationship with one of the other three, which could've made their death too shocking to overcome for a fight."

"Eldrack doesn't send Fallen on missions together if they're having a relationship," Chavali said.

"He sends you with Colby," Biholtz said.

Chavali glared at her. "I'm not in a relationship with him."

Biholtz arched an eyebrow in an annoying echo of Chavali herself. "If you say so."

Marcus coughed, failing to cover a laugh. "He has to know about it in order to keep people apart. They might've been having a fast-paced, passionate affair. The man can only keep up with so much, after all. If the rumors don't clue him in, he only has so much to go on."

Ready to leave this topic behind, Chavali returned to the real subject. "They may have been roused from sleep, which also explains the ease with which they were killed, and the lack of armor."

"Didn't the mayor say they rode out in the morning after staying the night?" Biholtz asked.

Marcus nodded. "They were found in a field, I think she said. So what were they doing there without their armor that morning? And how did someone sneak up on them in an empty field? I wish we'd have thought to check the field to see if the bodies had been dragged there. Except it's been a week. If the farmer didn't churn the dirt already, it's probably rained or been watered, and we wouldn't have found anything anyway."

"We may never know what happened to them." Chavali patted the horse's neck to check if it needed anything. The beast's simple, happy thoughts soothed her enough to drop the subject. "I'll make sure Eldrack hears about our speculation."

"Speaking of Eldrack," Marcus said, "do you have any thoughts for getting us back into Cloverdale without raising suspicion? I'm not eager to have the Princess's goons breathing down my neck, thinking I'm a traitor because we went to get fallen Fallen."

"I can't do what I did to get us out." She'd used Sean's powers of gossip to convince a significant number of mages to beg off patrols that night to hold a magical contest. To get Colby's shift rotated, she'd played the airhead for the soldier in charge of the schedule to convince him to allow Colby a few days off. The rumors of their coupling had preceded her. For once, that had helped.

"But we don't need to sneak all the way in," Biholtz said. "Right? It doesn't matter if they see us going across town, just if they see us coming in."

"It matters if they look inside the wagon and see dead bodies," Penny said. "But I can deal with that. We just need to get a giant white horse and a wagon close enough to appear that we're coming from another part of town to return it to the Kempers. These patrols don't seem to be talking to each other and keeping track of movements."

"We'll have to offload the bodies before returning it." Chavali considered and rejected a dozen options. Nothing seemed feasible. The patrols would have mages, and she had no idea how to get the bodies underground without hauling them past at least one of Aislynn's men. "Wait in the grove again. I'll ride in and get Eldrack's advice on the subject. He sent me on this mission without support. Finishing it should fall on his shoulders."

Marcus nodded. "I think that's a dandy plan. He doesn't get his hands dirty often enough anymore. You can tell him I said so. We've been here longer than him."

Chavali grinned and glanced at Karias. She had no idea how to justify swapping the horses with so much weight in the wagon. Their chat would have to wait. So long as he wanted her to keep his secret, he'd have to suffer being treated like a normal horse.

"You poor things," she said to the horses. "Just a little longer and we'll be home. You'll get some pampering soon."

She thought Karias's long look said he expected better than carrots and apples.

CHAPTER 18

Riding the gray horse meant Chavali's flight to the last line of houses carried less risk in the dark than riding Karias had. She watched the glowing mage lights accompanying the night patrols, counting their timing.

When she thought she could make it, she coaxed the spirits into providing a cloud of darkness, then thinned it until she could see through the murk. With Karias, this couldn't work. With the gray, it stood a chance.

As soon as the nearest mage light approached the closest vantage point, she urged the horse toward it. They closed the distance, then the patrol turned around. Chavali pushed the horse into a gallop.

The ease with which she slipped back into town convinced her to participate in the patrol setup if they ever needed to lock down the town again.

Colby or Teryk could have made deliberate mistakes in their reasoning to make escape and re-entry possible. The idea forced her to stifle a laugh. Colby couldn't and Teryk wouldn't. Either they'd made a mistake, or the Fallen hated the duty enough not to put much effort toward it. She placed good odds on the second possibility.

Dismissing her dark cloud once she'd passed a few houses, Chavali rode openly to the stable. She led the gray inside and secured him. As she turned to find a stablehand, she saw Eldrack stepping through the door.

"I didn't know you subjected yourself to fresh air."

Eldrack chuckled. "Not often. Give me the short version for now."

"I took the clan. We had a nice ride. They're waiting outside town on the south end with the bodies in a wagon. How should we get those inside, or do you wish to inspect them outside?"

"An excellent question." He gestured for her to follow him.

They entered the tavern. Chavali expected him to talk to Walt, but he led her down to the tower. No one else used the stairwell, a circumstance Chavali had never encountered before. She peered through archways, wondering if people milled in the halls, but saw no one.

"Where is everyone?" she whispered.

"Drinking, mostly." He held up a hand, asking for her silence. They descended to the thirteenth floor. She followed him into the last meeting room at the end of the hall. When she shut the door, he pushed a chair aside and ran his hand over the back wall.

"I'd rather not show you this," he said, "but I think the circumstances warrant it. If anyone asks, you know nothing."

"Of course. I have never learned anything of value from you."

He huffed a laugh. His Fallen ring flared with a dim glow. A seam appeared in the wall, revealing a door that he pushed open. "You won't have trouble getting anyone to believe that. This way."

"I rarely have trouble getting anyone to believe anything."

"So true."

She followed him into a stone passage small enough that Colby would have to stoop to traverse it. Eldrack and Chavali only had to duck their heads. The door closed on its own, plunging them into darkness. A soft glow along the bases of both walls showed them which way to go. They walked up a gentle slope, but the passage didn't turn, so far as Chavali could tell.

"Why is this here?"

"Emergencies." Eldrack kept a steady pace that Chavali found slow.

"Like needing to sneak bodies past soldiers?"

"Or escaping a siege or other disaster."

Chavali considered the foresight of including such a tunnel. She suspected the tower included others. Expecting so many people to escape through one narrow passage seemed too idiotic for those who'd thought to include one in the first place.

If this passage took them far enough to evade a siege, she suspected their walk might last some time. "Would you like to hear the long version now?"

"Go ahead."

She related everything they'd learned and surmised. "Had I not been so concerned with returning as soon as possible, I would've stayed to conduct a more thorough investigation or traveled on to try to meet the merchant."

"I understand." As with every other time he spoke these words, Chavali knew he meant them. "Aislynn is hampering us all in more ways than one. And we're no closer to finding the traitor than when she got here. But that won't stop us from finding these killers. Do you think you can get one of the children to draw the bird symbol?"

"Danel might be able to. I'll ask him in the morning."

"I want you to know that I don't regret sending you to find them in the first place. No matter how many rules it broke."

"Thank you. I appreciate that."

"You're welcome. We're coming to stairs, then we'll have to crawl a short distance. There might be plants in the way. I haven't come through here in some time."

"Would you like me to go first?"

"Please do." Eldrack flattened himself against the wall, and she edged past.

She climbed stairs and stopped counting at thirty-five. At the top, she found a wall glowing enough to see the lever to one side. Pulling it down caused a clunk. A round door swung in. Chavali heard animals chittering. Holding out her hands, she encountered shrubs, ivy, and branches, all of which she crawled through until she emerged in the clearing where her clan waited, watching her. The noise must have alerted them.

"It seems we aren't the first to favor this grove."

Eldrack wriggled into the glow of Penny's magical light. "No. Not the second, third, or twelfth either." He brushed dirt and leaves off his sleeves and pants. "Thank you all for doing this. I appreciate the help you've given Chavali with her mission. We can take the bodies through here. I'll handle them on the inside."

"And what about all of us?" Marcus asked.

"I don't think it'll make sense for all of you to leave the tower without coming in. Walt might raise an eyebrow at that. I suggest turning the horse loose and pulling the wagon into a field, then sneaking in on foot. Horses know how to find home. That's the best I have to offer."

Penny shrugged. "We can make like we came from the Kemper farm."

"I'll keep an eye on the horse," Chavali said. "I believe I can hide myself well enough to get into town."

One corner of Eldrack's mouth cracked into a smile. "It's almost as if they aren't trying very hard with these patrols, isn't it?"

"Some of them, maybe," Marcus said. "Others are downright surly."

"Let's all just be thankful Chavali isn't on the patrols." Eldrack grinned and went to help Marcus carry the first body.

"Yes," Chavali said with a smirk, "Let's. The patrols would be a thing to fear with my involvement."

"I think you'd spend all your time enjoying ordering Colby around," Biholtz said.

Chavali huffed and rolled her eyes. "You can stop anytime." She endured Biholtz's comments while they carried two of the bodies, one at a time, down the tunnel and into the meeting room. The last time they left, Eldrack stayed behind, giving Chavali a look that promised discussion later.

"I wish you hadn't said those things about Colby in front of Eldrack," she said when they reached the grove for the last time. "You're confirming rumors for him."

Biholtz shrugged. "You told me you missed him."

"When did I ever do such a thing?"

"Last night, at the inn."

Chavali stared at her. With how her dreams had continued to torment her, she considered the possibility she might have said something of the sort. "Was I awake?"

Scrunching her nose, Biholtz frowned. "I thought so, but maybe not. You woke me up, moving around."

"I had nightmares," Chavali said, hoping that laid the subject to rest.

Penny had already unhitched Karias. The clan worked together to push and pull the wagon onto the Kemper family's land without disturbing the already planted crops or drawing attention. Karias followed like an obedient puppy. As soon as they emptied the wagon, Chavali smacked Karias in the rump like she would with any horse who needed goading to move.

"Go home, Karias," she said.

Karias played his part, though she saw him glance back at her. She might have imagined his annoyance, but probably not.

"I'll come up as soon as I can, but I suspect the appearance of those bodies will put me in an awkward position." Chavali kissed Haizea and Danel on their foreheads, noting their worry about her. "It's nothing I can't handle. With luck, no one will realize I was gone."

Marcus patted her shoulder. "Make sure that horse gets back where it belongs. We'll see you soon." He led the clan as a good elder should.

Biholtz hugged Chavali. "Go see Colby," she whispered. Then she ran to catch up with the others.

Chavali rolled her eyes and turned her attention to taking a different route than the rest of the clan. If someone caught her, she didn't want them compromised. With a thin cloud to aid her stealth, she kept pace with Karias's weary walk. Despite appearing fine when she smacked him, he now walked at a slow pace with his head down.

A patrol noticed him, proving they had eyes. Four mounted people swarmed him. Chavali dropped to the ground and minimized her cloud, sure they'd notice her otherwise.

"What are you doing out by yourself?"

"Isn't this Colby's horse?"

"I don't remember seeing him in the stable earlier. Maybe he got loose and wandered."

"How did we not notice him before? He's huge and white."

"You and you, ride up the road and see if Colby or someone else is using him as a diversion to sneak out. Check that grove especially."

Two members of the patrol spurred their horses onward.

"I'll let Colby know his horse was out."

"No, we'll report this and the Princess can question him."

The woman snorted. "As if Colby, of all people, is up to something."

Chavali wondered if she'd rouse Colby's anger by telling him she'd stolen his horse and clouded him with suspicion. Considering the task she'd undertaken, she doubted it. He'd suffer the indignity of Aislynn's interview with honest confusion. After that, Chavali would tell him. If she needed to.

"It's always the quiet ones."

"Sure." The woman chuckled. "C'mon, big guy, let's get you back to the stables."

The pair escorted Karias into town, leaving Chavali with a clear path. She stopped wasting her effort on hiding when she'd passed a few houses. When she walked into the tavern, Walt watched her with his head cocked to one side and open curiosity. Chavali smiled and waved without stopping.

CHAPTER 19

Chavali opened the door to her room on the tenth floor to find Railan sitting in one of her chairs, reading from a folder and chewing on her pipe. Railan flipped the folder shut and scrutinized Chavali from head to toe with sharp, obnoxiously observant eyes. As always, the haphazard scars decorating the woman's face intrigued Chavali beyond measure. The struggle to avoid staring at them gripped her.

"Welcome back. I trust your extended visit with the clan was pleasant?"

"As usual, yes." Chavali hung her cloak and sat to unlace her boots. "Did Kelly send you?"

"Among other people, yes. I figured you'd need time cool off after how your interview went, though."

Chavali nodded, guessing Eldrack had been the one to alert Railan to her return. "I'm having trouble with Harris's memories." She saw no reason to play coy with the subject. "They've become mixed with Colby's memories and my own. My last few nightmares have featured elements of all three, along with some input from my more usual dreams."

Railan stared at her. "I don't understand."

"When I decided to prod Harris's memories, they mixed with what

149

I have seen of Colby's." She described the scene depicting both Colby's death and five pieces of Harris's life. "I've tried, several times now, to separate them, but things get worse each time. Now my dreams are bizarre combinations of three events at a time. One of Harris's, one of Colby's, and one of mine. I slept almost an entire day and still woke tired."

"But that's impossible," Railan blurted. She stopped herself and held up a finger. "Clearly, it's not impossible, because I believe you. What I mean is it shouldn't happen. Especially in a telepath's mind. You're not well trained yet, but you have enough of a grounding in the basics to be able to keep everything separate."

"Yet here I am. What do I do?"

"First, I want to ask you about the interview. Then we'll dive in and take a look. It's hard to offer advice without seeing things myself."

Chavali let her lip curl. "I don't like Aislynn."

"She doesn't like you either. But I'm more concerned about her opinion of Eldrack. Did she ask you about him and his decisions?"

"She asked if Eldrack had been negligent about the rules in not telling me I shouldn't have brought the children here. Then she asserted her right to question me about the clan. I disagreed. Interview over. Eldrack intervened to allow me to leave without consequence."

Railan nodded, rubbing her forehead with a frown. "That tracks with what I've heard from others. She's not coming out and saying it, but I think she's going to remove him."

"When she first arrived, she was quite clear that she would be assessing whether Eldrack required replacement or not."

"I heard that. What I'm saying is I think she came with the intent of justifying his removal, not determining if it's necessary."

"Ah. A subtle but important difference. What happens if he's removed?"

"They ask me to do the job, probably." Railan grimaced. "There's also the possibility someone's trying to get an administrator who wasn't Fallen. I don't think the King will allow it to become a political appointment, but you never know."

Chavali nodded. She disliked Eldrack on some levels. Despite that, she appreciated his approach to many subjects and respected his ability to manage the Fallen, including herself. "Politics," she spat.

"Exactly. Anyway, there's nothing we can do about that tonight." She held up a hand. "Show me the mess in your head."

Taking a deep breath, Chavali placed her hand in Railan's. Unlike their first foray into Colby's mind, Chavali controlled access to her own mind. She whisked Railan through her defenses and to the tangled heap in her head. They stood in a spot uncertain of its decoration. The walls rippled between the drab, dingy ones of Harris's childhood and Colby's more pleasant white ones. The furnishings likewise shifted, with the couch unable to decide if it had weathered many generations or had been recently re-upholstered with a floral print.

Colby's usual memory book lay on the couch. This one had a brown cover with a precise white spine.

"I don't know this memory for either man, but I see the influence of both."

As the words left her mouth, Harris appeared in the room as a boy. His face, though, had the wrong eyes. Colby's deep blue showed instead of Harris's soft brown. The hybrid boy clutched a man's sleeve. The man refused to fill in with detail, appearing as a vague figure of male authority in a suit.

"I don't need you to tell me there's something wrong here," Railan said. She laid a hand on the couch and ran it along the back. The pattern rippled under her touch. "This will be a lot like how we attacked Pale's manipulation of Colby's memories, except no one did it on purpose. The point is, look for the things that don't seem right in that specific way of being out of place. It'll probably be related to a shared theme between the two men, like justice or something. Your mind may have blurred the lines between them."

Chavali huffed. "Harris didn't care much for Colby's version of justice. And they have different ways of storing their memories. Them both being male hardly seems sufficient." She wondered if everyone's insistence on pairing her with Colby had influenced this. She didn't think she had such interest in Harris either, but the way she'd been mourning him for the past few days muddled the matter.

"If it's nothing more than gender and proximity, you'd see this problem with other memories too. Clan would merge with Fallen, and all kinds of people would blend together. You're not having these problems with anyone else, are you?"

"No. My nightmares have included me and my memories, though."

"I don't think that's critical. It'll be something specific to Colby and Harris. Something emotion-driven, like both of them having similar, strong memories relating to their first love, and that spiraled out of control. And I think you need a lot more training. Maybe we've glossed over some important basics, or they just aren't sticking. I know other ways to teach them."

"I'm not opposed to trying different techniques."

"Good."

"Please, I know she's innocent." Harris's mouth moved and made the sound, but a younger version of Colby's voice came out. Chavali recognized the accent and speaking cadence.

"I know you feel that way." The man spoke in an anonymous voice of authority, carrying grave weight. "She's your sister, after all. But the evidence is quite clear. The hearts of healthy men do not spontaneously explode."

Chavali frowned. "I don't know this memory. How do I have this?"

"Either you brushed against enough of it without paying attention, or it's some kind of bastard combination of things that happened to both of them. I don't see anything specific to tease apart."

Harris-Colby snapped his head around. The roar of an angry crowd pressed in, muffled by a barrier. He let go of the authority figure and ran, disappearing into the misty vagueness surrounding them.

The scenery shifted to a town square painted with exquisite detail, which pointed to Colby's tendency to notice small things. Chavali saw cracks between the stones covering the ground, bubbling with moss or thin dandelions. Brick buildings with storefronts formed the edges, each displaying different, specific wares.

In the center, a dry stone fountain held a woman's underclothes, rope, a thick log, bundles of kindling, and a scattering of blonde curls. Colby's book for this scene—a thick tome bound with red leather—lay on the stones ringing the fountain.

Chavali knew this scene too well. Pale had planted an anchor here.

To remove it, she'd seen the woman burning to death for a crime Colby believed she hadn't committed. After talking over the incident with him, she knew evidence had later surfaced to exonerate her, and the true culprit had, by then, escaped. The woman's screams still haunted Colby.

Harris ran into the scene, wearing Colby's armor and sword, and with his blue eyes. He stopped over the book and held his hands up. "Wait, please!"

Faint, gauzy lines formed the outline of an angry mob. The victim shimmered into existence as a ghost, weeping in despair.

"I take it you know this scene," Railan said. "Where was the anchor?"

"In the kindling."

"Fun." Railan headed for the fountain, which seemed a thousand miles and only one step away at the same time.

"You need to wait for us to finish the questioning!" Harris-Colby told the mob.

Another man in the same armor, Colby's squad partner for part of his first life, put a hand on Colby's shoulder and tried to pull him away. "There's nothing we can do," Edvic said, shaking his head. "They've judged her guilty."

Rabid, feral dogs flew out of nowhere to slam into Edvic. Though they stood several feet apart, the mad, writhing pile fell onto the woman.

Fire exploded into life across the pyre. Harris-Colby flashed to her side, shielding his face from the fire. Both the woman and Edvic screamed, except Edvic sounded like Harris's brother.

"Those dogs killed Harris's brother," Chavali told Railan. She bent to pick up the book.

"This is a mess," Railan said. She grimaced. Shimmering blue slime oozed out of her fingers and up her arm. Once it reached her elbow, she stuck her hand in the flames.

"Yes. That's the problem." Chavali touched the book, running her fingertips across it.

In Colby's mind, Chavali had never opened any of the books. She'd been able avoid intruding that much while dealing with the anchors. Logic told her she'd find something of value inside the books stored in her own mind, but it would take effort to decipher.

Railan withdrew a broken piece of wood and frowned at it. "This is from one of your clan wagons," she murmured.

Chavali looked up and recognized a wheel spoke. It appeared in gray instead of its true color, which meant it had come from her own memory. "There's the piece of me," she grumbled.

"Yes. So strange." Railan raised her knee and cracked the stick over it, shattering it into a dozen colored pieces. Carved runes decorated painted chunks of polished wood. Seer Marika had used these casting sticks. Chavali had kept two, but had replaced the rest with more interesting baubles over the years. She preferred the showier variety for her role as an entertainer.

She and Railan both crouched to inspect the sticks. Without touching them, Chavali read the runes, trying to puzzle out if she'd seen this arrangement before and what it related to. Fear, hate, pain, and danger showed. Marika hadn't used those runes. Hers had been different runes because hers had been used for a different purpose.

Railan bent closer. "Do these markings mean anything to you?" She reached for the one with the hate rune. As her fingers reached it, the rune shifted to fire.

Chavali blinked. "Wait."

Railan's fingers closed over the stick.

Flames from the pyre, which hadn't threatened them before, surged to Railan, engulfing her.

Railan squawked in surprise. Chavali turned aside, cringing from the intense heat. She saw more blue ooze slither across Railan's body, trying to smother the fire. Instead, the flames rippled across the ooze and danced through it.

The pyre exploded, throwing knife-edge shards of something pink in every direction. Railan screamed and curled into a ball.

Chavali lurched toward her and fell through a hole of blinding, white light.

Chavali opened her eyes in her room, slumped over the table. Beside her, Railan lay on the floor in a fetal ball, screaming loud enough to bring the whole tower to her door.

Desperate to ease whatever caused it, Chavali dropped to her knees and took Railan's hand again.

Searing agony split Chavali's head open. She opened her mouth and nothing came out. Railan's screaming made it worse. As intense as the headaches following a prophecy, the pain stole her breath and filled her vision with white starbursts.

Releasing Railan, she staggered to the floor and covered her ears.

The screaming didn't stop.

Even when she dragged in air, Railan still made an ear-splitting noise of terror and torture. Gritting her teeth, Chavali braced for the pain and took Railan's hand again.

She'd felt this pain before. Prophecies gave her this. None of those had broken her, and neither would this.

Powering through the agony, Chavali forced her way into Railan's mind. She fashioned herself a thick blade and chopped everything, heedless of the damage she caused. Delicacy couldn't survive under these conditions. Hacking through a jungle of thoughts and feelings, of pain and torment, she trudged onward.

In the center of the mess, she found Railan inside a large, plain shed lined with pottery pieces.

Railan hung frozen in a moment of time, her eyes wide, shards of metal and wood about to pierce her flesh and give her all those intriguing, distracting scars.

Railan had died when her pottery equipment exploded in her face? Compared to all the other deaths she knew details of—Colby, Eliot, Harris, Teryk, and herself, it seemed so mundane and ludicrous.

Seeing this moment also made Chavali curious about Eldrack's death.

The moment remained frozen, which seemed like it could be the problem. Chavali touched Railan's bare arm. All the agony she'd forced aside tried to flood her.

She snatched back her hand. If she wanted to solve this, she needed the ability to think.

First, she tried touching the exploding shards and pushing against them. That accomplished nothing.

She tried shoving Railan aside, but earned only pain for her effort.

Annoyed at Railan, she snatched a pot off the shelf and threw it at the floor. It shattered, then re-formed itself and flew back onto the shelf, as if Railan's mind couldn't accept her changes.

"Fine," Chavali snarled. "See how you like these changes." She twined her fingers through the spirits, calling them close. She didn't ask for a specific image, but rather a full-scale corruption of every aspect of this memory.

Later, if needed, she would help Railan fix it.

The spirits surged out of her body as hundreds of tiny, rippling streamers of purple smoke. They invaded the scene, roiling through the space. Purple stained everything they touched. With each passing moment, the scene grew darker.

The explosion shrank in tiny fractions of time, forcing the memory to rewind. As soon as Chavali realized this effect made a difference, she focused her will on forcing the memory into a box.

Inch by inch, the shards returned to their places. Railan had been opening the door of her kiln when it exploded. Chavali screamed from the effort of dragging the memory backward, until Railan jerked into motion. She stood and moved backward, leaving the shed.

The lines to the spirits snapped and Chavali fell onto her back.

CHAPTER 20

"**C**havali?" *Please be fine,* Kelly said inside her head. *I know healing has a weird effect on you.*

She opened her eyes to see Kelly hovering over her, worry lining her face. "I live." Her head felt fuzzy and thick, but nothing else seemed wrong. She noted dampness at the ends of her sleeves and hoped she hadn't thrown up bile on herself. With luck, it was drool.

Thank the Creator. Kelly removed her hand, cutting off Chavali's access to her thoughts.

Beside her, Railan groaned. Another white-clad healer tended to her. "That was the worst headache ever."

"What were you doing?" the new healer asked.

"Solving problems," Railan said. "The hard way, I guess."

Kelly peered at Chavali, her forehead crinkled with concern. "Are you all right?"

"I'm fine." Though she knew the spirits still clung to her, or else she couldn't have heard Kelly's thoughts, Chavali thought they seemed distant. Remote. Detached. She couldn't sense their usual whispers on the edge of her hearing.

"Let's get you moving," the new healer said. She offered Railan a hand.

With her head less than an inch off the floor, Railan groaned. She stopped trying to get up. "No, thank you. I'll wait. Give it a few minutes. This backlash is harsh. Have you met Chavali? Chavali, this is my healer, Maryna."

"I've heard you're difficult," Maryna said without a trace of humor.

"That's one way to put it," Kelly said. "Are we looking at telepathic backlash here?"

"Yes," Railan said.

"I don't like it." Chavali lifted a hand, found it too much effort, and let it fall to the floor. "Also, your death was...something. Very much something."

Railan laughed. "That's a word for it. The weird part is how that wasn't my death to m. Except it was, just altered. The kiln exploded like I remember, but then I got caught in a loop of being cut up by the shards. Except it was your feather. There's probably some deeper meaning, but I don't know what."

Chavali suspected she knew the reason. The mantle of the Seer passed through the feather. She didn't know exactly how it worked, but she'd used the spirits to free Railan, and the feather provided her connection to the spirits. "Perhaps you noticed how much damage I did to reach you. For which I apologize. Your screaming was far too loud for my ears."

"It was so loud your neighbor called for us," Maryna said.

Kelly patted Chavali on the shoulder. "Would you like me to get you some tea?"

Tea sounded good, but Chavali wanted company. With the spirits receded and her clan out of touch, the room seemed cold and sterile. She wanted to hug herself or run to her clan. Both exceeded her physical capabilities for the moment. "No, thank you. Please, stay for a while."

Kelly's brow flew up. "Are you sure?"

"Yes. I may be ready to speak with Alene. Not now. I'm too tired. But when I have some free time."

"Whenever that might be," Railan said with a sigh. "Do you mind if I lie here like a lump for a while?"

"No, I don't mind."

"And you're definitely fine?" Kelly asked.

"I can barely move, but otherwise, yes." Chavali rolled her eyes at her healer's incredulity. She knew she could be cold, annoying, and indifferent at times, but this seemed an excessive amount of concern over something so trivial. "Entertain me."

Kelly laughed. "Now I believe you're fine."

The healers sat with them for a while, chatting about who had blown up at whom over the past few days, and over what. Every petty squabble seemed more ridiculous than the last.

This tower had become a pulsing mass of frothing rage. When Eldrack had suggested drinking as the main activity tonight, he might not have been joking.

"I think there's a handful of Fallen left who haven't hit someone," Maryna said. "Surprisingly, Chavali is one of them."

"No, I hit Sean." While they talked, Chavali had sat up. She leaned against the footboard of her bed with Railan. "Sort of. I shoved his face."

The other three women laughed. Mad, frantic pounding on the door interrupted them. Kelly hopped to her feet and opened it to find Marjeline, the woman in the next room deeper into the floor.

Panic etched her heart-shaped face and she clutched her hands. Her dark hair stuck out at odd angles, and she wore rumpled clothes—a pair of light-colored pants and a shirt—without shoes. Chavali knew nothing of Marjeline's skills, save that the other woman could cause her door to open and shut without touching it. Some sort of magic ran through her blood.

"I don't know what to do." Marjeline covered her mouth as Kelly draped an arm around her shoulders.

"What's wrong?" Kelly urged her to a chair by the table.

"I can hardly breathe. I don't know why. I woke up with an awful pain in my chest." She rubbed over her heart like she needed to dig inside and massage the muscle. "It's not as bad now, but I still...it's like someone ripped me apart."

Chavali had no idea what could cause such a sensation. The two healers likewise seemed confused by the description.

Railan, on the other hand, swore. "That sounds like descriptions I've read of what it feels like when your healer dies."

Marjeline covered her mouth. "Kess, no."

Both healers paled. Chavali blinked. Tensions ran high in the tower, but no one would kill from anger. The spy might have killed a healer, but why now? Doing so increased their chances of discovery by a great deal.

She squared her shoulders, knowing *someone* needed to deal with this, and she had experience doing so.

"Do these reactions happen immediately?" Chavali asked.

"Yes."

Chavali turned to Marjeline. "How long ago did you wake with this?"

"I don't know? I've been too dizzy to stand for at least a half hour. I think it happened in my sleep and turned it to a nightmare for a little bit, so I don't know."

"We should check Kess's room." Without waiting for any of them to agree or disagree, she tossed the door open and strode out. All four women caught up with her on the stairs, Maryna supporting Marjeline. By the time they reached the twentieth floor, they'd passed a number of drunk and tipsy Fallen stumbling their way up the stairs.

Marjeline pushed her way to the front and led them to Kess's room. Chavali noted that she had no idea which room Kelly lived in. She could find Kelly's office, but had never sought to learn where she lived, or to see how the woman decorated her sleeping area.

Before Marjeline could open the door, Railan stopped her with a hand on her shoulder. "Let someone else see first."

Her breath catching, Marjeline nodded and stood aside.

Chavali bustled into the room. The small cell had less space than her own room. It contained a bed, a dresser, and a closet. They had much more spacious offices, so perhaps Chavali had seen where Kelly spent most of her time after all. Still, she should have realized her healer didn't sleep in her office.

"She's not here. There's no one."

"Then maybe it's a mistake," Marjeline begged.

Chavali shut the door and shook her head. She trusted Railan enough to hold no hope for Kess. "We'll have to search. When did you last see her?"

Tears welled in Marjeline's eyes. "A few hours ago? She was going to bed. So was I."

"Where was that?"

"One of the parties. The fifteenth floor."

"Is it common for healers to meet and share time in your bedrooms?" Chavali asked Kelly and Maryna. "Should we check other rooms down here?"

"No," Kelly said. "When we meet, it's usually in our offices, the dining hall or the healer hall. That doesn't mean she can't be in one of these rooms, but it would be unusual."

"We should go up, then." Chavali shut Kess's door and urged the group to the stairs. "Marjeline, perhaps you should take a seat in the dining hall. With one of you?" She looked from Kelly to Maryna.

"I'll stay with her," Kelly said. "I don't think I want to see— I'd rather you handle it."

Maryna's expression soured into a distressed grimace. "I'll stay with her too."

At the nineteenth floor, Chavali checked the dining hall first. She saw no sign of dead bodies and pulled out a chair near the door for Marjeline. The two healers sat with her. Railan nodded toward the kitchen door and Chavali headed in that direction.

A man screamed. The sound came from the kitchen. Chavali sprinted for the door. Railan followed. They burst into a long, narrow room filled with bright light and metal surfaces. Pots and pans hung from hooks in the ceiling. Shelves dominated one wall, with counters, sinks, ovens, cooking surfaces, and doors along the other. The shelves held a variety of cooking and baking implements, as well as serving dishes and hundreds of jars with labels. At least thirty people could work on various tasks at once without getting into each other's way.

Chavali saw a man's back halfway down the row. He knelt and sobbed hysterically over something large on the floor. Beside him, thin, light-colored liquid splattered on the floor surrounded an overturned bowl. Under it, she saw the thick, dark ooze of pooled blood and what appeared to be long sausages. As she approached, she saw a spray of more blood on the nearest cabinet door. With every step closer, the stench of copper, bile, feces, and urine grew stronger.

A woman lay on the floor, her healer white clothing drenched in blood. The blood seemed darkest over her belly.

Chavali avoided stepping in the mess as she circled around him. Once he'd seen her, she touched his shoulder and neck.

As expected, his thoughts raced in a jumble of confusion, grief, and fear. He'd known Kess and liked her. He couldn't believe he'd entered the kitchen and walked into the refrigerator without noticing this. Wild thoughts danced across his mind. He wondered if he'd narrowly missed the killer while inspecting the milk and eggs.

Chavali let go, satisfied he'd stumbled across the body and not killed her. "This is not your fault," she murmured as she crouched beside him, holding her skirt out of the mess.

The side of Kess's face had been burned by a something flat, as had her throat.

Death had come from the deep knife wound in her gut. Her attacker had disemboweled her.

"You can go," Railan told the man. "Clean yourself up and go see the on-duty healers." She helped him stand. "I'll be back shortly. Eldrack is on his way." She escorted the weeping man to the back door and left with him.

As Chavali reached toward the body, thinking to prod Kess's abdomen to find the edges of the wound, she noticed the polish on the nail of her ring finger had chipped. Unexpected dark grime lodged under it made her lip curl. She took better care of her nails than that.

Noticing it now seemed absurd, as if she needed to separate herself from the corpse's humanity to inspect it. The distraction kept her from vomiting over the stench, at least.

Chavali stood and found a pair of tongs. With them, she prodded the rumpled, drenched fabric of Kess's shirt and discovered a ragged hole. This told her little. Still using the tongs, she lifted the shirt to find the wound underneath.

Puckered flesh bathed in blood surrounded a hole wide enough to have been made by a sword.

Chavali thought of the wounds suffered by the four dead Fallen and shook her head. Their cuts had been smooth compared to this. She suspected a sawing motion, not a slice or stab.

Railan returned from the back. As the door swung shut behind her, Eldrack entered from the dining hall. For the first time, he seemed disheveled. His thinning hair lacked its usual flat adherence to his scalp and his clothes seemed hastily donned.

"What do you already know?" He covered his mouth and yawned as he closed the distance.

"This death happened long enough ago for the blood to stop and some to dry." Chavali gestured to the floor and cabinet. "It was messy.

Whoever killed her would have needed to wash up, but has had ample time already to do this. They stabbed through her clothes. This is not my expertise, but I think they used a smaller knife than a sword or dagger, perhaps one from the kitchen."

"Railan, please get Jacqueline down here. Aislynn is already on her way, so expect her soon."

Railan nodded. "Anyone else?"

"Wake Yvonne to do an inventory of the knives down here, and ask her to bring two people who didn't know Kess well to remove the body for cleanup so we can have breakfast in the morning." Eldrack crossed his arms and stared at Kess with a tinge of anger in his grave frown.

Chavali pointed to Kess's face and neck. "These burns are unusual. They suggest some kind of struggle, though I don't think she fought much."

"That surface she's next to is heated," Railan said. "That cabinet door gives access to the heat source."

"Ah," Chavali imagined someone slamming Kess's head on the surface to stun her. The throat burn may have been to keep her from screaming, or it may have been incidental to the point. With a subdued victim, the murderer could have stabbed Kess from behind to minimize the mess.

"If this was done in the heat of rage, it was very..." Chavali groped for the right words and found none. "I don't know. It seems convenient? Like it needed a plan, at least a few minutes in advance. There are no knives stored on the shelves in reach. All these hold herbs and spices. It would be more logical to smash a jar and stab with the broken glass if it were unplanned. Too much effort was spent on this, also." She pointed to Kess's intestines on the floor.

"It takes a lot of effort to kill a healer," Eldrack muttered. "Surprising they didn't slit her throat, though."

Railan crouched beside Chavali and peered at the wound. "It could've been a small knife, like the kind you normally carry, but I agree one from the kitchen is more likely, since we've been trying to get people to leave their weapons in their rooms."

"We have enough accidental injuries when fights *aren't* breaking out on the stairwell," Eldrack said.

Aislynn breezed through the dining hall door. She seemed as awake as usual, with no sign she'd been roused from her bed. Behind her, Eldrack's healer rushed in.

"This is awful," Jacqueline said. She stopped beside Eldrack, who touched her shoulder like he'd do for anyone in distress. They spent so much effort on keeping their devotion concealed.

Chavali only knew the truth from a brush with Jacqueline's thoughts. Otherwise, she never would have guessed.

"We need to know how long ago this happened," Eldrack told her, "and anything else you can tell us about her death."

Jacqueline nodded and shooed both Chavali and Railan. Chavali stood and set the tongs aside.

Nothing visible happened when Jacqueline touched the body. The spirits, though, resumed their incomprehensible whispering in Chavali's ears, loud enough for her to hear their agitation. With each passing moment, the voices faded until they resumed their normal, unobtrusive murmur.

"About two hours ago," Jacqueline said. "It was awful, but she was too stunned to feel it."

"And where we all of you at that time?" Aislynn asked with a bright, fake smile.

Jacqueline stood and straightened her shirt, her disgust at being asked plain enough to hit Aislynn with a brick. "On duty. Do you have any idea how many people have fallen down the stairs tonight? At least they aren't beating each other up."

"Chavali and I were doing some telepath training in her room."

"Telepath training." Aislynn flicked her gaze from Chavali to Railan and back. "At night. During this investigation. While everyone else is having an impromptu party."

Railan shrugged. "Telepaths don't drink much. It tends to make our gifts behave strangely."

"Drunk people are even more annoying than sober ones." Chavali shrugged. She always appreciated not having to lie to people who considered her suspicious. "And everyone knows I have been cursed with nightmares of late. She's been helping me with it at whatever random times we're both able."

Aislynn seemed convinced and turned her attention to Eldrack.

"I was asleep," he said. "And that's suspicious, of course. If you'd like, Your Highness, you can personally inspect my quarters to verify none of my clothes are missing or covered with blood."

She huffed and waved him off. "No, it's fine. Chavali, it sounds like you're the only experienced investigator I can trust right now."

Torn between slapping the princess or storming out to leave Aislynn floundering, Chavali crossed her arms and did nothing.

The dead woman on the floor deserved justice. Marjeline also deserved justice. Chavali hoped she never experienced the pain of Kelly's death. If she did, she'd want to murder the culprit.

"Do I have free reign to do this in my own way, or are there rules you wish to impose?"

"Find the person responsible," Eldrack said. "Don't kill anyone unless they give you no other choice."

"And don't leave Cloverdale without talking to me first." Aislynn huffed. "I suppose that's all the rules," she grumbled.

Chavali nodded. "I wish to know if the knife is ever discovered."

She stepped around the mess and left the room, secure that Eldrack would honor her request.

CHAPTER 21

In the dining hall, Marjeline still sat with the two healers. Even without color, Chavali could tell the woman had been crying. She stepped to the woman's side and put a hand on her shoulder.

"I'm sorry. I'll find who did this."

"Let me know if you need to talk," Kelly murmured. "As always. All of us are here for you too, Marjeline."

Chavali nodded, knowing she wouldn't have time to see Kelly again until she discovered the spy's identity. With luck, she'd figure out who did it and be able to let others handle that person. Then she could vent her rage to Kelly.

"Let me take you back to your room for some rest," Chavali said. She met the gaze of each healer, asking without words for them not to object.

"That's a good idea," Maryna said. She stood and helped Marjeline stand. "Drink plenty of water too."

Chavali supported Marjeline and helped her take the stairs at a slow pace. Weariness crept onto her own shoulders, but she pressed against it. "Can I ask, who was Kess closest to? Besides you, I mean."

Marjeline sniffled and nodded. "Isabella. Another healer. If there's anyone else, Isabella would know. Whenever I'm looking for her, I look for Isabella."

"Who is her Fallen?"

"Sean."

Chavali knew Sean well enough. Too well, in fact. She'd spent more time in his presence than she'd wanted in Eagle Falls. He'd married his healer, which meant Isabella probably spent most of her time with him. Funny how Chavali had met Isabella on multiple occasions without ever learning her name.

Regardless, she doubted Sean had anything to do with all this mess. If his healer said anything suspicious, though, she knew where to go next.

"Do you know the last time Kess left the tower for any reason?"

"She likes to go up for fresh air after her duty shifts. Usually around midday. Sometimes I go with her. We last went up after lunch today. Took a short walk around town in the sunshine. The patrols harassed us four times. It was annoying."

"The patrols are quite irritating, I agree. They'll stop soon, I hope."

They continued in silence, with Chavali uncertain what else Marjeline could tell her. At her door, she wanted to say something. Nothing came to mind. For a member of her clan, she had many ways to provide an outlet for grief. Outsiders didn't seem to believe any of the same things, so she doubted speaking about Kess's spirit or ashes would offer any comfort.

"When you wake, go see the healers," she suggested.

Marjeline nodded. "Thank you." She disappeared into her room.

Chavali paced to her own door and thought about sleep. She flicked the string of beads, making them clack against the wood. Waiting gave the killer more time to hide and prepare for discovery. Despite how much she wanted to rest, she shoved herself away from the door and forced herself to hurry down the stairs.

She encountered Kelly again by chance, and her Healer helped her find Isabella and Sean's room and wake the woman.

Kelly handled delivering the news. Thankfully, Sean wasn't around. Before Isabella could dissolve into tears, Chavali took the woman's small hand. Isabella's dark eyes remained wide with shock as she seemed to fail at focusing on Chavali.

In the time it had taken to reach the room, Chavali had decided that she wanted a better picture of Kess and her habits.

"I need to know if Kess often went to the kitchen."

Isabella nodded and pictured the pair of them ducking in to take bread, cheese, and jam because Kess wanted it. Isabella went along to provide an extra pair of hands. "She eats all the time. A little here, a little there. Some days, she practically lived in the kitchen between meals. The only place she spends more time is the library."

"The library? What did she read about there?"

"Old missions. She's helping with a cross-referencing project for older files in the restricted library. I guess there are old missions with incomplete notations, and she's been helping find what they reference in the main archive."

"You need special permission to step inside the restricted library," Kelly said.

"Who grants that permission besides Eldrack?" Chavali asked.

"Railan," Kelly said. "That's it. They give it to almost anyone who asks, though, so long as they have a real request and not just curiosity."

Chavali remembered Eldrack telling her they kept files regarding active Fallen agents there, then moved them to the regular library when those agents finished their service. In some cases, such as the wording of Chavali's prophecies, he'd said they keep those private until their release wouldn't cause any harm.

She had permission to visit and read her own prophecies anytime, of course. If she could read, she would have done so by now.

Killing someone to access the restricted library made no sense. Were that the motive, the killer would have targeted Eldrack, Railan, or their healers. Chavali saw no other reason for the restricted library to play a role in this.

"Was she involved with anyone?"

"No." Isabella covered her face. "She had a fling about a year ago, but nothing since then. And he's never bothered her after they broke it off. He wasn't a pain about it."

No other questions came to mind. Chavali doubted an old flame would wait until a year had passed before snapping and killing her. "Thank you," she said. "You've been helpful. I'll find this person."

Isabella dissolved into tears. Chavali excused herself, leaving Kelly to handle Isabella. Later, she'd apologize for that. Now, she needed to think. She climbed the stairs, weariness falling heavier on her shoulders with every step. Her thoughts focused on moving her legs.

Until she reached the wide expanse of the third floor, she hadn't realized she'd passed the tenth.

Standing at the top of the stairwell, she looked down. Already past the greatest obstacle, she chose to plod onward and spend another night with the clan. She trudged up the last few sets of stairs and waved to Walt as she passed through the tavern.

In the darkness, she walked with her head down. Two different patrols passed her, each asking for her destination. She told both "home."

She shambled through the door and kicked off her shoes. After walking outdoors in them, she needed to clean them. The thought trundled through her head as she shuffled through the dark, quiet house. Too tired to care about anything, she slipped into the bedroom where the children slept and climbed in with them. Haizea rolled over and commandeered her arm. Danel mumbled. Biholtz shifted and clung to her other side.

Her dreams flickered and sputtered, forcing together Harris's distaste for terrorizing villagers and Colby's distaste for wrongful executions. Chavali's own strange nightmares threaded through, adding flesh-eating plants and ice made of wagon wheels.

She woke when the children did, summoned to breakfast in the cozy, warm kitchen. Haizea claimed her lap while Danel sat in his own chair. Biholtz filled her plate with eggs, cheese, and apple slices. Penny handed her a mug of tea. Marcus sat and watched her with a grave smile.

"I understand there was trouble in the tower," Penny said.

"Yes." Chavali had no idea how they heard already, and didn't care. Not having to explain kept her spirits higher than they'd otherwise be. "Eldrack wishes me to investigate."

Biholtz opened her mouth, but Marcus shook his head and she shut it.

Penny didn't seem surprised. "They'll figure out you're the one in charge of that. Everyone'll know soon, if they don't already."

"And then everyone will either try to help or flee in terror." Chavali sighed. She'd have to fend off Sean again.

"The most important thing? What that person did is worse than it seems. Healers aren't ordinary people. They're connected to the Creator in ways we don't even fully understand. Someone who would—" Penny's gaze flicked to Haizea and Danel. "They're, in a sense, innocent, and their duty is..."

"Honorable beyond the call of normal?" Chavali suggested. "I've considered what Kelly does, and I understand what you're saying. Healers are like the Seer, only moreso."

Marcus scratched his cheek and squinted at her. "Kind of a chickens to goats comparison, but it's close enough. The word I'd use for the culprit is depraved. Evil. Killing a healer puts a blight on your soul."

Chavali wondered how anyone had managed to hide something so base inside themselves from Eldrack and Railan. "There is no pit deep enough to hide such a person for long."

Biholtz set down her fork and seemed ill. "Could...could the man who killed the clan have gotten inside?"

"He has a name, and we should use it—Robin. But I don't think so." Chavali pondered the possibility of an enemy to the Fallen somehow getting inside the tower. If he knew about any of the emergency tunnels, he could avoid Walt's scrutiny. To learn about them, though, he'd have to discover the knowledge from someone who already knew. Eldrack wouldn't have told anyone without a reason at least as dire as Chavali's, and his sense of who to trust had proven sophisticated.

She kissed the top of Haizea's head and set her aside. "I think I can't afford to waste time. I'll see you all again as soon as I can."

"Find them," Biholtz said. "And if it's Robin, I want to see his corpse."

Chavali squeezed Biholtz's shoulder and stood. "That's the only way I would allow him into your presence again."

She said goodbye and hurried outside. The patrol she encountered on her way to the tavern waved without stopping. A group of people ran through exercises in the town square. Chavali noticed their eyes on her until she entered the tavern. Few Fallen sat inside. All those who did watched her.

Walt waved her close. "I want to know who did it."

"I think everyone does." She patted the bar and left him without promising anything. On her way past the fourth floor archway, she heard her name.

Kiron, the smith, beckoned her into his workshop with a grim smile. "I've got something for you."

She followed him, wary of an ambush. The mild-mannered smith who wanted to help seemed a reasonable possibility for a killer's facade.

"You never did stop by after that announcement meeting, but I got a look at your hand and knife, so I got to work anyway. Minor adjustments to the hilt aren't too hard to make." He held up a long, thin dagger in a sheath. The dark leather wrapping both the curved hilt and the sheath matched the tone of her usual belt. Two narrow fingers of metal curled up where the blade met the hilt to form a delicate guard with etching reminiscent of a feather.

Chavali wrapped her hand around the hilt. The subtle curve fit her fingers as if he'd used a cast of her hand to craft it, and the pommel, capped with a smooth stone, jutted past her grip enough to use for punching without fear of incidental injury. She tugged off the sheath and inspected the curiously flanged blade half as long as her forearm, tapered to a deadly point. Pointing the tip at her face, she discovered a spiral running up the length.

"What kind of blade is this?" she asked with wonder. "I've never seen anything like it."

"You said you slit throats." Kiron's eyes twinkled with delight. "I guessed you might also stab people. This is ideal for both purposes." He ran his finger along the blade without touching it. "With a normal dagger, you have one or two angles you can use to cut a throat, plus the tip. For this one, you don't need to worry about whether you have the edge to flesh. It's as close as you can get to round and still have sharp edges. The point is designed for driving in and ripping out, causing as much damage as possible in both directions without making your job harder than it needs to be."

He pointed to the pommel. "And the best feature of all. The spiral attracts blood and funnels it into a reservoir in the hilt. Once it's drank the blood of a few people, this blade will become as close to indestructible as anything can be. More importantly, it'll never go dull. So long as the stone on the end stays silver, you don't have anything to worry about. If it ever turns black, you've let it go too long without a drink. I primed it for you on a few minor cuts."

Chavali frowned at it, wondering what sort of accursed magic created such an effect.

The spirits, though, seemed at ease with it. At the least, they didn't become agitated while she held it. Perhaps the effect had nothing to do with death. If they found it acceptable, she supposed she should do the same.

As Eliot had taught her, she swished the blade through the air to test its balance. The finer points of the action eluded her, but she had the basic idea. With this dagger, she barely noticed any weight at all. "This is... unexpected."

Kiron beamed. "I had a feeling you'd be hunting someone."

"And so I am." She wanted to find Eliot to show him this incredible weapon. He'd appreciate it more than most, she suspected. Smiling with true gratitude, she slipped it into its sheath and bowed to Kiron with a hand over her heart. "This is a magnificent gift for which I have no means to repay you."

Light pink tinged his aged cheeks. "I don't need to be repaid. Your thanks is more than enough to make my time worthwhile."

Sensing the type of man she spoke to, she bowed her head again. "Then I would make another request of you. Though she isn't Fallen, my niece is thirteen and has been learning to fight with a sword for some time. At the moment, she has only a practice blade, a length of metal barely passable as a weapon. While she has no need for something like this at her age, she could use a blade of quality."

Kiron swelled with pride. "I'd be honored to make something for her. Bring her to see me after you catch Kess's killer."

"I will. Thank you, Kiron."

CHAPTER 22

With Kiron's help, Chavali strapped the new dagger to her belt at the small of her back. She gave him the old one so he could repurpose it however he wished. Pleased for having improved Kiron's day, she headed deeper into the tower. Her mood soured at the sight of Fallen scuttling away from her along the way.

To her surprise, Portia stopped when she saw Chavali and waved her through the archway for the closest floor. She took Chavali by the elbow and turned her back on the stairwell.

"I know you're investigating Kess's death. Everyone knows."

"I gathered this."

Portia bit her lip, something Chavali had never seen her do before. "It's going to change how people treat you."

"This also is apparent."

"You have to remember we all want the same thing. But to everyone down here, you're Aislynn now. Her hand."

Chavali sneered. "This is one thing I am definitely not."

Portia huffed and rolled her eyes. "I mean that's how it looks. You're her pet attack dog now. And with all the rumors about you..."

"Wonderful." Chavali glared at the wall. Portia didn't deserve her irritation.

"I just thought you should know."

"Thank you." Chavali turned to go find Eldrack, but stopped. They hadn't talked since Harbor City. Chavali had spent her time wrapped in clan and herself. That Portia had made the effort to pass this along suggested Chavali needed to pay more attention to those she trusted.

Besides, Portia reminded her of Pasha. Their names even rang similar.

She set a hand on Portia's shoulder. "How are you handling this lockdown? You knew Harris and helped find his murderer."

"Oh." The corners of Portia's mouth quirked up in a sad smile. "I liked him. Not romantically, but he seemed like that kind of person you want on your team."

"I noticed that you seem to favor Teryk."

Portia's smile crept into a grin. "I guess that's one way to put it. I didn't think anyone had noticed."

"You think I wouldn't notice?" Chavali smirked. "You'd have to avoid me completely."

Chuckling, Portia nodded. "He's a good man. Like Colby. Kind of. No one is quite like Colby, but I mean he has that same sort of decency and nobility. Besides, he likes fine wine."

"Good. I'm glad you have someone to share your time and tastes with. I think solitude may be our worst enemy down here. When there isn't a traitorous murderer running loose, that is."

Portia sighed and shook her head. "I just can't wrap my head around it. I mean, killing a healer? Who does that? Teryk was livid when he found out at breakfast. I mean, first he was shocked, like anyone else, but then he dove head-first into rage. I sent him off to hit things and work that anger off."

"This seems wise. We should all see our healers today, I think."

"Good idea. I'll go see mine. If he doesn't see his, I'll send him there." Portia patted her arm and smiled again. "Good luck. Don't let everyone get under your skin."

"Thank you." Chavali squeezed Portia's shoulder and left her. She needed to know what Eldrack had discovered or not since last night. Two quarter turns of the giant stairwell later, she reached the tenth floor and considered stopping to change clothes. As she stepped through the archway, she saw Colby coming from the vicinity of her room.

She stopped, not sure how to feel about seeing him. On one hand, she knew she could trust him and found him capable and competent. On the other, the rumors caused a sideshow distraction she hated.

Besides, he cared about silly things, like her ability to sleep. Such things paled in comparison to finding a murderer.

He smiled with relief on seeing her. Her mouth curled up in a traitorous echo of him. As he approached, worry chased his relief aside.

"Did you sleep last night?"

Annoyed by his predictability, Chavali huffed. "Of course I did."

"There are dark circles under your eyes."

Taking his arm, she tugged him toward her room. People on the stairwell didn't need to hear this, whatever it turned into. "And? I'm busy."

"You're not too busy to sleep properly." He followed her willingly. "You haven't looked rested in weeks. I heard Eldrack has you investigating the murder, but he can't possibly realize how hard this is on you."

She stopped and stared at him. "What are you talking about?"

"Chavali, you're barely pausing to breathe and you're having nightmares. And you seem to be avoiding me, probably because I keep pointing these things out." He planted his big hands on her shoulders and met her confused gaze with concern. "Didn't you mention at some point that you're supposed to take care of your clan? How do you expect to do that when you can't even take care of yourself?"

At least he had no idea she'd taken Karias for two days. She preferred to keep it that way. In her current state, she wondered if she'd slip and tell Colby by accident for lack of considering him hostile.

Hurried footsteps heading toward them distracted her. She leaned to the side and saw Rennet running to them, determination etched in her features. The mage waved to her.

"This isn't a good time," Chavali told Colby.

"Chavali, I need to talk to you!" Rennet shoved against Colby as she reached him.

Though he likely could have resisted without trying, Colby let go of Chavali and hopped to the side. He sighed. "It's never—"

"Shut it, giant." Rennet looped her arm through Chavali's and yanked her toward the stairwell. "You can have her back later."

Pleased about her rescue, Chavali let Rennet haul her back to the stairs without a backward glance. Colby would, at some point, insist upon picking up that conversation later. Before then, she might find time to rest.

Or she might find a murderer. Either seemed a solution to the problem.

Rennet leaned close and kept her voice low as they ran up the stairs. "Last night, on my way back to my room after the party on twelve, I noticed someone in a cloak, being kind of shifty. At the time, I didn't think anything of it. People skulk down here all the time, for all kinds of reasons. Even I skulk. Lots of us do it to avoid the rumors. You should maybe think about that with Colby, but I guess both of you are pretty notable, so it probably wouldn't make a difference.

"Anyway, this morning, I heard when the healer died. Thinking back, this person seemed to be going up around that time. I mean, so was I, but I didn't wear a cloak and skulk. Looking back, it was suspicious. At the time, I followed them, thinking I'd find out who's seeing who without anybody knowing, but I don't know who's room it is and I didn't see their face."

She led Chavali through the archway for the eighth floor and took her down the first side passage. "That's the one."

Chavali frowned, not sure she believed Rennet. Not only did Eliot have no reason to pursue a liaison inside the tower, she doubted he had anything to do with either the murder of a healer or compromising information. He had too many reasons to keep his own secrets. Of course, someone who knew about Patrick could have pressured him with that knowledge. She liked to think her combat instructor would have asked for her help, or at least given her some hints.

"Are you sure this is the door?" To be on the safe side, Chavali touched Rennet's wrist and watched her think through what she'd seen the night before.

Rennet nodded. Unlike Chavali, she could see the numbers on the walls, and the twelve on this one matched her memory of a cloaked figure slipping inside. The figure seemed the right height to be Eliot. Rennet hadn't noticed the person's shoes and caught no glimpse of their hands or even a flash of bare skin.

With no other choice, Chavali approached and knocked on the door. Rennet stuck close to her. At least Chavali had a mage for backup if Eliot turned violent or had a problematic guest. They waited. Chavali reached for the doorknob, and it opened.

Eliot seemed rumpled, as if he'd been asleep until she knocked. "What?"

"Have you heard about the death last night?" Chavali asked.

His eyes shifted, darting his gaze to Rennet and back to Chavali. "Yes. Why?" He crossed his arms.

Sensing unease, Chavali tried to think of him as any other Fallen. "Were you at one of the parties last night?"

"No. Not my thing. You?"

"No. Did you otherwise leave your room?"

"No."

Chavali arched an eyebrow. His inflection, combined with the shift of his stance told her he had something to hide. "Where did you go?"

Beside her, Rennet jabbed a finger at him. "Was it the kitchen?"

Eliot rolled his shoulders. "No."

Chavali raised her chin, asking him without words to allow her inside.

"Fine. Yes. But I didn't see any healers there." He raised his hands in surrender and opened the door for them. "And I definitely didn't hurt one, let alone kill her."

"We'll be the judge of that!" Rennet strode in, her head high.

Chavali stifled her annoyance for Eliot's sake. "Rennet, we're all Fallen, and we have only a suspicion. Let him explain."

Eliot shut the door harder than necessary. "I'm so glad I get the chance to defend myself instead of being strung up without cause."

Rennet crossed her arms and glared at Eliot. Chavali tried to show him how little she approved of Rennet's tactics as she gestured for him to begin.

He sagged into a chair. "I had a thought to try to get out of this damned place and visit Patrick. The Princess won't even let anyone use carrier birds to send messages without reading them first. I don't really want her to read what I'd send to him. I swiped some food to bring gifts with me, and maybe bribe a patrol to let me leave. When I got to the stable, half a patrol was on their way out for some reason. I saw them, and they saw me. I realized I didn't have much chance of succeeding. So I came back."

"Who's Patrick?"

Chavali waved her dismissal of Rennet's question. "I know who Patrick is. You don't need this information."

Narrowing her eyes, Rennet scanned the room. "This is all convenient and suspicious. Where's the food you took with you?"

"I gave some to the stablehands and had the rest for breakfast. Search for it if you want."

Rennet dove into searching the room before Chavali could stop her.

"This is unnecessary, Rennet."

"Is it?" Rennet jabbed a finger at her. "I thought your job was to follow every lead. You are actually trying to catch this killer, aren't you?"

"Go ahead," Eliot said. "It's not like I have anything to hide anymore."

The defeat in Eliot's words and bearing hurt Chavali. She already considered him clan and wanted to fix the problem. But Rennet also had a point. If he'd done something inadvertently helpful to the killer or traitor, she needed to discover it. With a sigh, she turned her back on him and checked his dresser drawers.

Certain she'd find nothing of interest, she glanced through the contents of each drawer. As she shut his sock drawer, Rennet raised her hand in the air from beside the bed.

"Aha!" She produced a rolled scroll, small enough to attach to a bird. "What's this, Eliot?"

His brow knitted. "I think we all know what it is, but I have no idea how it got under my bed. I keep my supplies in that box." He pointed to a carved wooden box on his dresser.

Chavali popped the box's lid open and found pieces of paper, pens, ink, and the same kind of string used to tie Rennet's discovery.

"I haven't written any messages in at least a month," Eliot said. "I've thought about how to word one a bunch of times since this damned lockdown started, but I haven't done it."

Plucking the message out of Rennet's hands, Chavali wanted to toss it in the garbage. The stupid page could have anything written on it, including a love letter to Patrick that Eliot didn't want anyone else to read.

"We have to take this to Eldrack," Rennet said. "Just because you like him doesn't mean he gets a free pass."

"I was already interviewed," Eliot growled. "By the Princess. I've been cleared."

"Sure, you were cleared then, but this is different. The murderer and the traitor could be two different people!"

"Stop it," Chavali snapped. "We'll all go see Eldrack. Whether this is real or not, he needs to know about it. He's in the best position to see the overall picture. But in this, I do the talking, not either of you." She left the room, expecting both to follow her. Even if Eliot preferred not to, Rennet would prod him until he did.

At this rate, the day promised a great deal of unpleasantness.

CHAPTER 23

Chavali opened the door for Eliot and Rennet. They trooped inside and took the two chairs opposite Eldrack's desk. She shut the door and faced a comically confused Eldrack. The stack of papers on his desk seemed shorter than usual, which Chavali assumed related to the lack of mission reports to read and catalog.

"We found this in Eliot's room." She set the tiny scroll on Eldrack's desk.

"He's acting suspicious," Rennet said.

Eldrack untied the string and unrolled the scroll to read it.

"He's not acting any more suspicious than he normally does," Chavali said with a dismissive wave. "You might as well accuse me or Eldrack of acting suspicious. I could even accuse you of trying far too hard to accuse Eliot."

She noticed Eldrack's expression falling into a deep frown. "Who knows about this? Anyone besides you three?"

"No," Chavali said. "People saw us come here, but there's no reason they would know why."

"Should we have told Princess Aislynn?" Rennet asked.

Eldrack shook his head. "No, this isn't of concern to her. I was there for Eliot's interview. He's not the spy and he didn't kill Kess. It is, however, private, so we should keep this to ourselves."

Rennet blinked. "Private how? Is this about the werewolf stuff? Are they involved—"

"No." Eldrack smiled at her. The smile failed to reach his eyes. "This is not about the werewolves. You were a great help defending them, so I hope you understand that also needs to be kept private."

"Of course. I understand that. But what if Aislynn wants to know what's going on? He's been sneaking around." Rennet pointed at Eliot. "He almost left town!"

"Almost leaving isn't the same as leaving," Eldrack said. "Please believe me when I say Eliot isn't the problem here. Aislynn doesn't need to know about this. She isn't privy to every aspect of our lives here."

"What if she asks why I was in your office? I don't want to lie to her and trigger the Wasting."

"Should she ask," Chavali said, "tell her you assisted me with a matter relating to the investigation. If she wants to know more, she should speak directly to me or Eldrack because you don't want to confuse the lines of communication."

When Eldrack nodded his agreement, Rennet stood. "I understand. Sorry to bother you with this, I guess."

"You were right to come to me," Chavali said. "If you see anything else, please let me know."

Rennet nodded and left.

"You can go too, Eliot." Eldrack raised the scroll without letting either him or Chavali see it. "There's nothing on here that concerns you."

Eliot stood. "This happened because I want to see Patrick."

"I understand. I can't overrule Aislynn."

With a heavy sigh, Eliot nodded and left the office.

"What's on the scroll?" Chavali asked.

"A listing of names and descriptions for two groups of Fallen currently on mission. Both teams left before the lockdown and have yet to return."

Chavali sat in the chair Rennet had vacated. "Interesting."

"It's a clumsy attempt to frame Eliot."

She saw the truth of his words. Someone snuck around and used Eliot's own supplies to craft this message. They must have expected to be seen. "If the person wishing to frame Eliot had this information, they may have already sent it."

"I agree. I need to warn them. Aislynn shouldn't object to that."

"Is there anything I can do to help?"

"Keep searching for the killer. Focus on that." Eldrack tucked the scroll into a pocket. "There's one other thing. The werewolves are exposed, but it's vital we keep the blue flowers in Eagle Falls as quiet as possible. Aislynn doesn't need to know about them. No one needs to know about them."

"Of course. I trust you have the same opinion of information regarding my clan?"

Eldrack nodded. "Railan and I have taken great care with the decision of what goes in the archives and what goes into the restricted library. I should tell you that Aislynn has access to whatever she wants, including the prophecies and my analysis of the ones we've already seen come to pass. There's nothing I can do about that."

This revelation convinced Chavali that protecting the clan and their secrets remained a high priority. "And she understands the gravity of what she has read?"

"I believe so, yes."

"Very well. Has the murder weapon been discovered?"

"No. The head cook has confirmed a serrated bread knife is missing. I have no other new information for you. I wish I did."

Chavali stood. "I will find this person. It will be dealt with."

Eldrack bowed his head to her with weary, grateful smile. "I know."

She left and mulled over what she knew. The culprit had to make a mistake soon. Were she inclined to kill a healer, knowing she wouldn't be able to leave, she would've found a way to get rid of the knife as soon as possible, somewhere no one would think to look. In a place this vast, many such possibilities existed.

Ruminating on places suitable to dispose a long knife, she headed downstairs and sat alone for lunch. Whispers followed her. For several minutes, she thought the spirits had become agitated, then she noticed the Fallen and healers keeping their distance. They chattered, glancing in her direction over and over.

Chavali finished her meal and dumped her dirty dishes in the appropriate bin, then stepped into the kitchen. The blood and mess had been cleaned up. Five servants worked, though none of them used the stove that had burned Kess.

Waiting for someone to notice her, so she didn't startle anyone into chopping off a finger or worse, she imagined the attack.

Whoever killed Kess either followed or lured her into a meeting. Following seemed more likely at this point, though whoever managed to do that without being noticed had significant skills at stealth. The man who'd found her hadn't moved her. This mean the killer came from the door Chavali had used while Kess had her back to it. Luck seemed inadequate to explain the circumstance. The killer had some ability to conceal their movements or cloud the mind.

"Excuse me? Did you need something?" the nearest servant asked.

Chavali took a moment to remember why she'd come. "I am curious about the knife used to kill Kess. Do you have a twin of it?"

"Oh. We should. I think." He hesitated, checked with the next servant, who nodded, and bustled deeper into the kitchen. His discomfort made sense.

Making an effort not to seem impatient, Chavali waited. She had no other ideas yet. The murder hadn't been a mistake, but it might have been a product of circumstance. Had Kess been doing something the killer found threatening? If so, when did she do it? Marjeline had parted company with her at least an hour before Kess died.

The servant returned and handed her a long, lightweight knife. Chavali thanked him and inspected the blade. Serration ran from the tip to the handle. Unlike her new dagger, the wooden handle offered nothing of interest. The blade had full tang, with metal studs holding it place.

She held the blade how the killer would have, twisting her wrist to picture the attack. Once Kess had been subdued enough by the burning, the killer had the option to stab her from the front. Instead, they'd made the effort to stand behind her. This person had killed before and knew what to do. They probably had removed a cloak first and set it aside.

Chavali set the blade on the nearest counter, thanked the servants, and left, wondering about the cloak. What Rennet saw could have happened before or after the killing. If it came second, though, the killer would more likely have left the blade to frame Eliot, not a scroll. Planting the scroll must have happened first.

"Chavali!" Colby rushed to catch her as she climbed the stairs.

Startled by him, she squawked instead of falling. For once. "What?"

He took her hand and dragged her up the stairs. *Karias is upset, but I don't think it's about him. He should just be in the stable, so I have no idea what's wrong. I came for you because it might be trouble with the clan. If it's not, you're the one investigating the murder.*

Stumbling in his wake became running. Grateful she had the new dagger, Chavali kept her hand in his despite the variety of unpleasant scenarios he imagined. Most came from his experiences. Dead bodies, fire, large-scale fighting, even a mercenary army bearing down on the town all flickered through his thoughts.

The possibility of danger to her clan kept Chavali moving despite gasping for air and burning in her legs. Colby helped her scale the last few staircase, pulling her along. When they reached the tavern, though, and she couldn't run anymore. Instead of leaving her behind or waiting, Colby picked her up and carried her outside.

She panted as she waved to Walt, who watched them leave with curiosity. Outside, Colby darted around the tavern to the stable. The main door stood open. Chavali saw Marcus at the next building, checking around the corner. He called out Biholtz's name as if looking for her.

Colby slowed at the entrance to the stable and set Chavali on the floor. She leaned against the wall to catch her breath. Between gasps for air, she watched Colby try to open Karias's stall door and fail. Something wedged it shut. He spent a few moments trying to find it, then grabbed a metal bar and growled as he pried the hinges off the wall. The bolts holding each in place ripped out chunks of wood.

After giving the door a shove with his shoulder to no avail, Colby stood aside. "Kick it down, Karias."

The horse whinnied. Thudding landed on the door once, twice, and a third time before it flew open, spraying shards of wood across the aisle. Karias clopped to Chavali and tossed his head.

She pressed her hand to his side.

Biholtz and Haizea came to see me. I think they were playing hide and seek with Marcus. They giggled and hid in my stall. Someone came in, I didn't see who. Biholtz left the stall and asked them what they were up to without using a name. I heard a scuffle and tried to shield Haizea. Someone thumped me on the head hard enough to disorient me while I wasn't looking. When I regained my wits, Biholtz and Haizea were gone. I tried to open my stall door, but it had been wedged shut beyond my ability to kick it open. I believe the gray horse is gone. I can find him by smell.

Chavali paled. "Let me on your back."

"What?" Colby patted Karias's hind leg.

Tell him. Consequences be damned. Karias knelt his front legs for her to scramble up.

"Biholtz and Haizea have been taken. I'm going after them."

Colby stopped her in mid-jump. "How could you possibly know that?"

She glared at him. "I'm the Seer, not a carnival fraud. Help or get out of the way!"

Marcus rushed to the stable. "Dammit, I was afraid something had happened. I only stepped away for a few minutes."

"If they've really been taken," Colby said, "we'll need more help. I don't even have my sword."

"I'm going now." Chavali yanked her arm free and jumped onto Karias's back. "Do what you wish."

"I'll rouse the cavalry," Marcus said.

"Fine," Colby grumbled. "You're not going by yourself. But this isn't smart." He climbed up behind her and wrapped an arm around her waist.

"Find them," Chavali growled.

Karias leaped into action.

CHAPTER 24

Karias slowed as he approached a patrol in the late afternoon sunshine. Blooming flowers that should have been in full glory for the Spring Festival had it not been delayed lined the edges of the road between sprawling houses. Puffy cloud scudded across the bright sky, souring Chavali's mood further. How dare the weather choose to be pleasant at a time like this?

They took the children outside town. I don't know how they evaded the patrols, but we have no such luck.

Chavali scowled. "We don't have time for this. Charge through them."

"We're not charging through them," Colby said. "We're going to explain the situation." He tightened his grip around her waist.

I agree with him.

Overruled by both man and horse, Chavali glared at everything. She had no way to find the children without Karias, so she had no idea why Colby thought he needed to restrain her.

Her mood shifted sideways when she noted the two Fallen on patrol—Sivry and Algie. Sivry had proven herself a sensible and trustworthy elf in Harbor City. Chavali still had no idea what the wires connecting her earlobes to her jawline meant. At the moment, she didn't care what bizarre elf custom they represented. Algie, on the other hand, had no sensible bones in his half-elven body. His presence on the patrol promised delay and annoyance.

Sivry and Algie blocked the road with their horses. The two soldiers accompanying them, both wearing regimental armor with helms covering their faces, circled to box in Karias from behind.

"Is there a fire?" Algie chirped with a manic grin, his voice high-pitched and sing-song, as usual.

Chavali bared her teeth. "There will be—"

Colby covered her mouth with a hand. *Don't make things worse than they already are.* "We have reason to believe two children were abducted and taken from town. Let us through."

Knowing she had no chance of dislodging his hand by prying it off, Chavali elbowed Colby in the side. Though he grunted, he kept his grip on her.

"Oh really?" Algie tittered. "Is that what they call it these days?"

"What?" Colby said.

Chavali shared his bafflement. She considered biting Colby's hand, but didn't want to hurt him.

"Are you abducting Chavali?" Sivry asked, though she seemed confused by the idea.

"No. I'm keeping her from shouting at you. We really are in a hurry. These people are getting farther away every minute we waste here." *I'm really just trying to make this go smoother.*

Sivry snorted and grinned.

One soldier huffed in annoyance. "Do you expect us to believe someone hauling unwilling children snuck past the patrols?"

I'm going to move unexpectedly, Karias thought. *You do your thing.*

"It sounds farfetched, I know," Colby said, "but we're sure it happened."

Chavali tensed. Karias hopped. Colby let go of her mouth to reach forward and grip a handful of mane.

"This is not a joke," Chavali snapped. "Clear the path or we'll clear it for you."

"Tut, Chavali." Algie's mad eyes glittered as if he relished the chance to stop her. "I already know what you can do, and none of it scares me."

"You have no idea what I'll do to protect my clan," Chavali growled. She flung her hands down, causing darkness to bubble up from the ground.

"What are you doing?" Colby muttered in her ear.

Will this harm me? Karias asked.

Chavali ignored Colby. "No. Go."

Karias lurched forward with an angry trumpet demanding the other horses move. The bubbling darkness filled the road. Colby leaned to the side and did something with his muscles that Chavali paid no attention to. Karias galloped out of the darkness with the patrol still stuck inside.

Other patrols will have noticed all that. They'll come for us.

"Good," Chavali said. "We may need the help."

"I'm kind of ashamed to admit I've wanted to punch Algie for a while." Colby said.

He's adorable. Isn't he adorable? Karias slowed as he entered the forest at the edge of the fields surrounding town, sniffing the ground.

Chavali turned and leaned closer to speak to Colby. Her ear rested against his chest. "I have no idea why you should think hitting Algie, of all people, is shameful."

Colby shook his head and huffed. "I'm not surprised. And I still think this is a bad idea."

"I still don't care." She straightened away from him, seeking distance.

"I'm not even armed."

"You have two functional arms." She prodded the one around her waist. "One of them used a hand to cover my mouth. Again."

"There's something to be said for catching flies with honey instead of scathing tirades."

"We should have ignored the flies instead of trying to catch them."

I suggest worrying about why they took Biholtz and Haizea.

Panic flashed through Chavali's body as she imagined people targeting the clan. Had they gone to the farm first? Were Penny and Danel safe? Marcus would check on them. Wouldn't he?

He'd worry about them, knowing Chavali had gone to find the girls. Despite losing the two children in the first place, he'd settled into the role of clan elder well enough.

No, this had nothing to do with him. Marcus hadn't been at fault. This had something to do with her. Everyone knew she'd taken up the investigation. That made her a problem for the traitor. Targeting the clan to hobble her made her blood boil. If either girl came to harm, the perpetrators would die. They might die anyway.

"I don't believe you really think that would've worked," Colby said.

"I don't care what you believe. This is my fault, and I'll fix it."

Colby sighed. "How is this in any way your fault?"

"I should've warned Marcus and Penny, and stayed closer to them."

"Don't be ridiculous. You can't do your job with the clan stuck to your hip."

Karias took them off the road, following what appeared to be a game trail. Dappled sunshine, waning as the day turned to evening, cast shifting shadows. Leafy shrubs bordered the path with tall trees in the throes of early blooming. A breeze knocked petals off the branches, creating a false snow shower.

"They are my responsibility," Chavali snapped. "Their safety is my problem. I should have done more to protect them, especially from this kind of retaliation."

"Maybe you need more people to help with that responsibility."

"Don't be stupid. I'm the Seer."

"Was it your job to protect the whole clan by yourself before? So we're clear, I won't believe you if you say yes."

"Shut up," Chavali snapped. She twisted to wriggle out of his grasp. As she leaned forward, she heard a strange whistling.

Karias swore. Colby grunted and let go. Chavali straightened and saw Colby fall off Karias's back with something wrapped around his neck. He hit the ground with a groan. Everything around Chavali snapped into harsh focus. Karias whinnied as an arrow plunged into his hip.

I'm fine. We're surrounded.

"Kill all of them," Chavali growled. She raised darkness and drew her new dagger.

Karias charged the source of the arrow. Chavali held onto his mane as she kept his path visible. He plowed into a man with a dark beard, holding a bow and wearing close-fitting leather armor. The man flew into a tree and crumpled. Chavali knew common bandits, and this man was not one. His equipment seemed too well assembled and tended.

Hold on.

Chavali braced while Karias leaned on his front hooves and kicked behind them. Someone grunted and wood cracked nearby. Light exploded around them, ripping away the darkness. Two men, both as well-equipped as the first, rushed the horse with matching swords. Karias shifted fast enough to hit one with his flank. Chavali slashed at the other.

Mercenaries.

Her dagger sliced through the man's leather armor. No blood sprayed when it scraped across his flesh. Instead, runnels of dark liquid flooded up the sharp spiral and disappeared into the hilt. The man shrieked and stumbled back, clawing at the fresh wound in his shoulder.

Karias clamped his jaws around the other man's hand and tossed him aside. Chavali saw a woman, light-colored hair dancing around her head as if blown by an otherworldly wind, moving her hand in a wide circle to point at them. She nudged Karias with her knee and ducked. The woman pointed at the ground instead of them. Bubbles formed in the dirt under Karias's hooves.

Another woman, one with a sword in hand, threw a dagger. Karias danced to the side. The dagger sailed past, slicing a lock of Chavali's hair. A man lunged and grabbed her leg. She punched him with the dagger still in her hand. He let go with a grunt.

I'm getting you clear. Karias leaped over a fallen tree.

"Stop or he dies!" a woman shouted.

Karias stopped. Both he and Chavali turned to look. Two mercenaries had forced Colby to his knees. One held his arms behind his back. The other had a fistful of Colby's dark hair in his gloved hand and a gleaming sword held at his neck.

"Go," Colby grunted. The light stain of new bruises darkened his neck and cheek.

The man with the sword pushed it closer, nicking his skin. "Shut up." He watched Chavali with a vicious sneer.

"Turn your back on him and he's a dead man." The mage woman who'd caused the ground to bubble stood with her fists on her hips. Her hair hung to her shoulders, no longer teased by a strange breeze. She wore close-fitting leather armor and a smug smirk. "We don't need him for anything."

I might be able to escape and circle around.

Chavali needed to rescue her clan. No matter how much she cared about Colby and Karias, they weren't clan. She came for the children. Damn Colby for insisting upon coming with her. If he'd stayed behind to collect his armor and sword, this wouldn't have happened.

She met Colby's gaze and tried to imagine turning her back on him. The thought left her cold. "Where are the girls?"

"Girls?" The mage raised an eyebrow. "This is about him. Stop fighting or we'll kill him. Death is pretty messy, so we'd rather not, but force us and we will."

The idea of stalling kept Chavali from hurrying to obey. If she took long enough, Marcus and whoever he'd mustered would find them. This situation had no gray areas open to misinterpretation from the outside.

"How can I trust you about that? For all I know, the moment I surrender, you slit his throat anyway."

"Do you really think you're in a position to negotiate?"

Chavali sheathed her dagger and nudged Karias to turn around. "I feel I'm in a position to request clarity."

The mage waved her hand and the man lowered his sword. Colby still had no options. A thin, dark line of blood ran down his neck to his collar.

"Chavali—"

The man holding Colby's hair punched him. "That doesn't mean you get to talk," he snapped.

"Stop, please." Chavali slid off Karias's back. These people would all die. One way or another, she'd see to it. She raised her hands and noted Karias taking small steps away. "I surrender. Don't harm him."

"There. That wasn't so hard, was it?" The mage gestured for someone to collect her.

Chavali waited, expecting Colby to burst free of his captors or Karias to charge them. "Who are you people?"

Something hit the back of her head. Bones crunched. As darkness dragged her to the ground, she heard Karias scream and Colby groan.

CHAPTER 25

Chavali's eyes snapped open. Nothing changed. She hung in a blank, black void, with no sense of up or down. Shivering and sweating from chill and heat at the same time, she moved her hand, trying to find some reference. Though she felt her hand wave, she saw nothing.

She screamed. No sound came out.

Nothing like this had happened when she died. That time refused to stick in her memory, as if being brought back had erased it, but she knew she hadn't been terrified. She'd joined the spirits of her clan.

She stopped screaming. Or maybe she didn't. Without the sound, she couldn't tell.

Touching her own skin reminded her of swiping her hand across wet rocks covered with algae. Her joints popped and snapped with every movement. The weightlessness turned her stomach.

I'm not dead.

Nothing made sense. Her nightmares had never done this to her. Railan had taught her, though. She knew more now than she ever had before her death. Ripping through the panic threatening to engulf her, she focused on a singular goal—light. Her will pushed against the darkness.

The darkness pushed back. It clung to her, stubborn and sticky. Chill spread through her body. She remembered dying. Her hand had gone first. Robin had held her, trying to stop the bleeding. Cold had spread up her arm, too fast and too slow at the same time. He'd wanted so hard for her to survive she'd feared he might succeed in saving her. The fear had faded as the cold had crept to her heart.

I'm not dead.

Refusing to give up, Chavali struggled against the muck. Something brushed against her, malevolent and familiar. Not Robin, but like him. She couldn't place it, she only knew Robin had nothing to do with this. Niggling doubt left the possibility open. He'd said she would wish for death.

I'm not dead.

Pressing out with all the power of her mind, like Railan had taught her, she caught a glimpse of her own dark hair, floating in front of her face. She clapped her hands together and threaded her fingers through the muck, like she did with the spirits to make illusions. The simple power she commanded paled in comparison to the thick complexity of the gunk clinging to her.

Between her hands, spikes of light pierced the darkness. She tugged them apart, teasing the muck loose and growing the light. The irony of Chavali, someone with an affinity for death, using light to peel away darkness made her want to scream again.

I'm not dead.

Bringing the light closer to her face, she tried to press her head into it. The ground passed by. A horse's hoof clopped on packed earth. Beyond it, she saw another leg. Her hands hung toward the ground, except they weren't her hands. But they were. She hovered over her own body, outside it and possessing it at the same time. Her consciousness seemed shifted a foot to the left, holding on by tenuous scraps of memory or willpower.

I'm not dead.

The darkness pressed, trying to pull her back.

"Half the point of being a mercenary is not asking questions." This woman sounded like the mage.

"I'm just saying it's weird, that's all," a man said. "I mean, if I wanted to do something with my twin or cousin, or whatever they are, I'd, you know, walk up and say so."

"Maybe they're bitter enemies or something." This second man rode alongside the horse bearing Chavali's body. "That sort of thing happens."

"It doesn't matter," the mage said, annoyance plain in her voice. "What matters is we need to watch for that path so we can find the pass to Tila."

Chavali lost the battle against the darkness. The murky void sucked her back in. Knowing she could escape, at least partially, she struggled and thrashed with every ounce of power she could muster. The clan needed her. And who knew what had happened to Colby and Karias? Even if they lived, they hadn't succeeded in fighting these people off.

The idea of Colby dying stuck in her mind. He hadn't been killed, though. The mercenaries had come for her, or so they claimed. Killing him served no purpose. Leaving him alive to tell the tale of her abduction...no, that would've been stupid.

But he had to be alive.

Force, angry and hate-filled, punched her in the gut. Her body bowed and she screamed with no noise again. Malignancy hit her once more from the side, like a shark buffeting a victim to make her bleed. With each blow, dizziness circled her in a tightening spiral. The muck constricted until it dove into her mouth and down her throat, burning her from the inside out.

I'm not dead.

Warmth slithered across her skin and yanked her sideways. The gunk tried to hold on. It fizzled and popped. With one last heave, it released her.

Chavali blinked in sudden light. Wood surrounded her. Though she saw no bed, baskets, bins, or chests, she recognized the size, shape, and workmanship of a Blaukenev wagon. The planks lay in the right directions, the small window had the right edging, and the door had the right kind of knob. The lack of color pointed to a memory.

She sat, naked, on a wood stump with her elbows resting on a round table. Her Seer's table. The markings across the top, some of which she knew she couldn't see, matched her memory. Across the table, a woman with the clan's coloring sat in an identical chair, holding a cup of tea. She smiled at Chavali, wistful and sad.

I'm not dead.

"No, you're not." The woman sipped from her mug.

"I know you." Chavali laid her hands on the table surface and spread her fingers. "We met in Ket. Shared tea. The bartender claimed you didn't exist."

"Bah. What do men know?"

In another situation, Chavali might have smirked or chuckled. Instead, she scowled. "Is this madness your doing?"

The woman laughed. "You don't need enemies. You're enough to stop yourself. Come. Have some tea. Put on clothes. You'll feel better."

Until that moment, Chavali hadn't noticed her nudity as anything other than a basic fact. She felt exposed, like anyone needed only to look at her to take her secrets. The realization turned into linen settling on her flesh, covering her and concealing her thoughts, despite not touching her head.

She picked up a teapot and poured liquid into a cup, not considering where either pot or mug came from. The scent drifting to her nose brought tears to her eyes. Auivel's enchanting brew gripped her heart. Even with her tiny clan, she missed home so much it hurt.

Her first sip brought memories rushing forward, each riding the heels of the one before. Chavali leaned against a wagon, staring up at the stars with a cup in her hands. Pasha collapsed with her after dancing, picking up a cup someone had left behind. Marika told her the price of becoming the Seer over a cup and swore her to secrecy. Papá let her sit on his lap with a cup while they watched Marika tell a story.

"They were a good people," the woman said. "I miss them too."

The memories flickered and faded. Chavali sighed. "May I call you by a name?"

"If it makes things easier for you, call me Istal."

Chavali raised her brow. According to clan legend, that woman, the wife of the Estevior, First Blaukenev, was her ancestor. The stories claimed Estevior and Istal had populated the entire clan, though she knew they'd taken in strangers many times when the clan first began. At some point, Chavali assumed they'd mixed the blood enough to make it true.

"Are you Istal?"

Istal snorted. "Of course not. She's long dead, Chavali."

"I've spoken to the dead before."

"A fair point." Istal grinned. "But no, I'm not her."

"Very well. If you're not to blame for this situation, what do you want from me?"

Istal sipped her tea and sighed. She met Chavali's gaze with fierce intensity. "Strength. Courage. This is far from the worst thing that will happen to you. Expect your life to get harder, because it will."

Chavali dropped her gaze to her tea. "So I have things to look forward to."

"Sorting out your feelings for the various people in your life would also be a good idea. But I expect that to take time. You're not very good at it."

Rather than answer, Chavali sipped her tea. She needed to decide how much she liked Portia. Too many men swirled around her to know what to think about any of them. They could all go rot but for how much she needed people. Without clan, the Seer had nothing and no one.

Tabling the subject, she set down her tea. "Can you help me face what comes next?"

"My ability to interfere is limited. The others watch. We don't agree about everything. Whatever I do, they'll return three-fold. Things like this, I can do without being noticed."

The nature of Istal's answer raised a number of questions. Chavali had no idea who or what she shared tea with, other than holding absolute certainty Istal had nothing to do with the Creator. Despite Istal's protestation to the contrary, Chavali suspected this being might be the actual Istal's spirit.

"You spend too much time thinking and not enough talking," Istal said. "Have you at least given more thought to the matter of the Greatest Sin?"

"No. It remains a subject I care little about."

"That needs to change. The time of the Fallen is waning. They've served their purpose, but too many hands push too many forces against it now. Nothing can ever stay buried, just like Pasha's arm. Time is always a circle, never a straight line. Remember that as you choose your allies."

"What's that supposed to mean?" Chavali huffed, trying not to let her fear show. "Time isn't a circle. It doesn't repeat and cycle. Speak plainly! I have enough problems deciphering the prophecies without more symbolism heaped on top. What do you want me to do?"

Istal smiled at her, sad and sympathetic. "For now, wake up and save yourself. No one else will do it for you."

The wagon disappeared, and the darkness overwhelmed her.

CHAPTER 26

Chavali blinked and groaned. Fire crackled nearby. Shadows flickered across lumps she had trouble identifying. She smelled horse and dirt. Her arms refused to move. Something held her feet together.

"She's awake," a woman said through a yawn.

"Good," the mage said. "Take care of her."

A muscular woman wearing leather armor and with short, light-colored hair crouched beside Chavali, putting her sword scabbard into plain view. Fire light glinted off a metal decoration in the shape of a bird. The people who killed that group of four Fallen had taken Chavali prisoner. Maybe Aislynn had a point about the motive for those deaths. They'd picked a strange pattern of events to follow, though. If they wanted Chavali, why didn't they attack in Meckit?

The woman held up a waterskin. "Lift your head or I'll pour it on your face."

Chavali wanted more information. She played at more weakness than she felt and forced a cough. "Need help," she rasped.

"Fine." The woman lifted Chavali's head, the heel of her palm making skin contact. *You better be worth the pay. Missing this much sleep is a pain.*

Water dribbled down her throat, keeping Chavali from asking questions. The water helped, at least. She drank as much as the woman chose to offer, and grasped from her thoughts that they'd ridden on game trails through the night and a full day. They'd stopped short of the road leading to a mountain pass to rest and prepare for the possibility of encountering other travelers.

Still feigning weakness, Chavali rested her head as soon as the woman let go. Dark shadows of trees surrounded the clearing they'd camped in, "May I know your name?"

"No. Shut up and go back to sleep."

"I will choose a name for you. Cranky. This seems right."

To her left, near the edge of the clearing, a man chuckled. "Sounds fair to me, Cranky."

Cranky rolled her eyes and kicked Chavali's shin with steel-toed boots. "I said to shut up."

Chavli grunted at the sharp ache in her leg. She tried to curl around it, but her bindings interfered. "If I am this much hassle, you should let me go."

Several voices laughed. The mage approached from the nearby campfire and squatted in front of her with a smirk. "Don't waste your breath. We're being paid well to deliver you."

"To where?"

"Nope." The mage flicked Chavali's nose. Her brief contact gave Chavali nothing. "You don't get to know anything, princess. Where we're going is a surprise."

Chavali sighed and decided to trust the few things she'd heard

216

before speaking to Istal. "It's not Tila, then. We're just taking the pass."

"Can't say how you know that, but sure. Not like anyone's going to come looking for you." The mage stood. "Get some rest. You're walking tomorrow."

Seeing no other way to get more information at the moment, Chavali abandoned the effort. She needed to formulate a plan to free herself. Other topics would suit her better. "Did you keep your word? About the man your companions held hostage."

"He was alive when we left." The mage walked away.

From across the camp, a man chuckled. "Probably not for long after, though."

"Don't worry, sweetheart," another man called out. "He only had a few hundred feet to crawl to reach the road. Maybe he made it!"

Several voices laughed. Chavali clamped down on an irrational surge of grief and anger. She needed to count them. Aside from Cranky, the mage, and the two men who'd spoken, she guessed three more completed their troupe. For the sake of safety, she expected another two or three already slept.

Keeping her movements small, she tested her bindings. They'd tied her ankles, knees, and wrists, and bound her arms to her sides. All the ropes seemed tight enough to keep her from wiggling, but loose enough to avoid harming her. At least they'd bound her hands in front of her body. In Ket, Pale had cut her ankles and elbows to render her helpless. This seemed, at once, better and worse. She needed something sharp to rub the ropes against.

She also needed something to hide whatever she did. "May I please have a blanket or cloak against the chill?"

"Shut up," Cranky snapped.

"Aw, she said 'please' and everything," a man said. "Maybe we ought to reward politeness."

"Then you do it."

Cloth rustled and a man grunted. Boots kicked dust at Chavali, and a dark shape blocked her sight. Thin, scratchy wool drifted over her body. When the blanket settled, Chavali noticed the difference in warmth. She tugged it free of her face with her fingers and looked up at the man staring down at her. This was the man that had held Colby's arms. His expression left little doubt as to the type of interest he had in her.

"Thank you." She imagined stabbing him through the eye. At the same time, she smiled as if the small kindness made him attractive to her. Flirting might provide an opportunity to take the dagger sheathed at his belt or any of a number of pieces of metal decorating his person.

"Sure thing, sweetheart." He crouched by her side and touched the feather. "Weird ornament you got there. Some sort of freakish tribal thing?"

"Something like that, yes."

One corner of his mouth quirked up. "You actually like pink, or not get much of a choice in it?"

"I had no choice." She flicked her gaze away as if embarrassed by his attention.

He leaned close and whispered, "I'm not allowed to do anything to you, so there's no point trying to pretend you might like it. Besides, I saw how you looked at that big guy. I may be a mercenary, but I'm not stupid. And for what it's worth, you're definitely one cold bitch." Grinning, he patted her head too hard and left her side.

These people had been too well-prepared and well-paid. Whoever had sent them to collect her wanted her alive and unharmed, which pointed at Robin. He didn't seem the type, though, to hire people to do his dirty work. He'd led the attack on her clan and participated in it. Perhaps now that he knew what he wanted, he could get others to do this job.

Except she hadn't run into him. He had no reason to suspect she lived again. According to Eldrack, no one but the King of Shappa and his daughter knew the details of the Fallen. For everyone else in the entire world, death was final. If Robin had heard about Chastity and her feather, he might've assumed a cousin or other relative who'd somehow escaped the slaughter. He had no reason to associate her with the Fallen, if he even knew about the group.

Despite this, she had to operate under the assumption they planned to take her to Robin. With luck, the truth would turn out better. It couldn't turn out worse.

Istal had told her to save herself. Did that mean Colby hadn't survived whatever these people did to him? Or had these people taken her far enough to prevent him and Karias from finding her?

She needed more information, but had no hope of getting it tonight. Instead, she'd have to come up with a plan.

Her hip and shoulder complained. She rolled onto her back and stared up at the stars. Rope dug into her back. Her ability to craft illusions probably hadn't been compromised. Anything she created for others to see, though, would also be seen by her captors. They'd move and eventually determine the source.

Other illusions held promise. She knew how to craft convincing images of her favorite people. Her captors, though, might not be intimidated by anything less than an army.

The fire cracked and popped. She wondered if sounds might do enough on their own. If they did, how would she remove the ropes? Taking her time to avoid notice, she scanned what she could see of the camp. Horses stood to the side, out of reach. To her surprise, she didn't see the gray. Hadn't they taken the gray with the girls? Where were the girls, and why had the mage brushed off the question about them?

If they hadn't taken the gray or the girls, who did, and why had she encountered *these* people while Karias followed the gray's trail?

She determined a small shrub and a low tent blocked her view of the fire. From where she lay, she saw no one, which meant they also couldn't see her. Behind her, she noticed a thick metal stake in the ground with several lengths of rope disappearing inside holes riddling it. Each rope led back to her. The device confused her, but she saw no way to untie any knots.

Wriggling her hands down without tossing off the blanket and bringing her legs up, she patted the rope around her knees. If she wanted to sacrifice her skirt, she could tear it in half and pull her legs free of that one rope. The ability to move her knees didn't seem useful enough to destroy the only clothing she had out here. She checked for a knot and found one between her legs, too complex to understand without seeing it.

No matter how she twisted, she couldn't reach her ankles. Raising her hands proved she couldn't reach the rope on her wrists with her teeth —the rope around her chest prevented it. She rolled onto her side again, putting her back to the fire, and edged toward the metal stake to get a better look at it.

Though she couldn't tell how deep into the ground the stake had been anchored, she could see it stuck out a few inches. Through the holes, she saw the word "tube" seemed more apt. The hollow column of metal concealed knots for each rope holding her, making untying them impossible. The top featured a keyhole. Around the edge, she noted a hinge. This meant the top flipped up to access the ends of the ropes. A lock secured it.

These people had been prepared. They'd done this before, and knew how to handle keeping a hostage.

If only she'd allowed Colby to get his armor and sword, they might not have won that battle. She could've promised to wait, then urged Karias to leave without him. That approach might have worked, especially if she had agreed to leave a trail anyone could follow.

None of this helped her escape.

"Excuse me. I need to relieve myself."

"Go ahead," a man said, his voice sleepy.

They didn't care. Why should they? Such indignity didn't harm her, it only made her stink. If they wanted to fix that, they could dump a bucket of water over her.

Hopelessness crept in. She had no idea what to do.

Facing the possibility of Robin using her for prophecies for the rest of her life, she considered finding a way to meet her second death.

CHAPTER 27

Sleep eluded Chavali. She pictured Colby with horrifying injuries, able to crawl halfway to the road before collapsing. Karias hadn't been able to save him. Biholtz and Haizea suffered at the hands of some unknown, depraved man.

Everything had been her fault. She'd failed her clan. Again.

Tears blurred her view of the stars above. But she had no intention of obeying her way into a waking nightmare.

She threaded her fingers through the spirits and goaded them to scream the clan's rage. They rushed to fulfill her request, ruffling her hair with their passage.

Eerie, weeping moans whispered through the camp. Their volume raised with every moment. Shrieking screeches burst the waning quiet. Unearthly voices of rage, pain, and violence filled the air.

The mercenaries shouted and jumped to their feet. Chavali watched and waited. They batted at shrubs, weapons at the ready. As soon as one man drew close enough, Chavali swung her legs out and tripped him. He fell on top of her. His sword smacked her shoulder, cutting a shallow wound.

She squirmed, dragging the blade down her arm, not caring that it cut her flesh, because it also cut the rope. The man groaned and rolled across her legs.

Chavali sat up. She snapped the frayed rope over her arms with a growl and slammed her elbows against the man's throat. He choked and gasped. Desperation helped her slash the rope on her wrists.

Taking the sword, Chavali kicked the man aside. She sliced at the ropes on her legs.

With the noise, she heard nothing to warn her before something heavy impacted her shoulder from behind. Lurching forward, she smacked herself in the head with the flat of the blade in her hand. Another heavy thud knocked her to the ground.

The spirits ceased wailing.

"I knew it," Cranky snarled. She punched Chavali across the face, giving a flash of her anger at losing sleep.

Chavali dropped the sword and gasped for breath. Cranky grabbed her shoulder and jammed her thumb into the shallow wound. Unable to stop herself, Chavali screamed.

"Can we cut her up now? How about worse?" Rage painting her features, Cranky tore the slash open with her fingers. *I'll make you suffer, bitch.*

"Stop it," the mage ordered. "We get nothing if she's weak or sick. She isn't supposed to be hurt at all, other than bumps to the head. Check on Brigg. Koryd, clean and bandage our guest's wounds."

Cranky shoved Chavali to the ground. She dragged her companion to the side and patted his cheek with her blood-smeared fingers. The man who'd rejected Chavali's earlier attempts crouched beside her.

Chavali hurt too much to think straight. She clutched his arm and tried to pull herself up, intending to crack her skull against his face. Koryd slapped her across the face and pressed his knee into her gut.

On the ground again, she coughed and hiccuped, gasping for breath while tears streamed down the sides of her face.

"Settle down," he purred. "You're a feisty one."

"Excuse me!" Biholtz cried out, her voice pinched with pain.

Chavali snapped her eyes open. Biholtz had found her? How? Pain receded into the background. Koryd leaned close and clamped a hand over her mouth.

"You think things are unpleasant now," he murmured, "you ain't seen nothing."

"What do you want?" the mage shouted.

"I need help!" Biholtz shouted. "We were attacked. I don't know what happened to my parents."

"What? There's no one out here. How did you find us?"

Someone screamed. Horses shouted and stamped. Koryd sat up in time to catch a sword across the neck.

Karias pounded past her with Colby in the saddle. Colby turned his blood-streaked blade on Cranky and the man with her. He slashed both in one stroke. Koryd's head fell into Chavali's lap.

Chavali lurched up in time to see Biholtz dragging her short blade out of the mage's belly.

The teen spun and deflected a blow from a man behind her. Bones crunched as Karias slammed into another man. Colby hacked a different man in half. Karias kicked Biholtz's attacker, crushing his spine and throwing him out of sight.

Biholtz whirled, her blade ready. She saw Chavali and ran to her.

Determined and fierce, Biholtz seemed a warrior goddess and the embodiment of vengeance.

Her parents would've been so proud of her.

Too relieved for words, Chavali wept as she shoved the severed head aside and embraced Biholtz.

"Haizea is fine," Biholtz said. "We're both fine."

Over Biholtz's shoulder, Chavali saw Karias march through the camp, his legs stained with dark spatter. Colby followed on foot, stabbing his sword into the ground more than once. She suspected he ensured the deaths of mercenaries she couldn't see. He surveyed the area before trotting to her.

"Is any of that blood yours?" Colby asked as she approached Chavali and Biholtz.

Chavali covered her face, unable to stop hysterical tears. Shame roiled in her gut. She should be able to control this, but she couldn't. She should be able to save herself, but she couldn't. She should be the one rescuing them, but she couldn't.

Biholtz pulled away. "I think some of it's hers, but I'm fine. Ugh, this looks bad."

"You're right," Colby said, his fingers prodding the shoulder Cranky had savaged. *I'm so sorry it took me so long to find you.* "We should've abducted a healer. This needs bandaging before we go or she might bleed out. Grab whatever you can find to do that."

Colby wrapped his arms around her and held her close. "You're all right, Chavali. We found you. You're going to be fine. This isn't a dream or nightmare. We're really here."

Chavali nodded as she struggled to suck all the emotion inside.

Later, when she had time to herself, she would deal with this. "What happened?" she choked out.

"The people who ambushed us knocked me and Karias both out without hurting us much. I decided to go after the girls instead of you first because I knew that's what you'd want. We found them already beating up their captor. It was Teryk. I never would've believed it if I hadn't seen him suffering from the Wasting with my own eyes."

"Haizea kicked him in the shins," Biholtz said.

Colby lowered Chavali to the ground so they could wash her wounds and wrap them with clean cloth Biholtz had found.

"She's going to be fierce," Colby said with a smile. "And this is going to hurt."

"Just do it," Chavali said. She clenched her jaw while they worked.

"Once we dropped off Haizea and Teryk on the edge of town where a patrol would spot them, I tried to leave Biholtz behind."

Biholtz snorted. "Fat chance. Like I'm not going to come help save my Seer."

"I'm getting the feeling stubbornness is a clan trait," Colby said with a chuckle. "Anyway, Karias picked up the trail. We followed you all night, and stopped to rest as little as we could."

"I'm starving," Biholtz said.

Colby tucked the end of one makeshift bandage and started on the other shoulder. "Check the camp. I'm sure they have food. We should all eat before we go." *I don't know what I would've done if we hadn't caught up.*

Chavali wiped her cheeks. "I thought they'd killed you and Karias."

"I'm a little surprised they didn't. I guess they didn't expect anyone to be able to follow their trail. The path they took was challenging. It crossed water four times. Karias found it each time anyway. He's better than a tracking hound."

Biholtz returned with biscuits, cheese, and waterskins. "I don't think we should stay here long. I think someone fled instead of letting us kill them, and the camp is...kind of gross."

"I'm almost done here." Colby tucked the second bandage under itself. "Biholtz, can you wrangle one of those horses? Karias can carry all three of us, but he'll be happier if he doesn't have to."

"No problem."

CHAPTER 28

Chavali slept in Colby's arms while Karias and the second horse ran. She woke under cloudy skies with Colby's eyes drooping and both horses still moving at a good pace. Raising her arms hurt enough to make her gasp. As soon as they returned, she needed to see Kelly. Her head spun and she felt light and heavy at the same time.

That moment came sooner than she expected. They crested a hill not long after and saw Cloverdale only a little further up the road. As they neared the edge of town, Chavali saw a patrol stop and wait for them. Chavali recognized the two Fallen without remembering their names. Colby, on the other hand, greeted both them and the two soldiers.

"Thank goodness you found her," Sadie said. She waved them all forward. "That's a lot of blood."

Both soldiers seemed grumpy, but said nothing.

"Chavali was hurt," Colby said. "She needs healing."

The other Fallen, a man Colby referred to as Perrin, also waved them on. "Go ahead to the tower. We'll make sure the girl gets home and this horse is taken care of."

Karias sped to the center of town. *Now that you're awake, there's something I want you to know. Once again, we need to speak later, but I*

229

think it's important for you to be aware that I was able to track you through Biholtz.

Before Chavali could form a coherent response, Karias stopped and Colby helped her to the ground. She swayed on her her feet. Colby, despite his own weariness, scooped her into his arms and carried her. On his way out, he asked a stablehand to check Karias's food and water.

Colby stopped. Chavali raised her head to see four soldiers standing outside the tavern door, blocking passage.

"You can't go inside," one soldier said.

"She needs a healer. The healers are inside." Colby shifted her in his arms.

Though she'd adjusted enough to Karias's gait that the pain had faded into the background, Chavali groaned. She thought she sounded much worse than she felt.

"Do you see all this blood?"

Chavali slumped against him and fluttered her eyes shut.

"We have orders," the soldier said, though she sounded uncertain.

"I have a woman dying in my arms," Colby growled, "and you think I care about your orders? We're both Fallen. She needs a healer. Now, not an hour from now. Let us through, dammit!" He did something Chavali couldn't decipher with her eyes closed. The movement felt like he kicked someone.

"Fine! Stand aside and let them through."

The tavern smelled of simmering resentment and anger under its usual scent of hops and liquor. Chavali cracked her eyes open, finding it more challenging than before. Chairs scraped on wood.

"What happened?" Eldrack asked. "Haizea tried to explain, but she's only a child."

"I am not sure," Chavali slurred. She let her eyes close again.

"A group of people abducted her," Colby said. "It's not clear why. They've been taken care of, but she's lost a lot of blood."

"One of your agents was abducted?" This man didn't sound familiar to Chavali. "And a small child was the only report you had of it?"

"Eldrack, why didn't you say something about this?" Aislynn asked.

Eldrack sighed. "I did. I told you something had happened to her, but I wasn't sure what. That was the truth. She needs to see her healer, and then I need to get a report from her."

"I think Robin may be involved," Chavali whispered.

"What did she say?" a different man demanded.

"She's incoherent." For the first time, Eldrack touched her hand. *Be very careful what you say and around whom. I'm protecting you and your clan as much as I can, but you're going to have to watch yourself. These people are here from the capital, and I have suspicions about why. Please believe me when I say you can trust Aislynn, but only so far.* He pulled away his hand. "She's freezing, Colby, get her downstairs immediately."

"Yes, sir." Colby carried Chavali away.

"I thought Cloverdale was locked down," a woman said. "What kind of lockdown is this?"

The door shut, cutting them off from the conversation. Colby passed two more guards at the bottom of the stairs, and they let him pass without comment. He kept quiet through the defensive levels.

When they reached the spiral stair, he said, "I didn't like the look of that."

Chavali shook her head, but stopped because it made her dizzy.

"Sean! Find Kelly and send her to Chavali's room, please."

She blinked and saw Colby rushing down the stairwell. After another blink, she heard the beads on her door clack. The third time she opened her eyes, she saw Kelly, her eyes filled with concern.

Colby as a teenager chased wild dogs. Harris as a boy fled from them both. They leaped over burning shrubs. Istal barred their path with a clan spear. She spun the length of wood and used it to trip Harris. Dancing away, she laughed as the dogs pounced on him, tearing him apart. Colby shouted his agony at the sky.

Chavali snapped her eyes open, all the pain and exhaustion gone.

She sat up and blinked, trying to remember bits and pieces of Harris and Colby. Beside her bed, Kelly slumped in her chair. Colby sat on the other side, his hands resting on his knees and his body weighed down by weariness.

"Welcome back." Colby smiled at her.

Chavali ignored him. "What happened while I was gone? Who were those people in the tavern?"

"I need a nap," Kelly said. "Get something to eat and relax for little while."

Knocking on the door stole Chavali's attention. "What?" she called out.

The door cracked open and a servant popped his head in. "You're supposed to go to Eldrack's office as soon as you're able."

"Thank you. I will." Chavali scooted off the end of the bed and noticed the sorry state of her indoor shoes. They'd been through a lot. She needed new ones.

Colby took her hand. *It can wait. You've barely eaten for far too long.*

"No, it can't." She tugged her hand and he let go. "Thank you, Kelly." Without another word, she rushed out.

Eldrack needed to hear everything she knew. She hurried down the stairs, knowing she needed to spend time thinking. Eldrack could help. Not that he needed to hear most of it, but he could put some pieces into context and give her perspective.

Sivry tried to stop her for a word, but Chavali plowed past with nothing more than a wave. The elf deserved an apology from her, but not now. She passed Eliot without even a wave and plunged into the thirteenth floor. When she opened the door to Eldrack's office, she froze.

Aislynn sat in Eldrack's chair wearing a pained smile. Chavali stepped inside and scanned the entire office. Railan sat in her usual spot, frowning at a stack of papers in her hands. Eldrack's possessions remained, but not the man. Despite the absurdity, she checked the waiting area as if she'd missed him hiding behind a potted plant.

"Where is Eldrack?"

Aislynn sighed. "He's not here."

"I can see this." Chavali rested her hands on her hips. Doing so reminded her that she hadn't changed her clothes, which meant she still wore a dress with rips and blood stains.

"He's on his way to the capital."

Railan rolled her eyes. "Stop being cagey with her. Eldrack has been arrested. Politics has determined he's responsible for the information leak, a number of Fallen deaths, and Kess's death. Which is absolute crap—"

"It's not crap," Aislynn snapped. "It's reality. On his watch, someone turned traitor. Sitting in this chair made him responsible whether he had anything to do with it or not. The administrator is supposed to be in charge."

"Because there are no traitors at Court," Railan grumbled.

"That's different."

"Of course it is," Chavali said. She didn't understand what forces had arrayed themselves against Eldrack or why, but she knew how people worked. Power and the lust for it had been corrupting women for longer than the clan had existed. "You summoned me." She took as much of the angry edge off as she could, not wanting to give Aislynn a reason to do anything rash to her. "What do you want?"

Aislynn laced her fingers on the desk. The pose reminded Chavali of Eldrack, but not enough to trust the princess. "Where have you been for the past day, and what do you know about the Fallen bodies in the morgue?"

"I've been with my clan. And absolutely nothing."

"If I didn't know that both of those statements were bald-faced lies," Aislynn said with a sigh, "I'd believe you. Which explains a lot about why Eldrack gave you preferential treatment. Let's try that answer again. Pretend I'm Eldrack."

"You are not Eldrack. I will pretend no such thing."

Railan coughed. "Chavali, Aislynn needs to know what's going on. She's the acting administrator. She's read your files and knows what's going on."

"I doubt that." Chavali crossed her arms.

"Look," Aislynn said, rubbing her eyes. "The delegation from the capital wanted me to return as a witness with Teryk and his healer for Eldrack's trial, so they could install their own acting administrator. I told them to shove it because at least I care about what happens to the Fallen and am already looped in on everything. They think I don't know they just want to have someone go through the archives."

"To be clear," Railan rushed to say, "some random person shoved on us as acting administrator wouldn't have access to the restricted files without a very good reason. But them going through the archives is still worrisome."

Chavali glared at Aislynn. "You should have prevented this. He's not responsible for someone becoming corrupt just because some power is making a play for control over the Fallen. You're playing into their hands by allowing them to force his removal."

Aislynn let her hands flop onto the desk. "It's done. We need to move forward from here." She softened the edge of her anger. "Please tell me where you've been for the past day. I know you and Colby charged past a patrol, and I know it wasn't to go share a romantic picnic in a secluded meadow. People saw him drag you up the stairs and carry you outside when you faltered. I also know the little girl was found with Teryk, kicking his shins while he suffered from the Wasting. She claimed you were saving the world, because, and I quote, 'that's what the Seer does.' "

Allowing herself a smirk, Chavali thought about how to reward Haizea later. Someday, the girl would make a good Seer herself. "I do not understand the concept of a 'romantic picnic,' and am therefore unable to refute this notion."

Slamming her fist on the desk, Aislynn growled. "That's enough! Cut the crap. People are dying, and you were supposed to find the culprit.

We know Teryk didn't kill Kess, and neither did his healer. That means her murderer is still running around. We still don't even know why Kess was killed!"

Chavali shrugged. "Eldrack has a better rein on his temper."

"Eldrack isn't here. If we're all lucky, he'll be back, but that may never happen. Why did you leave, and where did you go? So help me, if you answer with anything other than a reason that explains your condition when Colby carried you in, I'll have you arrested too."

"Chavali doesn't really respond to threats like that, Aislynn." Railan set her papers down and faced Chavali. "She doesn't trust you because she doesn't trust anyone. She doesn't even trust Eldrack or me. She doesn't accept your authority either because she doesn't give a crap about royalty. As far as she's concerned, you haven't earned anything. Chavali's position as the Seer of her clan is something she was selected and trained for, if I understand correctly."

"This is a sufficient explanation." Chavali nodded. "I will continue to pursue this killer. Explaining everything is a waste of time."

Aislynn glared at her. "I'm not your enemy."

"Neither are you my ally. You and your men have threatened my clan and put an undue burden on the Fallen. Your approach to this situation has been heavy-handed and foolish, and I don't appreciate having to sneak past patrols to grant dignity to the dead. That mission should not have been one undertaken in a cloud of secrecy."

"So you *are* the one who collected them."

"Yes."

"How did you sneak in and out of town?"

"Using methods no one else could." This subject needed to change, because Chavali wanted to keep the option to sneak out if needed. With Aislynn in charge and the murderer still unknown, she doubted the lockdown would be lifted anytime soon. "Has anything of note been learned from the bodies?"

Railan nodded. "Jacqueline believes the four members of the team were killed by the same weapon. Beyond that, she said Niriya died last."

"I didn't know their names. Which wound was that?"

"The gut. The slit throat was first, then the back wound, the slashed one, and then Niriya. It seemed strange to her that the gut wound came last, because there was no other sign of violence, where the slashed one had been hit a few times. He should've been last. It doesn't really make sense that Niriya lived longer, because her wound was much worse, much more savage. It was a faster death than the back wound or slashing."

Chavali considered the situation and found this fact more baffling than the rest. Niriya couldn't have been asleep. She still had no idea why none of the team had worn armor, or why they'd been in that field after people in the town had seen them leave.

"Amazing. You can see the wheels turning," Aislynn said. "What do you think happened?"

Still annoyed with Aislynn, Chavali narrowed her eyes. "Someone killed them all with a sword."

"Chavali," Railan chided. "We're on the same team."

"I have no other conclusions at this point. Should I reach any, I'll let you know. When are you lifting the lockdown?"

"When the interviews are complete. Since Teryk didn't kill Kess, he obviously didn't act alone. His healer was questioned by a Truthfinder, so she's innocent."

"Wonderful. To improve morale, I suggest you proceed with the Spring Festival." Chavali turned to leave, but stopped herself. This woman needed to know the line she danced. "Do not summon me again without a good reason." She walked out, slamming the door on Aislynn's call to return.

CHAPTER 29

In the washroom on her floor, Chavali set a clean robe on the light-colored tile beside one of eight large bathtubs. A partial wall separated this half of washroom from the toilets and handwashing sinks. Though Chavali never bothered to pull closed the white privacy screens separating the tubs, someone else had used one to block view of the tub on the end of the row. She heard sniffles and the quiet sobs of someone who preferred not to be overheard while crying.

"It's Chavali," she called out. The other women living on her floor appreciated such simple courtesies.

"Is anyone else here?" Though she sounded terrible, Chavali recognized Portia's voice.

"No." Chavali turned on the water for her tub and stripped off her torn, blood-stained dress. "I won't be long."

Portia said nothing. Chavali stepped into the tub and scrubbed dried blood from her skin without closing the drain. She shuddered at the memory of that mercenary woman's fingers digging into her flesh. Lingering in a warm bath seemed like a pleasant idea, but Chavali didn't want to intrude on Portia's pain.

When the water ran clear through her hair, Chavali shut it off. She wrapped her robe around her body and sighed at the ruined dress. "I'm leaving," she told Portia. "No one else has come in."

"Wait for me."

Chavali heard the rush of water sluicing down a drain. "Are you sure?"

Portia pushed open the screen while tying her robe shut. "I've been alone enough for today." She saw the dress in Chavali's hands. "What happened to you?"

"The usual." Chavali shrugged, not wanting to discuss it. "This is normal for me, yes?"

For a moment, Portia seemed like she might laugh, then she covered her face and sniffled. "I can't believe I'm this pathetic."

Chavali hesitated, then she moved to her friend's side and draped an arm over her shoulder. "Betrayal is never easy to accept. Come." She urged Portia to walk, guiding her out of the room and down the hall.

"I just don't understand why I'm blubbering over it."

"You mourn the loss of something inside yourself. It's not about him. It's never about something as inconsequential as a man." Chavali opened Portia's bedroom door and escorted her inside. The mage's space remained tidy as usual, though she'd left her clothes and boots lying on the floor. Her woven rug had patterns Chavali found odd, probably due to not seeing all the colors.

They sat together on the edge of bed.

Portia wiped her face. "That makes sense, I guess. I could really use a drink, though." She pointed to a tall box on her dresser.

Chavali left Portia to open the box. Inside, she found three bottles side-by-side. Each remained sealed. Letters marked labels on the side, but they meant nothing to her. "Do you care which one?"

"Not really. Do you?"

"No." Chavali chose the middle one for no reason and picked up a corkscrew hanging on the side of the box.

Portia took both and removed both seal and cork with practiced expertise. "I just keep asking myself why I didn't see it. Am I stupid? He seemed so..."

"Genuine. Honest." Chavali sat again and watched Portia sniff the bottle. "I like Teryk. He was nice to me when I first arrived. There is undoubtedly a good reason he betrayed us all. To him, that is. No one forced him at knifepoint. Someone convinced him he did the right thing."

"And then he pretended to fall in love with me." Portia drank from the bottle. "Only I wasn't pretending back."

"He may not have been pretending."

"That almost makes it worse." Portia took another drink and offered Chavali the bottle. "Maybe not. I don't know. Why didn't I see this coming?"

Chavali declined the wine with a shake of her head. The taste of alcohol reminded her too much of a particular day with Seer Marika. "How long did you see him? A few weeks? I don't recall any sign of this before or during Harbor City."

"I've known him since I've been here. He's in his last year of service. Nine months to go. I've got about a year and a half left. There was a sort of fling when I was new, but it wasn't really right for either of us. A few months ago, he started making signals like he wanted to try again now that we'd both settled and made it past halfway."

Portia drank again and rested the bottle on her thigh. "When we got back from Harbor City, he said he'd been thinking about me while I was gone, and would I like to go for a ride, and then suddenly we're in bed. Creator bless, he's good in bed. Whenever you get to hitting Colby, I hope for your sake he's at least half as good."

Choosing not to fight this battle, Chavali remained silent. She again refused the bottle as Portia tilted it toward her before taking another swig.

"Then the lockdown happened, and he got all crazy claustrophobic. Wanted to be on the patrols as often as possible, always looking for an excuse to be outside. And I figured, he's that kind of guy. Half of everybody down here acted that way. I like being outside too. I mean, so do you, right? Going up to your clan all the time."

Portia sighed and drank deeply from the bottle. "Are you sure you don't want any of this? It's really good. I only get good wine. None of that cheap crap you get in the dives we always seem to end up in on mission."

"No, thank you. It interacts strangely with my abilities." The lie saved her from explaining about the last time she'd been drunk or the next time she expected it to happen.

"Shame that. Gives you warm fuzzies to cover over the gaping void inside. Everything is worse later, but that's later. Besides, it tastes good."

"I have found ways to deal with my disappointment."

Portia giggled. "Sometimes, you sound like Eldrack. He's always on about disappointment and finding ways to solve problems without whining about them. I mean, he doesn't say it like that, but you know that's what he means."

"I agree. He's annoying."

"And gone." Portia sighed and drank more. When she stopped, the bottle appeared half empty already. Chavali felt no need to police Portia's drinking, especially since the hangover would do the job for her. "How screwed up is that? How did those assholes from the capital even get here so fast? They showed up the morning after the Wasting hit him. The morning after! We found him and the girl around dusk. They got here so early with so many damned people, they had to know about it the night before."

"Curious." Chavali wondered how he got a message out while afflicted and in custody. It made no sense for him to have sent a message asking for such a mass rescue before then. As far as she could tell, he'd taken Biholtz and Haizea because they'd seen and interrupted him taking the gray horse. Knowing what he did about the patrols, she had no doubt he thought he could evade them.

"I don't even know why they came," Portia spat, her words slurred around the edges.

Chavali shrugged. "To protect their asset. We may see him among us again."

"And on that day, I'm gonna slap him across the face. Twice. Once for each cheek." Portia smirked. "So four times."

Chuckling, Chavali thought more about the message that must have been sent. Unless Aislynn requested their presence, which seemed unlikely, someone else had contacted those people. Someone else had a vested interest in removing Eldrack. He'd been concerned about news escaping of Eagle Falls' blue flowers, and the restricted archives probably had other such concerns. Such as the wording of Chavali's prophecies.

"You should shee your faysh," Portia said. She blinked and handed Chavali the bottle. "I my be dumb."

Her thoughts interrupted, Chavali took the bottle and found the cork where Portia had dropped it. "I have no idea what you just said, but I agree this is a good time to stop drinking. Rest would help, I suspect." She set the bottle and cork on Portia's nightstand and helped her climb into bed. "You're better off without Teryk. Men are usually the source of problems, not the solution."

Portia giggled. Chavali stuck the cork into the bottle and returned it to the dresser. She picked up the corkscrew so Portia wouldn't stab herself in the foot. Leaving it beside the wine, she rolled her eyes at the ridiculous laughter Portia seemed likely to continue for some time.

"Good night, Portia. I don't envy your morning."

CHAPTER 30

"**W**ould this morning be a good time to talk to Alene?" Kelly asked as she sat beside Chavali in the dining hall. As usual, her tray held a muffin, a bowl of cereal, and a glass of milk.

Chavali grunted through her oatmeal. Her night had been no worse than the previous few, and also no better. She wanted to decline on the grounds she needed more rest, yet wanted to agree to get something taken care of. Too many problems felt open and unsolved.

"Does that mean yes or no?" Kelly poured milk over her cereal. "I think it would be good for you, if that matters."

Considering she had nothing of import to handle for the day, aside from seeing her clan, Chavali sighed and nodded. "Yes."

His death may not have been her fault, but she held the key to his resurrection. This power sat ill with her. Jesting about holding his life in her hands seemed so distasteful when it was truth.

"Good. When I'm done eating, I'll get Alene. We'll meet in my office."

Half an hour later, Chavali paced across Kelly's office, wringing her hands. The swirled painting on the wall, usually a source of calm, refused to help her settle. She wanted to help Harris. Her stomach churned over what she'd managed to eat. He deserved her best, and she had no idea if she could deliver it.

The door opened. Kelly escorted Alene inside and shut the door. Chavali thought she should sit, but couldn't force herself to. Instead, she greeted both and kept pacing. Kelly settled into her usual chair. Alene took the spot Chavali normally claimed. She seemed small and young in the large chair. Her white clothes and light hair made her nearly disappear against the light-colored upholstery.

"You asked to do this," Kelly said.

"Yes." Chavali continued to pace, trying to decide what to say. She decided to begin at the beginning and see where it took her. "I met Harris when he tried to rob me on the road to a village in Mecalle. Even now, I'm uncertain why I spared his life and brought him back. Something about him made his death seem...wasteful, I suppose. He tested my patience over and over, and I thought several times about handing him over to the Mecalle authorities. Algie wanted to kill him.

"Which I understand. Harris is a foolish idiot. He deliberately failed to shoot me out of nothing more than lust. Typical man. He saw a woman and assumed I'd fall at his feet for being enough of a gentleman to avoid killing me. As if this is some kind of gift."

"Chavali," Kelly said. "I don't think you're helping."

"No, of course not." Chavali huffed and frowned at both women. They glanced at each other and seemed dubious. "I'm trying to say that I hesitated for a reason. A good reason. I think." She tried to think of the subject as a story. If she imagined Harris as a goat, perhaps the tale would come easier. No, that made no sense. Estevior's stories served as a better template. Tales of men all fell along similar lines.

"His father hit him. I know this. He grew up with disrespect for male authority figures. Though the memories are somewhat confusing, I believe his father also hurt his mother, which caused her to withdraw. They both left the picture for some unknown reason, which put Harris and his brother on the streets."

She saw a garbage-filled alley where the boys hunted for food scraps. Harris pined for the days when his mother taught him to read on the couch. He loved his brother too, though. The older boy, whose name she couldn't capture for some reason, found a bit of bread. He handed it to Harris rather than feeding himself.

"His brother died protecting him from a pack of feral dogs roaming the city streets. Harris escaped. This is not his real name, incidentally. I believe it's part of his surname, and he uses it instead of his given name to protect himself from the memories of his childhood. Which is a tactic I find interesting."

"You're getting side-tracked," Kelly murmured.

"Yes." Chavali rubbed her face and stopped pacing to stare at the swirled painting. "By himself, he found a gang of boys on the streets. They did all the usual things such children wind up doing to survive. Guardsmen became the enemy. So much death and abandonment in his life. He learned to shoot a bow and fight with a dagger. He can also pick locks and knows a fair amount about smuggling from his time as one. He's been a bandit and knows a great deal about how such persons operate."

She wondered if he would've known more about the bird woman. Such a tiny detail might have been enough for him to know her name or reputation. With his memories still in a tangled state, she had no way to find the information on purpose. Perhaps she'd stumble across it by accident later.

"This isn't really inspiring," Alene muttered.

"Let her go through her process. She hasn't properly mourned him yet."

"But he sounds like a terrible person shaped by terrible things," Alene said.

"He *is* a terrible person shaped by terrible things," Chavali said with a huff of irritation. She laid her hand on the painting and traced a dark swirl.

"I don't want to be bound to someone like that for the rest of my life!"

Chavali turned to see Kelly patting Alene's hand and urging her to stay without words. She hadn't realized what she asked of the woman, even though she'd been told. Alene had to be convinced to give up the chance for children she desperately wanted to bind herself to a person she'd never met. The girl needed to know Harris wouldn't hurt her, betray her, or take advantage of her. She had to feel she did the right thing.

"This is not the whole of him. He's like this painting." She patted the canvas and gave her attention to it again. "What I can see of it, anyway. Dark lines. Light lines. Together. Making a picture more complex and admirable than one or the other."

Tracing the edges with her finger, she continued. "He trusts and respects those who give him reason to. He's been hurt and betrayed, but hasn't let it turn him to darkness. As a boy, he defied his father. Every time life took from him, he licked his wounds and tried again. Though he's lost the people he cares about again and again, he keeps looking for someone new to care about. Instead of withdrawing and becoming bitter, he remains hopeful. Which is amazing and bizarre.

"His morals have some questionable gray areas, of course. I doubt most Fallen could claim otherwise. We are a peculiar collection of people, after all." She faced the two women, meeting Alene's gaze. "His loyalty, when given, is vast. He endured horrific torture and still never betrayed Eldrack."

Alene hung on her every word, her grimace betraying her discomfort with the idea of torture. "How do you know that?"

Chavali straightened and refused to allow that memory to replay in her head. "I know because I saw his death in the mind of his murderer. Harris crosses no one who doesn't cross him first, and he fights to the death for what he believes in. He surrenders when the cause is neither just nor heartfelt. And he's annoying in his attempts to be charming or virtuous, but in an amusing way."

"What did you do to the murderer?" Kelly asked, her voice quiet.

"Nothing. Colby executed him while I watched." At the time, this had frustrated and irritated her. Thinking back on the moment, she realized how much it had meant to Colby to perform a duty he felt belonged to him, and to save her from it. Despite the guardsman she'd killed out of mercy in the Lady of Ket's basement, he still saw her as someone in need of protecting from such base acts.

"He and most of his companions are dead," Chavali added. "Those who survived and escaped lost their base of operations. We burned it to the ground. This was somewhat accidental. Somewhat."

"You wish you'd killed the man yourself," Kelly said.

Chavali shrugged. "The situation was and remains complex."

"And your feelings for Harris?" Alene asked. With her eyes wide, she seemed even younger. Chavali wondered if she'd destroyed some of the girl's innocence. "I mean personally. Not your assessment of his character."

Looking away, Chavali didn't know how to answer. She considered lying in any of a dozen ways, then finally sighed. "This also was and remains complex. Suffice to say that I prefer him alive to annoy me in person than dead with his memories trapped in my head."

Alene covered her mouth and nose and seemed upset, though she didn't cry.

Kelly patted Alene's back. "Are you all right?"

"I don't know. I just—" She stood and hugged Chavali. "Thank you. I think I can do this now."

Not expecting the embrace, Chavali took a moment to return it. "No, I must thank you. Should he ever choose to behave like a wayward goat to you, tell me and I'll deal with him on your behalf. And if it isn't too much to ask, I'd like to be among the first to hear of it when he wakes."

"Yes, of course." Alene giggled and pulled away. She wiped her face, though Chavali still saw no tears. "Right after Eldrack."

"Thank you, Chavali," Kelly said. "I need to take her downstairs so they can begin the process."

"Of course." She gave both healers a buoyant, genuine smile.

Weight had lifted from her shoulders. At least something had been dealt with, even if Harris's memories still danced with Colby's in her head. After the last time she and Railan attempted to deal with it, she doubted Railan would be eager to delve again, but she thought she might ask anyway. Either way, accomplishing something else seemed within her reach.

CHAPTER 31

Finding Railan would take more effort than finding Eldrack ever had. The Administrator always seemed to know when someone needed him. Railan had no such tendency. Chavali paused at the landing for the thirteenth floor. She might find Railan in Eldrack's office.

Encountering Aislynn there seemed more probable.

Distaste for the princess turned her around in time to see Marjeline step into view, coming from above. As soon as Marjeline saw her, fury twisted her features. The moment reminded her of Niriya.

Marjeline rushed Chavali and jabbed a finger into her chest, shoving her backward until she walked into the wall. "You're supposed to be investigating! Why haven't you found Kess's killer yet?"

Filled with a strange relief, Chavali let out a heavy breath. Niriya had accused her of bewildering things before dying the next morning. Marjeline's question made sense. "I was attacked and had to recover."

"What?" As she'd hoped, Marjeline seemed confused.

"It's complicated. Please, know I haven't forgotten and I won't stop trying to find the person responsible. The most important thing you can do is send Railan my way if you see her. Can you do this?"

Her brow furrowed and her anger blunted, Marjeline nodded. "I guess so. I...don't have anyone to talk to about this. Who should I trust?"

Chavali patted Marjeline's arm through her sleeve. "Jacqueline. Eldrack's healer will do whatever she can to help you. Especially with Eldrack gone. Having you to talk to may help ease her worries also."

"Oh. Yes. That's a good idea. Thank you." Marjeline flashed to frustration and pointed her finger at Chavali. "Find the killer."

"I will. This is my only concern now."

She watched Marjeline nod and hurry downstairs. Still not wanting to see Aislynn, Chavali considered her options. She had no leads for the murderer. They'd cleaned up too well. With the knife missing, no one seen with blood, and nothing near Kess's body to suggest a motive, she had nothing.

Except for Kess's job in the restricted library. That one fact stood out, bright and shining, like it ought to matter. How could it, though? Someone with access there should have been a prime target for cultivating as an accomplice, not for death. Unless they'd approached Kess and been too clumsy?

Chavali trusted Eldrack when he said Teryk hadn't killed Kess. If he had an accomplice, and that person both summoned the people from the capital and killed Kess, they might have extended an offer to Kess and been rebuffed. In a panic, the accomplice could have killed Kess rather than face unveiling.

This line of thinking led her to those associated with Teryk. Chavali doubted Portia had been involved. Her reactions had spoken volumes, and she lacked the ability to lie convincingly about such major things. Their chat last night had cleared any doubt from Chavali's mind. Teryk's healer had been cleared by a Truthfinder, and she'd accompanied him to Todan anyway.

She needed to question Teryk. Even if he didn't know who killed Kess, he knew the identity of his accomplice.

How convenient those people from the capital arrived before she did.

They may have even orchestrated her abduction, though that seemed unlikely.

"Chavali!" Sean bounced into view and looped his arm through hers. Too tired to resist, Chavali let him sweep her down the steps. "You look terrible, but better than I heard. Someone said Colby carried you inside, covered in blood and barely conscious, which is so romantic. He's not talking to anyone, which is so typical. He's not too bright, is he? Not that I think you've only got a chance with men like that, but let's be honest here."

"What do you want?"

"I want to help! Rumor has it Kess's killer hasn't been caught yet, and I know you're the lead investigator. What can I do?"

Other than leaving her alone, Chavali blanked on any task to set him on. Not even a useless one came to mind. Until she considered who she had at her disposal. Sean knew every rumor about everyone. He also knew how to spread new rumors. This capability had potential to help her in the future. For now, she had questions.

"What do you know about who Teryk spent time with, other than his healer and Portia?"

"Oooh. Tricky. He didn't parade around with anyone else. I do know that he came down to see the healers a lot. Like, more than most of us. I mean, I do that too, but I'm married to one. Isabella is absolutely torn up over Kess. She said you asked her a few questions, so I know you know that. I'm just reminding you."

Chavali frowned. "Healers? Why would he spend so much time with the healers?"

"I suspect he was seeing one. Romantically. Which is even worse for Portia, of course. But this whole thing is so tragic all around. The Wasting! It's awful. I saw him as they carried him down to Leilya."

"Who?"

"His healer."

"Ah. I think I need to check on something. Keep your ears open for me, and see if anyone knows who he might have been meeting."

"Oh, definitely." Sean puffed his chest. "You can count on me." He let go of her and dashed upstairs.

With him out of the way, Chavali once again had no idea what to do. She shrugged and kept going down, figuring she ought to see the restricted library. Eldrack had invited her to visit it and examine the written records of her prophecies, but she hadn't yet done so. Perhaps knowing what the rooms looked like would somehow help.

She passed the twentieth floor for the first time. At the next archway, she saw rows upon rows of thirty-foot-high shelves with rolling ladders. Books filled the shelves. The room held no interest for Chavali, so she kept going. At the next archway, a gate barred passage. Through it, she saw hazy clouds.

Uncertain she had the correct level, she continued downward. Around the corner, a large iron door blocked the way. She didn't remember passing this door on the way up for the first time with Eldrack, but she'd been disoriented from her binding. Convinced this didn't lead to the restricted archive, but rather to the place they stored the corpses and those between resurrection and waking, she turned around and approached the gate.

The walls had no sign of a keyhole or other place to insert something. If she needed such a thing, Eldrack should have given it to her when he invited her down anyway. Perhaps a person guarded the gate, and she needed to inform them of her presence. Hopefully, neither Eldrack nor Railan needed to accompany her inside.

The gate had no bell or button. She reached out to touch a thick, solid bar. Her hand passed through it. Blinking, Chavali pushed her arm through. When she met no resistance, she walked into the bars.

On the other side, she found rows of ten-foot-high metal shelves stacked with books. Glittering cords ran from each book to its shelf, where it fused with the metal. A shiny tag of something like paper dangled from each cord. The room smelled of paper and ink, time and deliberation.

"Chavali." A woman with papery skin sat beside the gate, looking over a pair of half-circle glasses. Something about her set Chavali's teeth on edge, but she didn't know what. The filmy sheen over her eyes seemed pale compared to the contained menace of her overall presence.

"Hello." Chavali had no idea how the woman knew her name. "I wonder if you can tell me about the project to index restricted archives with the open ones?"

"Ah. Yes. There's a team working on that. You'd think all of them would want to bury themselves in that kind of work while the tower is locked down. You'd be wrong. Only one continued the work after that nasty business started. I haven't seen her in a few days.

"They're cataloguing the contents of the main archive, something that has been handled on and off throughout the years. The last librarian passed about two decades ago, and no one took up the position until last summer. He's been sorting all of it. The restricted archive, of course, has been kept in good order, but the cross-referencing is supposed to happen upstairs. As a result, it's been spotty. Eldrack is a good man, but he hasn't been on top of that."

Chavali nodded like this provided valuable insight. "The one woman. Is that Healer Kess?"

"Yes, that's her."

"Do you know what she last worked on?"

"Files in the back corner." The woman waved to the right. "Near where your prophecies are stored." Despite her unfamiliarity with the room, the woman seemed to think that provided enough direction.

Kess working near the prophecies seemed suspicious. Chavali didn't need to see the location, but she did need to think. She imagined Kess telling someone about shivers when she worked near genuine prophecies. That person, overcome with greed or ambition, asked her to collect them. When she refused, they killed her to prevent exposure.

The scenario made sense, though it offered no explanation for the mercenaries or the dead Fallen group. She also had no suspects. Isabella couldn't have done this. Sean lacked the capacity to do anything worse than spreading rumors. A cold-blooded killer didn't live inside his harmless exterior.

"May I ask," Chavali said, "how do they do this work? Physically, I mean. How is it carried out?"

"Using the catalog from upstairs, they go through the files down here and mark what has a cross-reference in both the main catalog and the restricted file."

"Do the files down here ever leave?"

The librarian's eyes widened with horror. "Goodness, no. The files never leave here. Even the Administrator comes down here to look at whatever he wants."

"How is this enforced? What prevents their removal?"

"Me. The chain is only there to keep each file where it belongs. I can spot a liberated page from twenty feet away, though." The librarian narrowed her eyes at Chavali. "So don't you think about removing those prophecies."

The woman's stern, piercing gaze made Chavali squirm. Agitated whispers from the spirits confirmed her opinion. This woman looked human, but had something else to her, much like Walt the bartender. Whoever founded the Fallen had been clever in finding ways to collect guardians throughout the centuries.

"No, I have no wish to. Thank you for your help." She left the archive behind and climbed the stairs, wishing she could speak with Eldrack. She rounded the stairs at the fifteenth floor and saw Colby, on his way down.

He smiled at her. "Chavali, I was just looking for you."

The one thing Chavali didn't need was a distraction. "Oh?" She had to get rid of him without making that obvious.

"Have you eaten today?" He reached her and took one more step down, putting them nearer to the same height.

"Yes."

He held out a hand to her. "Come have a cup of tea with me anyway?"

She stared at it. His thoughts didn't bother her, but she didn't want them now. "Perhaps later. I'm on my way to see Aislynn."

His smile faltered and his hand fell to his side. "Have you heard she's decided to hold the Spring Festival even though she's not lifting the lockdown?"

"No, I had not." Ideas circled in her mind. Plans formed. "I need to go. It's important."

"Right. Of course it is." He turned his back on her and descended.

The exchange bothered her. Colby had an annoying habit of distracting her no matter what she did. She considered changing her mind and joining him, but this murderer pressed on her mind. Whoever did it had to be dealt with. Teryk couldn't have caused Harris's death. This other person had.

She ran to the thirteenth floor, determined to push past her annoyance with Aislynn in the name of solving this abominable crime. Once there, she tossed the open door to Eldrack's office. Aislynn jumped, which pleased Chavali. She slammed the door shut as she strode in.

Aislynn clutched her chest and grimaced. "Knock or something."

"This is about the prophecies. I'm certain of it. Someone knows about them and wants access to the transcripts. They killed Kess because she wouldn't get them while working in the restricted archive, and she must have threatened to reveal their interest."

"That's a compelling motive, but who is it?"

"I don't know, but I have a way to find out. It involves the Spring Festival."

CHAPTER 32

Crafting the rumors for Sean to spread took more time and effort than Chavali liked. Over the two days until the Spring Festival, she fed him information in measured doses while pretending to care about the useless gossip he offered in return.

Between preparing a decoy, dodging Colby, Portia, Marjeline, and anyone else she didn't need to see, skirting around near-brawls in the stairwell, and evading requests to assist with festival preparations, she visited the clan as much as possible.

The day of the festival, Chavali stood in the washroom near midday, staring at herself in the mirror. For the trap she'd constructed to work, everything had to happen in the right order and everyone had to be in their place. Few of those involved knew their role, making the chances for mistakes daunting.

She'd done all she could do until nightfall, and now had a chance to enjoy the town-wide party.

She'd chosen to wear her Seer's costume for this day. The dress, complex and many-layered, had survived her death as well as she. The soot, dirt, and blood had been scrubbed out, but she remembered it all. The sleeve cuff had been spattered with her blood. Robin had smeared it there when he tried to save her.

As far as she knew, the brown shades of the outer layers matched her hair, and the pink embroidery matched her feather. The blouse, edged with delicate lace, hung off her shoulders, leaving her neck and upper chest exposed. Like the day she died, she wore her golden Seer's pendant on a golden chain. Unlike that day, she wore her Fallen ring on her finger—doing so carried no risk here.

"I am the Seer of the Blaukenev clan," she murmured to her reflection. "And I am also Fallen. I will not allow any of this to go unpunished." She smoothed the front of her dress, then patted down the thick waves of her hair. Squaring her shoulders, she took a deep breath and strode out of the washroom.

Several other Fallen mingled in the hall, headed aboveground at a leisurely pace. The festival began whenever people arrived and started it. Kitchen staff brought food outside instead of serving it downstairs, ensuring the denizens of the tower surfaced early. Chavali moved at the pace of the crowd. She joined Fallen, Healers, and servants on their way up, slowed by the narrow, twisting passage on the second floor.

The endless line of people marched up the last set of stairs and poured through the packed tavern. Chavali noticed Colby at the bar and slipped out before he could stop her. She needed her head clear, and her thoughts about Colby caused too much distraction. Likewise, she had no desire to face Marjeline's continued wrath and pain or Portia's guilt and heartache. At least Sean had his wife to keep him distracted.

Outside, she strolled toward the clan's farm. Sunshine warmed her, chasing away the bite of a cool breeze. She passed people hurrying to finish last-minute decorating. The flowers intended for the festival had already faded and withered, so they filled pots with colored glass, paper decorations, and simple handicrafts.

When she reached the Whitefield farm, Biholtz leaned against the house with her arms crossed, watching Haizea and Danel inspect and pick dandelions. Haizea seemed to have fallen into a basket of ribbon. Biholtz and Danel wore matching vests with satiny trim over shirts and pants. Biholtz had pulled her hair into a ponytail and wore her sword tied to her waist with a sash.

Chavali grinned at the sight of them, each doing their best to represent their clan. "Biholtz, it's a grand party, you don't need a sword."

"You're armed. Why shouldn't I be? What if some other Fallen decides to try attacking us? No one is knocking me down again. Not like that."

"You have a point." Chavali nodded and gave the girl a quick hug. "You remind me of your mother today."

Biholtz smiled. "You remind me of everyone today."

"Chavali!" Haizea offered her a dandelion bloom. "Penny said we're having lunch in town."

Danel handed her two more flowers. "She said we can have anything we want!"

Chavali tucked the flowers over her ear. "We always listen to our elders."

"Eliot is here," Biholtz said. She jabbed her thumb over her shoulder. "They're grilling him for induction into the clan."

"He needs to get going." Chavali left the kids to their work and stepped inside.

Eliot, Marcus, and Penny all laughed in the kitchen with the scent of coffee in the air. Chavali bustled in, not wanting to overhear them discussing her. Whatever they felt they couldn't say to her face, she thought she didn't want to know.

The three of them sat at the kitchen table, Marcus with his back to Chavali. All seemed comfortable, which didn't surprise her. Eliot had a knack for fitting in with people when he wanted to, and the two elders got along with everyone, so far as she'd seen.

"Should I take the vote now?" Chavali stopped in the doorway.

"Sure." Penny patted Eliot's hand. "I think he's a fine choice for the clan."

Marcus nodded. "The kids like him, and so do I. Biholtz told us we needed to choose yes."

Eliot chuckled, looking more at peace than he'd been since the lockdown started. "I haven't been able to talk to Patrick yet. Which you know." He checked his mug and sighed. "I need to get going. Thank you for the conversation this morning. I've been about ready to stab people. You helped."

"You're welcome anytime, son," Marcus said.

Chavali nodded toward the door. "I'll walk you out."

After depositing his cup in the sink, Eliot followed her to the door. Chavali waited for him to pull his boots on, then they stepped outside and followed the walk to the road.

"You're sure you're fine with this?" she asked, keeping her voice low.

"I've handled decoy duty before. This one is extra-special because everyone seems to know my team is on a decoy mission. You have no idea how irritated the others are about everyone finding out we're a decoy, and then still running it anyway."

She smirked. "This is worth it."

"You should know that I told them it was your idea." He grinned.

"Wonderful." Chavali snorted. "Watch yourselves. This person killed a healer, so they're capable of anything. And thank you."

"Enjoy the festival. I'll try to remember you're risking your life while I'm leading a bunch of grumbling Fallen to the Creator's Tower and back." Eliot flipped her a salute and jogged toward the center of town.

Marcus and Penny stepped outside. Chavali took Haizea and Danel's hands, amused by the excitement and joy in their thoughts.

Together, her clan wandered through town. Everywhere they went, flowers, glass, and paper decorated buildings and fences. Like the children, many people had picked dandelions and other weeds for the celebration.

The smells of frying dough and coffee drifted across the town. Over a dozen people juggled various items, from wrinkled apples to sharp knives. Fiddle and pipe music goaded revelers into bouncing, and drums beat alongside and between them. From Haizea and Danel's thoughts, Chavali knew everyone wore bright colors. Wherever they went, they found people determined to enjoy themselves.

"It's like a carnival," Biholtz said. "Only bigger. And free."

They passed a woman handing out small tarts without asking for payment. Another woman offered lengths of ribbon to those with none. A man offered Haizea a stick with a glittery star tied to the top. He gave Danel a sword made of sticks and twine. Both children accepted the gifts with grace.

The group stopped to eat tiny sandwiches and strips of fried potato. Biholtz found someone offering chocolate-covered gingersnaps.

Beyond that, she encountered a teenage boy who made her blush. Chavali joined a group of adults raising and lowering a large sheet while young children ran in and out.

Later in the afternoon, they found a gathering of children in front of a wood pile where someone used puppets to put on a show. Haizea squealed with delight, having never before seen any such thing. She let go of Chavali's hand and ran around the back to tackle the person responsible. Biholtz darted after her and apologized to the woman—a healer—who laughed.

"You watch from here, Haizea." Biholtz set her down among the audience.

"I want to watch that!" Danel pointed with his stick-sword at two Fallen on the roof of a nearby building. They acted out a silly, acrobatic duel with thin, wooden blades.

Marcus scooped up the boy and settled him on his shoulders. "How's this for a perch?"

"Best view in town!" Danel laughed.

The healer brought out a dark dragon puppet. With the help of a second puppeteer, they acted out a knight challenging the dragon for supremacy over a town. At the climactic moment of truth, Algie burst out of the crowd, wielding a mop dripping with dark liquid. He brandished it at the puppets like a spear.

"Foul beast! I'll save this village from such a vile creature." As he whipped the mop around, it spattered the children with the liquid.

Kids squealed with glee and danced in the strange rain. Several leaped to their feet and attacked Algie, knocking him to the ground and tickling him. Chavali stood by and watched with a grin. Haizea wrestled the mop away and raised it with a whoop. The puppet show stopped in favor of everyone laughing at Algie's plight.

When he finally broke free, Algie couldn't stop giggling. He reclaimed his mop from Haizea and dashed off to cause more mayhem. Several children ran after him, causing their caregivers to scramble. Haizea ran to Chavali and Penny.

Holding up her arms, she asked, "What is it?"

"Paint," Penny said. "Green paint. It'll come off in a bath."

Haizea wrinkled her nose. "Or I could stay green."

"You can take your bath tomorrow," Chavali said.

Biholtz picked up Haizea. "They're going to start the puppet show over. Do you want to watch, or find something else?"

"Something else!"

They wandered off, leaving Marcus and Danel behind.

Drums called to Chavali. She guided the group toward a pulsing, beating rhythm that reminded her of clan bonfires. Before Marika chose her, Chavali had learned to dance. After, she'd helped Pasha practice. She glanced at Biholtz as they neared the drummer, but the girl hadn't been picked for dancing in her youth.

Chavali didn't know the three men beating their drums. People around them bounced and swayed, but left a space on the grass in front of them. Penny stopped to get Haizea a drink. Chavali remembered dozens of bonfires and how the dancers had always thrown writhing, mesmerizing shadows on the ground.

She yanked off her boots and handed them to Biholtz with half a grin. The grass cooled her feet. Stepping into the empty space, she clapped a few beats with the men, then let the rhythm move her.

The last time she'd danced, Pasha had been there. They'd played with the beat and each other, reveling in the freedom of movement.

In her mind, Pasha danced with her now.

They mirrored each other, clapping their hands together and jumping on the beat. Their hips and heads snapped to one side and the other. Spins twirled their skirts. Tears slipped down Chavali's cheeks as she raised and lowered her hand, her wrist flicking in time to the drums. She remembered smacking Pasha's foot to make her point her toes when they did handstands and flipped over.

When the drums stopped, so did Chavali. She stopped and panted, facing the drummers, who all stared at her.

Behind her, applause seemed distant and strange. Rather than say anything, she touched her hand to her chest and bowed to the drummers. All three smiled at her. She wiped her face as she fled the crowd.

Biholtz found her before she went far. "The clan lives in us."

"Yes. That's how it works." Chavali slipped her boots on.

Haizea wrapped her arms around Chavali's waist. "Just like Mamá."

Chavali touched Haizea's head. "Just like many of them. When you get older, I'll teach you. You can teach others yet to come."

CHAPTER 33

As Haizea pointed to the next thing she wanted to see, Penny stepped to Chavali's side. She set a hand on Chavali's shoulder and nodded behind her. "I'll watch the girls."

Chavali turned to see Colby approaching. He seemed conflicted about seeing her, but headed for her. She didn't want to deal with him now. Not with Pasha so fresh on her mind.

Not when he'd probably watched her dance.

"This is not necessary."

"Don't be stupid." Penny nudged her toward Colby.

Chavali stumbled a step. People nearby gave her knowing smiles and smirks. She wanted to shout at the top of her lungs to make everyone stop pairing her with Colby. These people all had nothing better to do than busybody matchmaking for someone who wanted no match. For a brief flicker of a moment, she considered slipping into the crowd and disappearing. The sun hung low enough in the sky now that he might delay her.

Biholtz waved to Colby. Chavali surrendered to inevitability. She closed the distance and kept going at an angle so he could walk with her. If they talked on the way back to the tower, she could keep more careful track of the sun, and get inside around dusk. Did she have an hour still? Maybe. Maybe less.

"I didn't know you could dance," Colby said, his smile strained. He seemed the same as always, though she noted he'd left the button at the top of his shirt undone and tucked a dandelion into its hole.

She remembered telling him once, but he'd probably forgotten. Small, simple details faded when nothing reinforced them. Her behavior never pointed to this skill. "Most of us could."

"Ah." He opened his mouth and shut it, leading Chavali to wonder what he wanted. "You look nice."

"Thank you. Is Karias cooped up, or have you let him run loose?"

"He's loose. Somewhere. I last saw him surrounded by a gaggle of cooing children." He pointed to direct her away from the crowds, guiding her between buildings with a light hand on her back. "I need to talk to you," he said as the noise faded.

"I gathered this." She forced a smile. Given the choice between Colby and Karias, she'd have preferred to discuss many things with the horse tonight. "I don't have time. The sun is setting soon, and I have things that need doing."

"You never have time lately." His sullen overtone made her frown.

"You, of all people, should understand that killers don't catch themselves."

Colby sighed and stopped her. They stood in the deep shade of a shed. The festival hadn't touched this part of town, leaving them in quiet. Perhaps because of that, he kept his voice down. "Was that dance part of your carefully crafted plan to catch them?"

"Of course not. Don't be ridiculous."

He held his hand palm-up between them. "You gave that much time to strangers. Why am I wrong for asking the same?"

"Your timing is awkward." She stared at his hand, not sure she wanted to know what he thought about anything at the moment. "I need to go soon."

"I tried to find you earlier. Were you avoiding me on purpose?"

"No." She started to snort at him, but saw his face and stopped. He seemed hurt or angry. For some reason, reading him lately had been a challenge, and this moment proved no different. "I was with clan. They come first. You know this."

"It feels like you have been." He let his hand fall to his side and looked away from her. "You've skipped all your reading lessons since the lockdown started. We used to share a meal once a day or so by pure accident. Chavali, you haven't even asked for help to catch this killer. You're trying to do everything yourself, and you've barely been eating or sleeping lately."

Chavali didn't see the point of this conversation. He dragged her away from the festival to chide her about not managing her time properly? She crossed her arms and forced space between them. Everything about him seemed opaque tonight, which annoyed her. Of all people, Colby normally took the least effort to read.

"I've had to deal with Harris." Her face felt grimy all of a sudden. She rubbed her cheeks and wished he'd waited until tomorrow to corner her.

"Harris." Colby frowned. His gaze dropped to the ground. "I didn't realize. I thought— But I should've asked." His wounded, apologetic tone made Chavali want to slap him.

"Stop it. None of this is about you."

"No, I suppose not. I just thought, after everything we've been through—"

"That nothing else would matter? Someone killed a healer, Colby! Should everything else sit aside while they run free?"

He looked up, blinking. At least she could still read confusion when she saw it. "What?"

She raised her hands and had to restrain herself from trying to strangle him. Taking a deep breath, she lowered her voice so it wouldn't carry. "What do you think I have to go do soon? I set a trap. It springs tonight. At dusk, the restricted archive librarian will leave that archive unguarded, and the servant tasked with holding the keys to Eldrack's office will 'accidentally' leave them lying out.

"Eliot and a team left earlier today with a book of false prophecies as a decoy. Another book of false prophecies now lies in Eldrack's office with a group tasked to watch them, and they are unaware this book is false. The real book remains in its place.

"Do you have any idea how much effort it took to not only convince Aislynn and Railan to be up here where everyone would see them, but also to get the restricted archive librarian to leave her post and set up the competing rumors on these things so the culprit could be caught without risking them? Even with those precautions taken, I still plan to be in the archive in case they go looking, but I also have to be seen out here for as long as possible."

Colby stared at her, his brow furrowed. "That's...a pretty good plan, though maybe a little overcomplicated. You could've put the real ones in Eldrack's office to minimize potential damage to everything else in the restricted archive."

Chavali waved him off. "There aren't enough trustworthy people to go around. Even those I asked to guard Eldrack's office might have noticed the difference when I left them there and inadvertently told someone. Besides, I thought leaving them in the archive would minimize the possibility of loss while moving them from one place to another."

"That's reasonable. If you'd asked, I could've helped plan this."

"I didn't even explain it all to Aislynn or Railan. The more such things are said aloud, the more chance it gets overheard."

He nodded and crossed his arms. She thought he struggled through something, but, to her irritation, she had no idea what. "What's going on with Harris?"

"They found a healer for him. They wanted me to convince her to bring him back. I took his memories at one point, so I had insight." She thought he wouldn't let her go until she explained, and she had time left. "When I tried to delve into them, they tangled with your memories in my head. It's still something of a mess. I haven't been sleeping well because of it. This is the entire problem."

"That's it?"

She narrowed her eyes. "This is quite enough, thank you."

For whatever reason, his shoulders tensed even though he seemed relieved. "I need to ask you something. Or tell you something. Or something. I'm not sure."

"Figure it out and do it already," she snapped.

"You're so difficult." He huffed.

Chavali growled and turned to stalk away. She could deal with this sort of thing anytime.

Colby caught her arm. "That's not what I wanted to say."

"Get on with it. The sun won't wait."

He let go and rubbed his mouth, showing more signs of nervousness than she'd ever before seen in him. "The other day, when those mercenaries abducted you. They knocked me out. When I woke up, the first thing I thought about was you. Whether you were safe or not. Not Karias. He came to mind right after, but not first. I've been bonded to Karias for several years. Eight or nine now. I've known you for a few months. Nine, if you count the first time we met." He paused and looked at her like that explained everything.

"And? Is there a point you plan to reach with this?"

He huffed and held up his hand for her again. "When I saw you, with all that blood, I thought— It doesn't make sense. Because you're everything I thought I hated. I mean, honesty is the most important thing to me, and here you are, flinging lies around. To everybody, about everything, all the time. None of this makes any sense to me, but that doesn't make it less real."

Suddenly, Chavali had a feeling she knew where his thoughts led.

She didn't want to go there. Not now, not tonight, not ever. "I can't do this."

"I won't force you. I know how you feel about that. Just tell me what Harris means to you."

The change of subject confused her. "What he means to me? I've already had to explain this to his healer."

He gave her a forced smile. "Humor me?"

"Fine. I prefer him alive to dead. I trust him enough to leave him alone with the clan. Whether I trust him enough to ask him to join it is another matter entirely. It depends on how he behaves when he wakes."

One corner of Colby's mouth twitched. His shoulders tightened more. When he spoke, his voice seemed strained. "What about me?"

"What about you?" She growled at him, then she took a deep breath and let it out to force away the frustration he'd spawned. With it, she tossed her anxiety, because it wouldn't help anything either.

He'd either say it or he wouldn't. She hoped he didn't.

"I prefer you alive also. I trust you with the clan. I would already have asked you to join us if I didn't worry so much about how it will affect your bond with Karias. This seems a thing we should speak on for more than a minute or two, and this is all I've had to spend on you of late."

Colby went through several rapid shifts of expression, too fast for Chavali to follow, which still bothered her. She caught his shoulders relaxing, though, and he nodded. Again, he raised his hand for her.

Continuing to ignore his hand seemed rude. "I would rather wait until tomorrow, when this is done. These things are complicated."

"It's not complicated, Chavali." He reached toward her, stopping his fingers short of brushing her cheek. "You only want it to be so you don't have to deal with it. Before I died, I thought I'd live forever. I'd get through anything because I wanted it enough. If I've learned anything from my time as Fallen, it's that life is short and precious, and tomorrow might never come. You want to wait, but something else will come up, then something else. Again and again."

Her fear surged despite her best efforts to bury it. Half of her wanted to duck and flee. The other half despised her cowardice. She met his gaze with as much steel in her spine as she could manage and pressed his hand to her cheek.

When I look at you, I see a partner. Someone I trust, someone I know I can depend on. There are times I want to protect you, but you don't need that. You need a shoulder to lean on, not a defender. You need an equal. Someone you can talk things through with. Someone who cares about you. Someone loyal to you first and the Fallen second.

"Clan comes first," she whispered. She remembered Keino failing at understanding this. Maybe if she'd explained it more instead of expecting him to figure it out, he would've made her happy. He'd still be dead.

Colby stood in front of her, alive and a better man than Keino had ever aspired to be. Given the need, she'd kill to protect him.

No. The Seer comes first. Then clan.

"I can't."

You can't what? Trust me?

She stepped back, and he let her. Covering her face, she groped to keep herself together. Colby wrapped his arms around her and held on. His body warmed her. Her forehead rested on his chest.

"Stop holding it in," he murmured. "You always hold it in. You're going to burst if you don't let something out. Let yourself feel."

"I don't have time for this."

"Yes, you do. I won't let you take too long. I promise. Let me be your partner. Lean on me."

She thumped his chest with a fist, annoyed with him for being right and good, honorable and decent. Her eyes burned with tears she didn't want to shed. "I hate you."

"I love you."

"Why?"

"I have no idea."

She laughed, or maybe she cried. She couldn't tell which, only that tears streamed down her cheeks.

CHAPTER 34

"We need to go if we're going to reach the archive in time." Colby's voice rumbled in his chest, resonant and soothing.

Chavali stared to the side, watching the shadows deepen against the nearby wall. Colby's steady, grounding heartbeat thumped in her ear through his soft, smooth shirt. When had she forgotten how much she needed to be held? Keino had always rushed these moments more than she'd liked. Her parents had stopped holding her when she became the Seer. Pasha had given her random hugs, but not like this.

"We?"

"Do you really think I'm going to enjoy the party while you go down there by yourself and potentially face someone willing to kill you? Right after I told you how I want to be your partner? In my place, I think you'd call me an idiot for that."

"Probably. But others are helping already. Portia is in Eldrack's office with Railan and one of Aislynn's Truthfinders. They believe they guard the true prophecies. My hope is the culprit goes to them. My fear is they call my bluff."

"So you've tasked yourself with making sure someone is there if they do."

"Yes. I trust me. And you. We only need to get down there without rousing suspicion."

"We can use all those rumors to our benefit for once." She heard the grin in his voice. "Everyone will think we're sneaking off for privacy."

Chavali had abused the rumors before, but kept her mouth shut. He hadn't noticed Karias's two-day absence, and she had no intention of revealing it. "In that case, I should lead."

"And scowl. Roll your eyes a few times along the way."

She pulled away to meet his gaze with an arched eyebrow. "I don't do these things that much."

He ran a thumb over her eyebrow, his grin broadening. *Saying all of this out loud is such a relief.* "This too. Add some of this. No one will believe you if you don't."

Rolling her eyes, she broke free of his embrace and marched toward the center of town. Those who noticed her caught sight of Colby in her wake. Their expressions oozed with assumptions. She tried to react like she always did, with annoyance and exasperation, but it seemed empty and flat.

They reached the tavern and found the establishment full of patrons. Violet waved to Chavali. When she saw Colby, she turned away to giggle behind her hand with someone else. Chavali glared at the door, then at the stairs, then at the false shelf, then at the wall. When they reached the top of the spiral stair, each step echoed in the tower's emptiness.

"Should we go to your room or mine?" Colby asked, failing to contain his amusement. "Yours is closer, but mine has my sword."

"I am not participating in a conversation about your sword."

Colby laughed. "That's probably for the best."

Chavali huffed, thinking she might've created a monster. "I didn't wait before, and that turned out poorly, so I'll wait this time while you fetch it."

"You're truly gracious, m'lady."

"Don't make me regret telling you about this." She led him to his own room on the eleventh floor, but let him open the door. When he stepped inside, she saw another Fallen stepping out of a room down the hall. As little as Chavali wanted to do anything to confirm all the rumors, she ducked into Colby's room, pretending to be both furtive and unaware of Bernard's observation.

She shut the door and pressed her ear to it. Colby opened his mouth, but she touched a finger to her lips and waved for him to be quiet. In the hall, she heard nothing until Bernard reached the door.

"Nothing going on between you," Bernard said with a chuckle, his voice muffled by the door and difficult to discern. "Sure. I believe you, Colby." His voice faded into the distance, but she caught two more words. "Reading lessons."

Straightening with a sigh, she shook her head. At least the rumors held some truth now. "We have certainly been spotted."

Colby held two swords. One, she recognized as his usual giant, two-handed blade. The other, he'd brought when he and Biholtz rescued her from the mercenaries. "I think maybe the shorter one for this. We're expecting cramped quarters."

"Where did you get it?"

"Teryk. I was unarmed, he wasn't. No one asked for it back when we returned, so I kept it."

"With you carrying a sword, anyone we pass will know this is no covert liaison."

Colby tied the sheath to his belt. "I think they'll figure that out anyway. No one uses the meeting rooms for that."

"Then we must avoid being seen." She put her hand on the doorknob and listened through the door again.

"How are we going to hide in the archive?"

"The same way I did at the Harbor City palace to catch Bricene. Once we stop moving, I can conceal us behind an illusion." She opened the door and led him up the hallway.

Colby caught up after closing the door and kept pace with her. He rested a hand on her back as they slipped to the stairs. She welcomed his reassuring presence. They hurried down the stairs together. As they neared the thirteenth floor, he stopped and pulled her to the center column of the stairwell.

He pressed her against the stone. Chavali heard voices nearby without understanding the words. They faded into the distance. A distant door shut. Colby took her hand and headed deeper at a more hurried pace.

I think I saw Portia and the Truthfinder who sat in on my interview. His thoughts showed her the backs of two people entering the thirteenth floor archway with a purposeful stride. Chavali suspected the man to be Orlin, who'd also been present at her second interview. Aislynn seemed to place more trust in him than the other Truthfinders.

"Good," Chavali murmured. Portia knew her job. That group hoped for a peaceful intervention followed by an interrogation. Railan had Chavali's permission to contact her telepathically if they caught someone in their net. She'd convinced Railan that her own presence would spoil the trap. Everyone knew she hunted the killer. No one expected the same from

Portia.

Chavali slipped on a step at the nineteenth floor. Colby caught her. His thoughts processed voices coming from below and showed her his plan of action a moment before he carried it out. He whisked her through the archway and held her against the wall. The way they stood, the wall now hid Colby's sword.

To her surprise, the voices came from the healer's hall, which shared the floor with the dining hall. He'd heard them wrong. She nodded behind him.

I can only think of one thing to do. He kissed her.

She lost the thread of her own thoughts as his swirled around her. He noticed the softness of her skin. Two people approached. Her hair tickled his neck. He wished he'd told her how he felt a week ago. If either of the people attacked, he'd take the hit and Chavali would have to act first. She tasted—

"Chavali?" Kelly sounded startled and aghast.

Colby broke off the kiss. Chavali didn't need his thoughts to show her that he had no idea what to do.

"Kelly. Maryna." She resisted the urge to wipe her mouth. Her mind felt more scrambled than when she woke from a mashed up nightmare.

"What are you doing down here?"

In her current state, Chavali had no idea how to read Kelly's tone or Maryna's expression. She giggled. "Acting like foolish teenagers?"

Kelly huffed and gestured for Maryna to head upstairs with her. "I can't believe how easily you can lie to me, Chavali. How many times have you told me that you don't have a relationship with Colby?"

"She didn't until a few minutes ago," Colby said. He had the sense to sound sheepish, and to cross his arms in discomfort.

"This happened in the fashion you'd expect, I think. After an argument."

Blinking at them both, Kelly opened and shut her mouth, then she broke into an amused grin. "Well. Then. What are you doing down here? You both have rooms, don't you?"

Colby coughed. "She mentioned an argument."

Maryna rolled her eyes and tugged on Kelly's arm. "Take it private. We're going up to the party now that our shift down here is over."

"Of course," Chavali said. "This was not intentional."

Kelly waved and fell into step with Maryna.

"While we're down here, I'll get us something to drink," Colby said, loud enough that both healers would overhear.

"Good thinking."

He took her hand. *I'm sorry about that. We could've kept going.*

She waved him off and pictured how her next chat with Kelly would go. Or anyone, for that matter, because she had no doubt the entire tower would hear of this incident by morning. Kelly might not consider this within the boundaries of her confidentiality promise. Maryna had no reason not to tell whomever she pleased.

So much for keeping things in the realm of rumors. Colby leaned out to check the stairwell. With no one coming, he tugged her along. They ran down the next three flights of stairs and slipped into the restricted archive.

No one sat at the librarian's desk, which meant they'd taken too long to reach the archive. Chavali took the lead, ready to spin out an illusion if the culprit had beat them here. They darted down the outer aisle and discovered the outer edges of the shelves formed a curve away from the stairwell.

At the last row of shelves, Chavali slowed and peered around the books. The far end held books and more books, all secured with chains, but no people. She ran down the aisle to find the right book for her prophecies.

"I don't know if we beat them or not," she whispered. "It should be here someplace."

Colby tapped a tag on a chain for a thin book. "This is it." He flipped the tome open and showed her thin, crinkly pages of tidy handwriting. "It's still here." He scanned a few pages, his brow furrowing more with every passing moment. "Look, here's the one with the lines about the dragon devouring and the cat out of play. So it's real, not a fake someone swapped in."

Before the words on the pages could distract him, she snapped the book shut and returned it to its spot. "Stand there. Quiet now. Read later." She threaded her fingers through the spirits and projected an image of the back wall to conceal them both.

Colby opened his mouth. Chavali held up a hand and put her finger to her lips. He took her hand.

I should read those prophecies. If I understood Eldrack correctly, I'm referenced in some of them.

Chavali had no way to answer without making noise. She shrugged. The text of the prophecies interested her in a detached way. If she could read, she thought she would look them over to indulge her curiosity. Not knowing, though, didn't bother her.

Don't you want to know?

She shrugged again. The prophecies used enough metaphor and symbolism to be almost worthless, in her opinion. Warnings helped little when the recipients had no reliable way to decipher them. If the spirits could say what would happen without abstraction, she would see more value in them. Despite this, she had accepted the burden of protecting them.

I want to tell you that I didn't mean for the first time I kissed you to be like that. It seems fitting, somehow, but it was rude. And not really how I pictured it. I kind of thought we'd find some real privacy first. This was the opposite of that. In every way imaginable.

Waving to shut him up, she tugged her hand out of his grip. Unlike Keino, he let go. Every time she wanted space, Colby let her have it. That alone earned forgiveness for many sins. "Later," she mouthed, barely making any sound.

He went still. A few moments later, he touched her bare shoulder. *I hear footsteps. Someone's coming.*

Chavali nodded and rested her hand on her dagger's hilt while Colby moved his hand to his sword. She cocked her head to the side and listened. Soft shuffling neared them, moving fast. The sound moved closer and closer until someone in white rounded the corner.

CHAPTER 35

Maryna, Railan's healer, hurried down the aisle to the prophecies. She picked up the book and checked the first page. "I knew it," she muttered. Setting it down again, she reached under her shirt and withdrew an identical tome. She snapped off the chain and clamped it to the replacement book.

Colby rushed out of the illusion to knock Maryna to the floor. She squawked and landed with a thump. He flipped her onto her stomach and pressed a knee to her back. Though she struggled and flailed, she had no hope of dislodging Colby.

Chavali dismissed her illusion and stared at Maryna. For some reason, the culprits in these situations always defied her expectations. Her ideas about the traitors had been ill-formed, but she'd never expected a healer to be behind the death of an agent or another healer. Maryna knew how much they sacrificed. She understood the goals and hardships.

"I should've known you weren't down here for a tryst," Maryna spat. "Lying to your healer, Chavali? That's despicable."

Sitting out of reach of Maryna's fists, Chavali arched an eyebrow. "How does it compare to killing one?"

Maryna stopped struggling. "I didn't kill Kess. I don't know who did."

"And I should believe this because you claim it? Do you take me for a fool?"

"Of course not. I didn't kill her! Bring a Truthfinder. I'm not afraid of them. I had nothing to do with that."

Colby set his sword aside and removed his belt. "I don't think we're going to risk you grabbing a weapon."

Chavali frowned. How many traitors could the tower hold? "Who are you intending to deliver the prophecies to?"

"I don't have anything else to say. But I did *not* kill Kess. I would never harm another healer."

"Fallen, of course, are another matter entirely, yes?"

"No." Maryna groaned while Colby shifted to wrap his belt around her wrists. "No one was supposed to get hurt or killed. I'm doing what's right for Shappa."

Chavali slapped her. "Those deaths are on your head. Whether you held the knife or not."

Colby looked up from fastening his belt around Maryna's wrists. "Chavali."

Biting back a growl, Chavali stood and took a step back. She slipped and fell into dark, sticky muck. Clawing for the surface, she broke loose enough to see, but nothing else. From one step to the left, she watched her hand grip the hilt of her dagger behind her back.

The Chavali that wasn't Chavali drew the blade and plunged it into Colby's back.

He cried out. Chavali froze, horrified. Her body ripped the blade across his back, drinking his blood and tearing him apart.

Colby slumped. Blood gushed from the ragged gash.

Maryna wriggled onto her back. "What are you doing?" she shrieked.

Chavali swooped on her and dragged the blade across Maryna's neck, slashing open a wide, smooth slice.

Her mouth still moving, Maryna stared at Chavali without comprehension. Blood flowed down her chest, staining her white clothes. Kiron had made a blade perfect for slitting throats, as Chavali had requested.

"Stop," Chavali whispered.

"I don't think so," Chavali's mouth said with Chavali's voice. She inspected her blade and grinned. "This is a really nice dagger. An excellent addition to this prize." Stooping, she snatched the book of prophecies and checked to make sure she had the real one.

Chavali didn't know what to do. She didn't understand any of this.

Someone stole her body and ripped out her heart with her own weapon. "Save him," she mewled.

"Oh, get over it, Chavali." She jogged to the gate and passed through it. "You're better off without him. He's too soft and sentimental for you. Someone like Robin, on the other hand," she gushed, "is exactly what you need. He's strong. Real strength, not muscles that wither away. His priorities are straight too. Honestly, Colby's a waste of your time and energy. Big, dumb, like a giant puppy."

If she had her body, Chavali knew shock and grief would paralyze her. Instead, she rode along with the entity claiming it, unable to do anything but follow up the stairs.

Colby had been right, and so horribly wrong.

If he hadn't said anything, if he hadn't persisted, she would never have known. How long did he hold her? Half an hour? She got that, and a kiss with half his attention on the audience?

"If only I'd had this dagger before," Chavali's mouth said. She sighed. "It would've made so many moments so much cleaner."

Chavali groped past her pain to try to think. Not many people knew about Robin. Even fewer idolized him. She flashed on Niriya's sense of violation. Tangled memories. Murder.

One name linked everything, and that person didn't have a body anymore. Because Chavali had killed her while linked to her.

"Pale?" she asked, her mind-voice breathless and shaking.

"You finally figured it out?" Pale snorted. "It only took you forever and a half. That asinine twit Keino got in the way for a while, I'll admit, so you maybe haven't had as long to notice as you could have."

The clatter of running feet made Pale look up. She ducked into the nearest archway and hid around the corner.

Chavali sputtered with questions. She needed to know how this had happened.

The why questions mattered less, though they hurt more.

Pale had killed Colby for obvious reasons. Maryna had witnessed too much. The reasons Chavali had come up with for Kess's death made enough sense to apply to Pale, and the librarian had acted like she'd seen Chavali before.

She remembered the dampness on her sleeve when she woke with Railan. Had Pale washed blood from her clothes? "How did you cause my memories to tangle?"

The noise receded below. Pale dashed up the stairs to the thirteenth floor. She ran down the hall to the meeting room at the end.

"Bravo, Chavali," she said as she shut the door. "It took some time, but I had plenty before you even tried to get into that stupid chest. You need to work on how you compartmentalize everything, sweetie. Shoving all your feelings and memories into boxes makes them easy to tamper with."

Pale pressed her hand to the wall as Eldrack had done. Chavali's Fallen ring glowed. The door swung open. They dove into the darkness.

Nothing would stop Pale from here. Nothing *could* stop Pale from here.

Chavali had no control, and no one knew what had happened. The death of Railan's healer would leave Railan stricken and unable to think. Chavali had no idea how Colby's death would affect Karias.

Trying to detach herself from her feelings for Colby squeezed her chest. Nothing else mattered.

Except clan still mattered. Biholtz needed her. They all still needed her.

"Oh, Chavali. You're so much more sentimental than anyone thinks. But you know what? You and I are going to be best friends. You'll see. Robin will fix this mess and we'll share. You can handle your power and I'll handle mine. But first we need to make sure you're not going to mess everything up. Until then, this is my body, and you get to sit in the corner."

"What did you do to Niriya?"

Pale giggled, the sound high-pitched and more unhinged than girlish. "She sent a message for me. To Robin. He knows you're alive, sweetie. Even if we just sit here, he'll come to us. And you know what, he doesn't even know there are written prophecies! When we turn up on his doorstep with this book, he'll be so pleased."

Chavali wanted to throw up from pain and rage. "Niriya killed them and herself. Because you told her to."

"Yes. Such a waste of talent, but then, witnesses are witnesses. If you want me to explain why they didn't have their armor on, I have no idea. Maybe I implanted a little too much of a suggestion." Pale giggled again. "Who knows? Niriya was a talented wench, after all."

Chavali remembered Biholtz saying she'd moved around and spoken at night in Meckit despite not remembering it. "And all this time, while I've been struggling to sleep, you've been walking around, doing things in my body, and keeping me from resting enough."

"Obviously. You're really quite firmly entrenched here while you're awake. Well, you were. Now, not so much. Opening up to Colby gave me an excellent lever. All that silly emotion swirling around, and you have no idea what to do with it. Until that happened, I figured I'd just wait until Robin showed up to collect us. Besides, it was funny to watch you search for a killer you'd never find."

Pale climbed the steps to the door. "And the best part? If you'd just submitted to a telepathic scan, someone would've noticed me. But no, your precious clan secrets have to be protected. You're obsessed with that, Chavali. No one cares about the spirits. You can scream from the rooftops that the souls of the dead cling to you and no one will care. Well, Robin might care. I'll bet they can do way more than you've managed to convince them to do. Illusions are chump tricks."

"I would rather be dead than watch you abuse the spirits."

Pale giggled. "You'll change your mind for Robin. Maybe he'll think some of this crap is useful, I suppose. Your weird need to protect your language is stupid too. No one cares how many different words you have to describe how goats behave, or about all the stupid stories you have access to."

Chavali splashed in the gunk, finding it stickier than before. The muck clung, not offering a crack or gap to exploit.

"I will admit," Pale said as she reached the glowing door, "Karias is interesting. Robin might be able to use that knowledge. I guess if the horse-spirit-thing survives Colby's death, then we might be able to take him too, but not until later. For now, we have a long walk ahead of us. This would've been simpler if you'd just let those mercenaries deliver you, but, in hindsight, I suppose that was really too much to ask. Especially with Colby around."

Pale pulled the lever and crawled through the foliage. Nothing stood between them and Robin. Between Chavali's endurance training and Pale's willingness to take whatever she wanted from anyone, they'd reach Robin.

He'd see her in this dress, the one she'd worn that day she'd killed herself.

Though she wanted to stay strong, Chavali closed her eyes and wept. She should've stayed dead. So much pain had been loosed on the world because of Eldrack's choice to bring her back. The children would've suffered for a great deal longer, but in the end, they would've been released through death.

One way or another, the clan was lost that day last summer.

"You're so morose." Pale straightened in the darkness and brushed leaves out of Chavali's hair. "Is it going to be like this the whole way?"

"Drown in stagnation," Chavali sobbed.

Pale giggled. "That's really the most vile curse in your whole language? Your clan is adorable. Well, it was. Like you so rightly think should be done, we'll take care of what's left of it once we have you under control, because that clan is really just a problem for everyone. Then you can be happy. Won't that be wonderful? I can hardly wait until we're best friends."

CHAPTER 36

Pale tucked the book under her arm and set off down the road. She walked with a cheerful bounce in her step.

Chavali stopped struggling against the muck. With Pale able to monitor her thoughts, she had no hope of escape. Oblivion would hurt less.

"Do you hear something?" Pale stopped and turned.

Not sure she wanted to know but unable to curb a flicker of hope, Chavali stopped sinking. She scrambled to keep the ability to see. Through a dark gauze of slime, she saw the blazing light of bonfires in the distance. The moon, full and bright, cast a pale glow on the packed earth.

Laughing and clapping, Pale skipped away from Cloverdale. "Made you look! Oh, this trip is going to be so much fun. It won't even take that long, because we can use the Creator's Towers. Three days, I think."

When she thought Pale could sink no lower, she made everything worse. Chavali wished for someone to cross their path and kill them both. Ridding the world of Pale ranked higher in her priorities than survival.

Pale huffed. "Boring and repetitive." She hummed to herself as she strolled.

With nothing else to do, Chavali distracted herself by sorting through Harris's memories. She did it for no other reason than having something to do.

Either she'd die or Robin would force his control over her.

Under his thumb, she suspected he'd either straighten all this out for her or make it worse. Robin would do whatever he felt contributed to his control and her utility.

Harris memories went to the left, Colby to the right. Without Pale actively keeping them entwined, Chavali found the threads and fussed with the knots. Colby stood proud and strong, in command of his men. Harris hugged his knees and rocked back and forth, reeling from his brother's death. The two memories had nothing to do with each other, except she'd loved each of them in their own way.

Thundering hoofbeats on the road behind them made Pale pause and turn. A white ghost bore down on them at high speed. Pale scrambled off the road. Chavali let herself hope Karias would see only the lie and kill her.

Dropping the book in the grass along the side of the road, Pale tried to summon the spirits. She rippled her fingers through the air the same way Chavali did. Her will formed a sharp spike of demand. Then she pictured the illusory screen she wanted.

The spirits buzzed. Chavali felt pressure around her. They knew. Pale had no connection to the clan. Her body bore the mantle, but Chavali's soul carried the link.

"Make them obey," Pale growled.

Chavali snorted. "No."

Karias hopped to a stop with three people on his back. He crossed the grass to her.

"Chavali, are you hurt?" Kelly slid off Karias's back and rushed to her. She took Chavali's arm and frowned.

Penny and Biholtz helped each other reach the ground. "Karias was insistent about bringing us here," Penny said. "He's a peculiar creature."

"You don't know the half of it," Pale said with a smirk.

Kelly turned and stared at the space where Chavali hung, tethered to her body. Furrowing her brow, she shook her head like something didn't make sense. "What's wrong?"

Pale shrugged. "I don't know. Maybe it's you."

"It's Pale!" Chavali screamed. "It's not me!" She thrashed to free herself again. "Tell them!" she shouted at the spirits.

Biholtz cocked her head to the side. "Why are you out here?"

Looking around as if she hadn't realized her location before, Pale shook her head. "I don't know. Where am I?"

"What happened?" Kelly murmured. She touched Chavali's neck, taking her pulse.

Chavali noticed the spirits fed her and Pale nothing. They buzzed louder with agitation and failed to devour Kelly's thoughts.

"Bring Biholtz closer," Chavali whispered. "Summon clan."

Pale squirmed away from Kelly. "Stop touching me. It's annoying."

Biholtz drifted closer. Penny turned her head like she heard something nearby but couldn't place it.

Karias stepped closer and nudged Pale with her nose.

"Get away from me," Pale snapped. She backed away from the horse and shoved Kelly aside.

Kelly stumbled and fell to the ground.

Biholtz, Karias, and Penny closed in, sending Pale scrambling backward.

"Stop it." With every word, Pale sounded more shrill. "What are you doing? You're acting creepy and weird. It's me, Chavali."

"You sound funny," Biholtz snatched Pale's hand.

The spirits flooded down Chavali's arm, pulling her with them. She didn't resist. They swirled and spun, and dragged her free of the thick ooze. Crowding around Biholtz, they seethed with triumphant rage. They shoved Chavali forward.

"It's Pale," Chavali snarled through Biholtz's mouth.

Pale stared at Biholtz. Chavali felt her trying to infiltrate the girl's mind. "She's lost her mind," Pale ground through her teeth.

At Chavali's command, the spirits formed a wall between Pale and Biholtz. They rebuffed Pale's assault and threw it into her face. Pale jerked her head as if she'd been slapped.

Penny raised a hand and drew a sigil in the air.

Pale fell. Instead of scrambling to flee, she froze in place.

Chavali felt nothing else from Pale, as if Penny's magic and the spirits colluded to keep a barrier between them.

"That's about enough of that," Penny said. "She's immobilized and stuffed. Now what?"

Chavali wished she had the power to become visible. She saw only one way to solve this problem. If only she could show them how much it hurt. "You have to kill the body."

Biholtz's hand flew to her mouth, covering it in horror. "No!" she screamed. "We need you!"

"She's taken over. I can't win against her." Chavali covered her face and wanted to weep, but she had to save the clan.

"We'll see about that." Railan stepped through the nearby trees, supporting Colby's weight as he stumbled with her.

Colby gasped for breath and his skin seemed pale, but he'd somehow survived Pale's attack. "Nobody is killing Chavali's body," he wheezed. "I don't care what's in it."

"It's Pale." Chavali didn't know what to think or feel. She'd been ready to kill herself again because she thought she'd lost the most important part of her second chance. Then he walked back into her life.

Kelly scrambled to her feet, prophecy book in hand, and rushed to Colby. Her hand glowed as she took his arm. "She doesn't get to take my Fallen," Kelly growled. Chavali had never seen her angry before. "That— That woman is dead and needs to stay that way. She's already done more than enough damage and killed more than enough people. Railan, you finish this. You deal with her and you save Chavali. I refuse to give up my Fallen to someone as— As terrible as that."

Railan nodded. "We're not going to kill Chavali's body. We're going to kill Pale. This time, she's going to stay dead."

As his flesh knitted, Colby straightened with a sigh of relief. "Send me in."

"Send you in? I—" Railan stopped in the face of Colby's fierce, determined anger. "—will have to think about how to do that. Give me a minute."

Chavali released her hold on Biholtz enough to avoid saying anything. She wanted to touch Colby and make sure he was real. At the same time, she wanted to keep Biholtz out of the middle. The clan came first, no matter what anyone said.

Biholtz sucked in a breath. "Send me too. I can help. You have to send clan to deal with this. She needs an anchor."

"I can fulfill that," Penny said. "There's no need for you to face this danger."

"I'm thirteen, not five! I can do this. You need to do magic stuff. I need to help Chavali. We share blood, and that will always be a stronger bond than just being in the clan."

"By that logic," Kelly said, "I should also go. The more connections we offer to Chavali, the better off we'll be. Besides, Pale is obviously strong enough to cause serious problems. We need to pile on and help each other."

Karias whinnied and stamped a foot.

Railan raised an eyebrow at him.

Colby and Kelly both seemed intent on Biholtz. She crossed her arms and glared at them.

Railan's mind-voice fluttered on the air. *Chavali, I know you're there. Latch on and I'll reel you in.*

Chavali followed orders.

"Fine," Railan muttered. "Either I can go in, or all of you can. It's pretty clear all of you aren't going to stand by and do nothing, so you can all go together. Since none of you have done this before, the most important thing to remember is that it's your will that controls everything. Muscles don't help. Focus on your goals and worry about how to meet them with your mind. I'd like to do this someplace controlled, but I think we're better off going for speed here. Any questions?"

"Will Chavali be there?" Colby asked.

If good intentions could win, Railan told her, *you'd be a sure bet.*

Watch yourself and remember your goal is to force her out of your body. The environment is your primary concern. Focus on controlling it and unbalancing her. Help Colby and Biholtz create swords from their will. I can't do anything more than throw you all in and keep Pale from escaping. Later, you and I are going to talk about the fact you've been keeping Karias's dirty little secret from me.

"I understand," Chavali said. She wanted to joke with Railan, or tell her something cryptic, but couldn't find the words. "Trust him to watch over us."

I got that part, thank you. Be swift. I can't keep this up forever.

"Yes," Railan said to Colby. "She's here, she's just not there. If there's no other questions, all of you lie down and get ready for an experience you'll never forget. Or want to repeat."

CHAPTER 37

Railan raised her hands and held her thumbs and forefingers together. Chavali suspected she did it for focus and concentration, not because she had to. She took a deep breath in. Bright, golden tendrils spiraled from her hands. One reached for Chavali. Five more plunged into the foreheads of everyone else except Karias.

Chavali wrapped her fingers around the tendril and let it whisk her into an inferno. Brilliant red and orange fire blazed in a ring, surrounding her on scorched, barren ground. Colby stood at her back with Penny, Kelly, and Biholtz. The roaring flames twisted upward, closing off any avenue of escape.

Parts of wagons, painted in bright colors, smoked and burned on the ground as anchors for the blaze. Across from Colby, a doorway blocked by debris offered no exit.

The spirits slithered over Chavali's body in wispy bands of purple. She raised her arms and watched the thin lines. Tiny hands and screaming mouths reached out and receded. Unintelligible murmurs crowded around her.

Heat stole her breath. She wanted to take hold of Colby and never let go. Business and clan came first. She touched the outside of his leg. He covered her hand with his own.

The spirits didn't feed Chavali his thoughts. This meant nothing, because the spirits clearly operated differently here.

"In this place," Chavali said, "your will is your weapon. Focus on what you want with as much force as you can."

"Sounds like magic," Penny said.

"Also like healing." Kelly touched Chavali's shoulder. "The connection between us—"

Chavali cleared her throat. "It should also be noted that Pale can hear and see us. I'm uncertain whether she can detect any of our thoughts. Mine, probably. Yours, I can't say."

The air rumbled with distant, sonorous thunder, the repeating noise battering against her chest. After three booms, Chavali realized it matched the rhythm of Pale's annoying giggle, issued from a creature a thousand times bigger than them. Knowing that made her want to punch Pale in the face. Except it would be her own face.

To her left, Biholtz frowned with concentration. Purple light coalesced in her hands, forming a rough blade shape. Tendrils writhed along the flickering length.

Glancing behind, Chavali saw Colby had already created a shining, silver replica of his usual sword. He may not have been able to resist Pale in Ket, but forging his will into a weapon seemed to come naturally enough.

Kelly held a large shield so white it defied the concept of color. "I hope someone else has an idea. I've never been in a battle before. Unless crossing verbal swords with Chavali counts."

"If that counts, we've all got plenty of experience," Penny said with a grin.

Chavali snorted. She restrained the urge to keep a hold on Colby to make sure he was real. Nothing here was real. Everything they did here happened in Pale's head. "Pale is the environment. We need to take that away from her."

Penny raised her hands and drew a bright blue sigil in the air. Chill air surged in, providing a barrier against the heat.

"If she's the environment," Colby said, "but it's your body, how do we do that without hurting you?"

"This should be your last concern." Chavali took Kelly's hand in hers and reached for the fire.

"Stop being such a damned martyr," Colby growled. "I'm here for you, not for the rest of the world."

Chavali's chest filled with something warm and foreign. "I appreciate this, but it doesn't change the fact that Kelly can heal me. And if she can't, I would rather be dead than under Pale's control."

She pressed her fingertips into the fire. Searing, agonizing pain scorched her flesh. Kelly's hand glowed in Chavali's, repairing her fingers. The fire crackled and sizzled.

Colby yanked her out of the fire by the shoulder of her dress. "Knock it off. Are you trying to get hurt?"

"I'm trying to determine how this situation functions." Chavali rubbed her hand against her skirt.

"We can do that without melting your hand."

"If you have an idea, make it happen."

"They sound like a couple," Biholtz said to Penny.

"A young couple," Penny agreed.

"Shut up," Chavali snapped. She pushed Colby's arm to get him to stab the fire.

The sword tip cut into the flames with no effect.

Kelly stepped forward and touched her shield to the fire. Though it created a small void in the flames, they reached over the shield to reconnect above it.

"Water," Biholtz suggested. "I remember when—" She shuddered and shook her head. "Chavali's fingers sizzled."

"Not just water, though," Chavali muttered. Pale knew that water stopped fire. This barrier had nothing to do with fire. Memories formed it.

She'd taken the memories she'd seen while riding in the back of Chavali's mind and when she'd rifled through Colby's head a few months ago. The doorway pointed to Colby, and the wagons pointed to Pale's interpretation of the attack on the clan. In both cases, the fire had been insurmountable.

An insurmountable obstacle couldn't be defeated. No matter how much she wanted to overcome this, her efforts made no difference unless they all overcame it. Colby could hold them back. Biholtz could hold them back. One moment of belief in the futility of trying could hold them back.

She grabbed a fistful of Colby's shirt to get his attention. He met her gaze with firelight dancing in his blue eyes. His sense of failure lurked in the rigid set of his jaw and tension across his shoulders.

"You can defeat this memory," Chavali said. "It doesn't define you. One time, you didn't succeed. One time. Pale used this memory against you in Ket because she knew you hadn't dealt with it. Not properly. She set those triggers where she did because those memories are too painful for you to face. But you have to face them. You have to believe they aren't your future, only your past."

Colby looked away. "It's not that simple."

"Of course it's not as easy as snapping your fingers and refusing to let it hold you hostage." Chavali touched his cheek but didn't force him to look at her. "These things always take time. That time begins when you take the first step. Until then, you'll never heal." She turned to Biholtz. "This is as much about you as him. The wagons make that clear. I never saw the fire. You did. And you could do nothing about it. They stopped you. You watched them all die and burn. Your escape from the fire came at the price of your freedom."

Biholtz dropped her unstable sword and covered her face. "Why did he let me live?"

Kelly hugged the girl. "He let you live so Chavali could rescue you. Now it's your turn to save her."

The fire flared into the cleared space, lashing at the group with long fingers. Penny drew another blue sigil, creating a protective sphere around them. Colby flinched from the fire. Kelly pulled Biholtz closer to the center.

Convinced Kelly would help Biholtz and Penny would protect them all, Chavali returned her attention to Colby. "I forgive you for failing."

He blinked at her. "What?"

"I forgive you for failing. I forgive you for not saving those children. I forgive you for leaving Karias behind. I forgive you for the sacrifice made on your behalf that eats you up inside and reminds you of how you failed that one time when it mattered."

He seemed lost between confusion and distress. Though he opened his mouth three times, he said nothing. When his gaze drifted back to the fire, Chavali rose on her toes to cover his eyes with both hands.

"This can be overcome," she said. "Believe it. This is not the fire that killed you. It looks like that fire, it even feels like it. But it is not that fire. You're in Pale's mind, which resides in my body. She knows our memories. She's seen me think. But she wasn't here, and this isn't real. None of this is real. Nothing we see here will be real."

Chavali watched him gather himself. When he took a deep breath, she removed her hands. He kept his eyes closed. His shoulders straightened and the tension smoothed away.

"Point me," he whispered.

She slipped out of the way, giving him a clear path to the fire. "Go," she said.

Colby held his sword pointed at the flames. Water beaded on the surface and dripped from the edge. He took one step at a time.

Behind Chavali, Biholtz roared her defiance. Chavali turned in time to see Biholtz rushing the fire with her purple sword out and ready for violence. She slashed through the flames as Colby's sword pierced the writhing curtain. Sizzling filled the air, along with the smell of burning goat hair.

Penny leaned close. "You need to fight this too," she murmured.

With a firm nod, Chavali raised her arms and pictured one of her old nightmares. As she reached the part with the flood, water beaded on her fingertips. One drop fell, then another and another. The dripping sped until brackish water pooled at her feet. Nightmares soaked through her boots and chilled her toes.

Kelly scooped water with her shield and flung it at the wall. The spray sizzled and smelled of rotting flesh. Penny set her hands on Chavali's shoulders, providing physical support. Biholtz slashed at the flames, cutting pieces off. The bits of fire fell into the ring and died in the water. Colby's sword carved wide swathes.

The water flowed around the wagon parts to reach the fire. Pale's rumbling giggles stopped. Water met fire, clashing to create a wall of steam. Colby stopped and stepped back, panting harder than Chavali had ever before seen.

"No, Colby," Penny said. "Keep fighting."

He swiped an arm across his brow and lifted his sword to hack through the steam. "It's more exhausting than I'm used to."

Biholtz had lost her rage, but kept stabbing at the wall anyway. Her shoulders drooped and her blows lacked precision.

"Pale is working against you," Penny said. "She's making it harder than it needs to be."

Chavali clucked her tongue in irritation. "Muscles are an illusion here. The sword is only as heavy as you make it, and you don't need to breathe. Pale wants you to give up. She's making you think you have no other choice. Surrender and she wins. There may never be another chance to fight this battle."

She distanced herself from the potential outcome. Pale winning meant either death or torture. The clan might collapse without her. None of them knew how to pass on the mantle. Biholtz was two years old when it passed to Chavali. Estevior himself had discovered how to do it, and had passed the knowledge down over the centuries. No one remained to explain except Chavali. The mantle required actions no one could blunder into.

With the future of the clan on the line, her focus narrowed to channeling her nightmares. For once, they served a purpose other than torment. Water rushed from her hands and surged at the fire.

Colby flung effort at one more swing, chopping through the doorway. The beams fell and knocked him down. Kelly dashed in and shoved the broken wood off him and into the water.

Water surged over the flames, drowning the fire to nothing and soaking Colby. He sat up, coughing and spitting. "This isn't water, it's vile."

"It's the stuff of nightmares," Chavali said.

CHAPTER 38

The steam cleared, revealing a gray, drab cobblestone street. Dark clouds threatened rain. Crumbling buildings on either side leaned together overhead. Black iron fences lined the road, constraining blackened vines and branches.

For a moment, Chavali thought she'd lost color again. Then she saw the violent violet glow of Biholtz's sword and noticed Colby standing with Kelly's help, both in full color. She glanced at Penny, still holding her shoulders from behind.

"Harris spent time here," Chavali murmured. "This was how he saw a place he—" No one present needed to know about the smuggling he'd done in that town. "A place he lived for a while."

"She's not terribly original, is she?" Penny asked.

"It doesn't seem so."

"Is that good or bad?"

"I think it means we know some of the rules already."

Biholtz turned around in a circle, gaping at the tall buildings. "What should we do?"

The air rippled with a deep, booming roar of anger. Chavali noted that Pale sounded less huge than before. If every scene they punched through reduced Pale's size in some fashion, she felt confident they'd eventually reach some center location with a version of Pale they could kill. Until then, they had to dance to the enemy's drumbeats.

Chavali wondered what damage they'd do to her own mind in the course of this escapade.

At least they'd brought her healer. "Destroy it." Harris had wanted to smash this street, but never could. It loomed in his memories, as foreboding as his abusive father.

Colby glanced at her, still panting. "Are you sure?"

"Yes."

Both he and Biholtz jammed their swords into the cobblestones. Chavali raised her hands over her head and called upon her nightmares again. Blood rained down, splattering red over them and cracking stones. Kelly held up her shield to protect herself.

"I'm not sure how much use I'll really be after all," Penny said. "I'm able to use magic here, but it's more tiring than usual. Like I'm weaving through sludge. I think it's because the rules are different here."

"Hold onto your power," Chavali said. "Save it for dire need."

"I can do that." Penny squeezed her shoulders and let go.

Stone melted apart with each sword stroke. The blood rain reduced the remaining rock to rubble. Colby scooped a handful of stones aside to reveal sharp white crystals, glaring in their brightness. He examined the gray rocks in his hand.

Chavali recognized the crystals. Once, she'd found them under grass and flowers, and bled on them to destroy them and escape a mind-prison.

"This seems kind of mundane," Kelly said. She inched closer to

Chavali. "Easy."

"Pale is being smart," Penny said. "Walking out and greeting us would be stupid. Throwing things in our way to wear us down is smart."

"Yes. These are outer defenses. She is spending little effort—" Chavali saw Biholtz raise her sword while standing over the crystals. "Wait!"

Biholtz stabbed. The crystals exploded, tossing Biholtz into the wall. Colby lurched toward her but missed with a swipe for her. The girl hit the nearby wall, punching a hole through it. Rubble fell on her and she landed halfway inside the building.

Chavali forgot about everything else. She ran for Biholtz. Colby reached her first. Another peal of giant Pale's laughter shook the ground. The building collapsed with a creaking crack, crushing Biholtz under a hail of wood, brick, and plaster. Dust billowed in a gray cloud, obscuring Colby. Chavali cringed back, as did Penny and Kelly. All three women coughed and sputtered.

Stones and bricks clattered around her feet. Without waiting for the air to clear, Chavali dove at the pile of rubble, flinging stones aside to reach them. "No, you don't," she growled. "You aren't taking them away from me."

Railan hadn't explained the finer points of how this worked. When two telepaths engaged in battle, the loser died, she knew that much. That very thing had killed Pale when Chavali triggered one by accident. Chavali's first true lesson for using her gift had involved avoiding that in the future. In this situation, she didn't know if it still worked the same.

Kelly used her shield to scoop debris away. "They're fine," she said.

"Of course they are." Chavali ignored the sting of cuts and scrapes on her hands as she moved jagged shards.

Penny cleared her throat. "Ladies, I think we have another issue."

Chavali paused to check on Penny. The elder knelt at the edge of a small, dark hole. Pink flares, the same shade as Chavali's feather, writhed and pulsed inside a ring of pale pink crystals. Watching it for several moments, Chavali realized the pulsing matched the rhythm of a heartbeat. Her heartbeat.

She looked at her hands. Blood streaked her palms and fingers. Had she been thinking, she would've stepped in sooner and stopped Biholtz. Though the crystals had nothing to do with this street, the message so far had been one of mining everything in Chavali's memories for the battlefield.

"I don't understand," Kelly said as she scooped more debris aside. "Colby should be here. I don't even see a trace of him."

Penny frowned. "Telepath stuff is outside my knowledge. I've met a fair few, but we never traded expertise. My usual go-to these days is Railan."

"And she's out of contact," Chavali said with a sigh. "We will assume they've been ejected. Neither has any sort of magical or telepathic ability, so this makes sense."

She hoped this explained their disappearance. Losing Colby again would hurt too much for words.

Knowing that made her want to rage at the sky. No one but clan should matter this much. And yet, here she stood, torn by not knowing his condition, but not as much about Biholtz.

"I hate you," she grumbled under her breath. Crouching beside the hole, she smeared her blood on the crystals, careful to avoid further injury on the sharp edges. The pink deepened a tiny amount.

Kelly knelt beside her and touched her hands. "Let me do it."

"Why? I already bleed."

"Because this is about you. It's your body. Your mind. Your life. You're the one who can't afford to fail." Kelly smiled at her. "I'm just your healer."

Chavali frowned. "There is no 'just' about the sacrifice you made."

"I'm so glad you understand that." Kelly sliced her hand open on a crystal. "I didn't really understand what I volunteered for. Then or now. There have been moments when I've regretted being your healer. So we're clear, this isn't one of them."

The crystals pulsed with darkening red.

"I wish—"

Still bleeding with one hand, Kelly touched her arm. "Jacqueline told me that all Fallen have a problem with regret. It's something you have to learn to live with. You died. Someone sacrificed to bring you back, but you can't return to your life as it was. That life is gone. Trying to recapture it never works, even after your service ends.

"And I know. You've only been back for a few months. The world kept going while you were gone. My life kind of passed me by while I sat with you in the basement, too. I'd already left home and been brought in, but I wasn't prepared for staying underground all day, every day, for five months. So I understand that part."

Chavali took her hand. "I've been terrible to you."

"A little." Kelly smiled again. Her eyelids drooped. The crystals glowed with deep red.

"I'm sorry."

"You'll be terrible again. It's part of who you are." Kelly's words slurred and her entire body sagged with exhaustion. "But I'm ready for it now."

Quirking an eyebrow, Chavali wanted to refute her. She decided not to argue with her healer for once. "This thing is taking too much. Let go."

"You have to..." Kelly's eyes fluttered shut. She mumbled something incoherent.

The crystals burned dark crimson. They folded into the hole, dragging Kelly with them. Chavali, taken by surprise, dove in after her.

She fell.

CHAPTER 39

Chavali hit a ramp of ice and slid down it. Frigid cold burned her skin. The spirits seemed thicker around her. She saw no sign of Kelly, but Penny followed behind her.

Kelly had been thrown out of Pale's mind. Belief in this simple fact kept Chavali from screaming.

The ramp leveled out, becoming a flat plain of ice stamped with a wagon wheel design. Chavali chose not to waste her time trying to slow herself. When she reached the end of her slide, she sat up and scraped her arm across the ice.

Beneath, she expected to see the faces of clan long past, or perhaps clan she'd known.

Nothing lurked beneath the ice. Pale's scream rent the air. As before, it seemed closer and smaller than the first rumble. Chavali recognized her voice with less effort. This layer lay close to Pale's sanctum.

Penny neared her, crawling across the ice. "What's that smell?"

Chavali sniffed the air and caught a sweet, minty flavor. "An herb we use for tea. I haven't found any yet and don't know the name, or I would've gotten some for you to try."

"Why do we smell that?" Penny sat on her boots and twisted to check in every direction. "There's nothing but miles and miles of ice."

Thumping the ice with her fist, Chavali shrugged. "For the same reason anything else happens here. Pale wants to win, but can't make it impossible for us to find a way. No matter how much she wishes to be an impregnable fortress, she's still a spirit masquerading as a person."

"You certainly get into some strange predicaments."

Chavali laughed. "Yes, I seem to." She examined her arm and noticed the spirits had thickened, creating a gauzy film around her body. The effect reminded her of the armor she'd worn the last time she and Pale battled.

Penny patted the ice with her hand. "Judging by the first two scenarios here, we should either break this or melt it."

"Yes, that seems logical."

"But you disagree."

"I don't know." Chavali groped to explain something lurking on the edge of her thoughts. "Something about this seems...predictable? Pale is not like this. Not what I saw of her. Is she constrained by my memories and nightmares, or just using them to annoy me? Why is none of this about Pale?"

Penny nudged the ice with an elbow to no effect. "Maybe it can't be about Pale. Like you said, she's a spirit masquerading as a person. We don't know that much about spirits. Maybe they can't form new memories and have new experiences."

Chavali raised her brow. Despite making this point herself, she hadn't considered treating Pale like a spirit. She studied the wispy coating over her body and wondered how to leverage it against Pale. Did she have no better option than armor?

Somewhere in this journey, she expected to meet Pale and fight her. The last time they met, Pale had been overconfident about her power. Would she make the same mistake because she had no other choice?

Despite all the pain and suffering Pale had caused, Chavali pitied her. She hated Pale for everything she'd done, but still pitied her. A swift end to her madness seemed the best answer. Robin had made Pale, after all. He bore the true responsibility.

"If you have an idea for getting through the ice, please try it."

"Nothing special." Penny reached out for Chavali's hand. "I was just going to shove power at it. If you have an idea, I'll feed you power for it. Kelly was right. This is really your fight. The rest of us came along to help, not to win it for you. We all thought our connections to you would matter, that they'd make a difference. But in the end, it's your body and your fight."

"I don't believe I would have made it this far by myself." Chavali took her hand. Warmth surged into her.

Penny squeezed her hand and smiled. "I think you would have, but by now, you'd be spent and still have to face Pale. She did everything she could to stop you, but she couldn't stop us all."

In the end, she'd face Pale alone. She knew that now. Chavali pressed her palm to the ice and remembered the nightmare with lava. Molten rock oozed from her palm. Intense heat pressed against the ice, creating a flickering edge of flame.

"My dreams and memories haven't controlled me for a long time, Pale! They won't do it now, either. The nightmares I know live in my mind, and you can do nothing worse."

Pale roared in rage again, her voice vibrating the air and ground.

Cracks formed in the ice. The lava coiled, snakelike as it sank deeper. A crack ripped between Chavali and Penny. Penny scooted across the crack. Chavali pulled to bring her close.

The cracks fractured, creating small islands of ice. Penny wrapped an arm around Chavali's waist, keeping them close. Their chunk of ice wobbled, threatening to flip them into the water.

"Close your eyes," Penny whispered. "Focus. Ignore the ice." She rested her chin on Chavali's shoulder. "I always wanted a daughter, but we only had sons. I hope you get to meet them, and their wives, and the grandkids. They visit once in a while. In a few more years, there will probably be great-grandkids." She sighed. "No matter what happens, and aside from the reason why, I'm glad you came into our lives."

"I feel this too. Thank you for everything." The exchange felt like saying goodbye. Chavali clutched Penny's weathered hand until she thought she'd break the elder's brittle bones.

Penny slumped. The ice pitched. Chavali let go of the lava to clutch the edge. Heated ice burned her hand. They flipped over. Green frigid water shocked Chavali. Though she scrabbled to swim up, she sank lower with every stroke. Bubbles streamed up as she fell down. When she hit the silty, sandy bottom, she realized she no longer held Penny's hand.

Fish swam past her. Plants with flat leaves disappeared upward and swayed with a gentle current. Chavali knew this nightmare. She breathed the water because it wasn't water. If she moved in one direction, she'd find ruined husks of houses. In the other direction, she'd find a dark, foreboding shadow. When she faced this in her dreams, she always fled from him.

Pale wanted to manipulate her by playing on images she feared when she had no control over them or herself. Despite living in Chavali's mind and rifling through her memories, Pale hadn't taken the measure of her.

She bounced her way to a plant and gripped its slimy stem. Her hair drifted across her face, obscuring her vision. Pushing the dark locks aside, she noticed a smudge of white and yellow gliding through the murk. The strange object neared and she recognized Kelly's halo of blonde hair.

Kelly bumped into her. White cloth strained to cover a bluish, bloated body. Her purple lips hung open, baring her rotting teeth in a feral grimace. Maggots swarmed her lidless eye sockets. Gobbets of blackened meat clung to bones sticking out of ragged wrist stumps.

Grimacing in disgust, Chavali shoved the body away. "I know that's not real, Pale." Her voice burbled in the fake water. "Even if they're all dead—" She paused to choke down a bite of grief for the possibility. "Railan is watching over them. So is Karias. They aren't going to fall into a lake and become like this. Not in the amount of time we're spending. Come out and fight me."

Pale's giggle sounded almost normal, though the water forced it to warble. Her voice came from everywhere and nowhere, crowding Chavali. "You're right. They're all dead. While you've been busy in here, I broke free. Railan was occupied. And you have this delightful dagger. It even kills horses. They haven't been disappearing because they sacrificed to save you. They've been disappearing because I slit their throats and our dagger drank their blood. We're on our way to see Robin now!"

"You're lying." Chavali's voice cracked. She had no reason to believe Pale. She also had no reason to disbelieve Pale. Hugging herself, she told herself they lived. They all hovered around her body, waiting for her to wake so they could tell if she won or lost and act as necessary.

"Am I?"

The slippery plant grew, carrying Chavali upward. She didn't want to see whatever Pale wanted to show her. When she let go, the plant stuck its leaves to her and carried her. Her struggles accomplished nothing. Suckers on the leaves wiggled with her, keeping her encased.

Chavali grunted as the plant used her to punch through wood. Splinters stabbed through her flesh. Broken boards flew in every direction. She smashed onto the ground, surrounded by trees in the dim, pale light of the silvery moon. The scent of crushed pine needles filled the air.

Groaning at what felt like broken bones, Chavali rolled onto her side.

Colby lay on the ground beside her, drenched in glistening blood from a deep slash across his neck. He stared past her shoulder, his eyes open and glassy. Stillness consumed him.

Startled, Chavali scrambled to flee this horrifying nightmare. She hit something. When she turned, she saw Penny's body in the same state.

Railan lay nearby, her throat cut. Biholtz and Kelly had suffered the same fate. Karias's bloodstained shape lay beyond them all.

"No," she whispered. She clambered to Colby and knelt beside him. Tears welling in her eyes, she touched his cheek. "This isn't real."

Her fingertips brushed his stiff, dark stubble. Beneath it, his flesh radiated a chill.

"Oh, it's real. They're all gone now, Chavali. You have nothing left to live for. Submit and I'll shield you from the nightmares. For once, you can rest. How long has it been since you truly rested? Almost eleven years? No more waking up screaming. The best part is you never have to suffer through anyone else's thoughts ever again if you don't want to."

Chavali covered her face. Biholtz never should have come. If only she'd stayed behind.

True adulthood began at seventeen in the clan. Four years too early, Bihotz had been forced into responsibility she didn't need, and it killed her.

Penny never should have come. Chavali could imagine her protesting that she'd lived enough.

But Marcus needed her. The children needed her. Chavali needed her. Without her own mother, she needed the wisdom of elders and the warmth of cookies.

Kelly never should have come. Her healer had already given too much for Chavali. She didn't deserve what Kelly had sacrificed.

All the terrible things Chavali had said and done to Kelly before she knew the truth had to be repaid. And she had to admit she liked Kelly. The woman had done too much for her. Chavali couldn't hate her.

Colby never should have come.

She'd killed him twice in one day. He'd held her the way she needed holding, the way no one had done for so long.

If only she'd denied him until tomorrow, he'd still be alive. As if she'd ever had trouble keeping her feelings locked away.

"They all deserved to live far more than me," Chavali murmured.

Pale sighed. "That may be true, but here we are."

Chavali wept.

"Yes, yes. This is all horrible." Pale hummed the same wretched tune from before. "Let it all out. When we reach Robin, it'll be best if you're done with this."

Chavali lay on the ground, curled into a ball and squeezing her eyes shut. "You didn't have to kill them all."

"Of course I did. They would've followed us otherwise. I can't have that."

Pale killed them all for no reason other than escape. Like her master, she had no capacity for grace or decency.

Both of them needed to die. A second time, in Pale's case.

Colby wouldn't want her to give up because he failed. Biholtz would demand she get up and face down Pale to save what remained of the clan.

Nothing mattered more than clan. Only a few short months ago, she'd spent weeks believing herself a clan of one. Though it had been terrible, she didn't have to suffer that again.

Marcus, Danel, and Haizea still needed their Seer. They deserved her strength, not her weakness.

She could defeat Pale. In her own body, she'd killed Pale once before, and she could do it again. Her mind knew how to do it.

Anger roiled in her belly, yearning to punish this vile creature who'd dared to attack the clan. Just as her master had found defeat at Chavali's hands, just as Pale herself had found defeat at Chavali's hands once before, Pale would not win.

Not now, not ever.

"You poor thing," Pale said with cluck of her tongue. "Are you exhausted already?"

Chavali lay still. Pale couldn't read her thoughts. If she feigned weakness and submission, Pale might relax and leave herself open to attack. "Please remove the bodies," she whimpered, her voice as meek as she could manage with so much rage surging in her blood.

The scenery vanished, leaving Chavali lying in a grassy field under moonlight. Pale knelt beside her. She tucked a lock of Chavali's hair behind her ear.

"I'll take good care of you," Pale said, her voice soft and sweet. "We'll be such good friends. I promise nothing bad will ever happen to you again."

Chavali had never wanted anything as much as she wanted a knife to stab Pale. She sniffled, keeping up the facade. "Can I have him here?"

Pale smiled, sad and sympathetic. She reminded Chavali of Eldrack at his most annoyingly nice, except he always meant it. This instead smothered, thick and cloying. "I can't do more than an image, sweetie. Robin can give him to you, though. He'll fix everything."

Sniffling again, Chavali watched Pale, waiting for the right moment. She'd have only one chance to take Pale by surprise. After that, it would become a battle.

To keep up appearances, she made a small, helpless noise.

"I know it hurts, sweetie." Pale sighed and looked away. "Everyone always wants—"

Solid purple flame sprang from Chavali's hand and she stabbed Pale. Though Pale hadn't expected it, Chavali could only reach her leg. The purple shard pierced her calf and thigh at a diagonal, punching through the other side.

Pale screamed and leaped away, taking the flame blade with her. Chavali leaped at Pale, tackling her. They fell through the ground together. The sky rippled. Pale shrieked about treachery and squirmed. Chavali punched her, able to hit only her shoulder.

Dark clouds billowed above. Chavali knew what she wanted to see.

In response to her, choppy waters surged below. She'd won already. Pale had lost control.

"No!" Pale screamed. "This body is mine!" She wrenched Chavali around.

Chavali resisted. They spun. Pale growled.

Instead of responding, Chavali sneered and did the one thing she knew would irritate and shock Pale the most. She changed her shape. Her will, in her body, forced Pale to follow suit.

Pale's eyes grew wide as Chavali became a purple goat with dragon scales and wings, shrouded in writhing black armor.

"No," Pale breathed.

"Yes," Chavali bleated. She lurched at Pale, slamming her hooves into the interloper's dracogoat chest.

Because Chavali wanted ice, the water crackled as it froze over. She rode Pale to the ground, breaking her back on a frozen peak. Her wings raised and pumping for power, she stomped on Pale's broken, twitching form.

"This is my body," Chavali snarled.

She shifted again, back into her own shape, formed a fresh purple blade of flame, and slammed it through Pale, pinning her to the ice. "This is my mind."

She wished she could kill Pale ten, twenty, twenty thousand times.

As she sliced the blade through the body, Pale whimpered and faded. Her cry of denial died as Chavali summoned a cleansing breeze.

Chavali remained on one knee, her purple blade blazing with pulsing light where it stuck out of the ice. She didn't want to face reality. Too much blood had been spilled and too many lives had been lost.

But she was the Seer of the Blaukenev clan, and if anyone had to accept her fate, Chavali did.

She closed her eyes.

CHAPTER 40

*P*lease, Creator, if you have any mercy in you, let it be Chavali who's waking.

She opened her eyes. Colby loomed over her, his hand around her neck tight enough to keep her under control. Pressure held her wrists over her head. Aching pain blazed in her skull.

"Pale is dead," Chavali rasped. Tears filled her eyes and she had to blink rapidly to see him.

Prove it.

"I cannot."

His grip eased. *What's wrong? That's a stupid question, but why are you crying? You never cry.*

"This is a lie," she chided. "But she showed me your dead body. She said she killed you. Everyone. Even Karias." Turning her head, she saw Railan massaging her own temple, Biholtz hugging Penny, and Kelly holding Chavali's wrists down with the fabric of her skirt between their skin. Karias watched over Colby's shoulder. "She was...convincing."

Colby smiled. In his thoughts, she saw a flash of him waking and checking on Biholtz. As she'd hoped, they'd all been thrown out when they "died" in her mind. He let go of her neck.

"Are you sure it's her?" Kelly asked, frowning at Chavali.

He brushed hair off Chavali's forehead and touched the feather. His gaze held hers, and she wanted never to forget this moment. "Yes, I'm sure."

Kelly shifted to the side, releasing Chavali's arms. She took Chavali's hand and squeezed it. *Everyone is fine.*

Terrible heat surged through the connection, seeking her pain and attacking it with brutal force. Chavali's mouth fell open. She heard nothing but the roaring of blood in her ears.

Then it stopped. Kelly let go. Chavali panted. Her head felt fine, but exhaustion threatened to overwhelm her. As much as she wanted to sit up, she couldn't. She tried and failed to move her arm.

Colby scooped her up and held her close. *I knew you'd beat her.*

Slumped with her chin on Colby's shoulder, she smiled at Karias. She had many things to discuss with the horse, most of them unpleasant. For now, she suspected Railan would monopolize his time.

"Twice tonight" she murmured to Colby, "I thought she killed you."

"Maryna didn't die when Pale cut her throat," Colby said. *Despite betraying us all, she saved me. She didn't even heal her own wounds fully before reaching out and healing me. I don't know what to think of that.*

"Healers are difficult to kill," Kelly said.

Railan sighed. "She's in a lot of trouble. I will be too."

"I need to speak to Aislynn," Chavali said.

"Before we return to the tower," Railan said, "I need to ask all of you keep this escape tunnel to yourselves. I know you clan people can keep secrets, but Colby and Kelly, you can't say anything about it either. Not even if asked directly. This is a direct order on your honor as Fallen. And a Healer. While I still have the ability to give direct orders. Consider it to be coming from Eldrack."

"I think I can manage," Colby said.

Kelly nodded. She touched Chavali's shoulder. *Come see me whenever you can. We should discuss things. Lots of things.* When Chavali nodded, she withdrew her hand. "Penny, Biholtz, would you like to come back to the festival with me? I hate to walk alone in the dark."

Biholtz hugged Chavali from behind, forcing Colby to shift aside. "We were all so worried you wouldn't be you," she gushed. "Pale is really dead this time?"

"Yes." Chavali reveled in the embrace of clan. As much as she craved Colby's touch—a strange thing in itself—he wasn't clan. They'd fix that soon. "She's gone. There is nothing more of her left. The clan is safe from her, as are the Fallen."

Penny ruffled Chavali's hair. "It took me long enough to get off the ground that I'm not getting back down there again. I'll give you a hug later. At a sensible height."

Chavali grinned. "I would stand now if I could."

"I know. We'll see you soon. For now, I think Marcus and the little ones are probably fretting, assuming they're all still awake. Haizea looked about ready to fall over after so much excitement today." Penny tapped Biholtz on the top of her head. "Come on. Colby's going to have to carry her, and we all know what happens next."

Biholtz stood with a melodramatic sigh. "Our bed isn't big enough for him. How are we supposed to learn anything if they go off and use their own?"

"There are some things I will never understand about this clan," Penny said with a chuckle.

Colby's cheeks burned warm enough that Chavali felt it through her hair. He coughed and squirmed. *I'm not used to people discussing that so...bluntly. Even the worst among the gossips use innuendo. Subtlety. Knowing looks.*

Too tired to form a proper laugh, Chavali giggled.

"Make sure she eats something, Colby. It'll help her recover." Kelly draped an arm around Biholtz's shoulders and looped her other arm through Penny's. "The festival isn't over yet. They haven't done the sky display yet. Wait until you see it, Biholtz. They blow things up that make colored sparkles."

The trio headed down the road to town. Railan stood and watched them, her hands on her hips.

Would you like me to take you to your room, or to the farmhouse?

"My room, please."

As Railan turned, she caught Chavali's eye. Her gaze flicked to Karias, then back. Chavali understood and nodded. Karias had asked Railan to continue keeping his secret from everyone else. They'd discuss it later. Without Colby present. Perhaps she'd steal Karias again and meet Railan for a ride in a few days.

"Railan, could you make sure Karias has food and water in the stable? If you don't mind, I'm going to take Chavali back through the tunnel."

"For what it's worth, I'm sorry I didn't see what was going on with Maryna. And I'm also sorry for not picking up on Pale. A lot of pain could've been avoided, and I should've been the one to prevent it. That's my job." She looked away, into the darkness. "It *was* my job. We'll see if I get to do anything more challenging than folding laundry after this."

Chavali held on as tightly as she could while Colby stood with her in his arms. He did most of the work.

"What will they do to you?" he asked.

"Not sure." Railan patted Karias's neck. "I didn't do anything wrong that I know of, so we'll see. Maybe I should steal your horse and flee. Except I know they'd find me, and that would probably trigger the Wasting anyway." She shook her head and sighed. "Get some rest, eat, and report to Aislynn, probably in that order."

"What about Eldrack?" Chavali asked.

"No idea. He might be done here for good. In that case, Aislynn will probably stay until another Administrator is appointed. Even if I'm cleared, it won't be me. I don't want the job, especially with having to muddle through without my healer."

Weariness and the dim light kept Chavali from taking Railan's measure, but she thought the telepath needed some time and space to handle Maryna's betrayal.

"I will say this much. What little I know of the clan, your powers, and the prophecies," she held up the book Pale had stolen, "is as safe as I can keep it."

"Thank you. As we'll be going directly inside, we can take the book and leave it in Aislynn's care."

Railan nodded and tucked it under Chavali's arm. "I have no doubt you can keep it safe. See you soon. I hope." She snapped in the air for Karias to follow her.

The horse clopped to his master and pushed his nose at Chavali. She lifted a hand to touch his soft hair. *I'm relieved you're fine and safe. Please, take care with Colby's heart. I warned you once before—if you break him, I have to pick up the pieces, and I hate doing that.* He paused before adding, *Also, Railan is more annoying than you because she can contact me from a fair distance. Come see me soon so we can talk about this notion of joining your clan. Among other things.*

"Follow Railan," Colby said. "I'll come brush you tomorrow."

He's damned right he will. Karias whickered and left, following Railan like a giant puppy.

Chavali giggled again, too tired to stifle it.

"Maybe food first," Colby said as he pushed his way through the shrubs and branches to reach the escape tunnel. Chavali thought him too big to fit, but he stepped through as if the plants parted for him.

"Aislynn first."

"You're too punchy to explain things to her. She can wait."

"No. Aislynn first."

He hurried down the stairs in darkness. "You can't walk. If I decide not to take you there, you're not going there."

Chavali grinned, enjoying the frivolous argument for no reason. The light tinge of exasperation in his tone amused her. She thought her own weariness explained this. "Aren't you tired? Aislynn is probably in Eldrack's office. It's closer. You can sit while I explain."

"I can take you to your room and leave you there while I go explain. I think I have a handle on what happened."

"Bah. Just because you were there means nothing."

Colby chuckled. "No, not a thing. Though I will admit there's one thing I don't understand. Why didn't Teryk suffer the Wasting until he tried to flee? Why didn't Maryna suffer it? Passing information betrayed us all and got Harris killed. That seems like it should have triggered it."

All Chavali's amusement fled. She considered the possibilities and realized an important fact. "Maryna said she was serving Shappa, and she believed that. Do you remember the oath we swore? We bound ourselves to the Creator and Shappa, and to pursuing Reunion. Not the Administrator or other individuals. The Wasting struck Teryk when he panicked and took the girls. Until then, he believed he was doing the right thing for Shappa or the Creator, or Reunion. He never betrayed our mission. Maryna likewise never betrayed the Fallen, only Harris."

Colby didn't respond until they saw the glowing door at the other end of the tunnel. "I don't find that comforting."

"Neither do I."

He breezed past Eldrack's office without a word and carried her to her room. The beads on her door clacked, offering the comfort of familiarity. After kicking the door shut, he laid her on her bed and took the book.

The pillow seemed to cast a spell on her, forcing her eyelids shut. "Can you help me with my boots?"

Colby untied the laces and tugged them off her feet. "I'll bring up some food for you."

"Stay." She forced her eyes to crack open long enough to see him watching her.

"Are you sure?"

"Yes."

Chavali fell asleep in a cocoon of his warmth.

EPILOGUE

If he lived a hundred years, Robin would never grow tired of the Harbor City Palace Chef's ability to turn Hardrun perch into a light, delicate meal worthy of the Creator. He closed his blue eyes and savored the hint of lemon and herbs in a bite of fish mixed with a soft, butter-suffused root native to North Cascain. This food demanded lingering. Happy to oblige, he sighed with pure pleasure.

"I love watching you eat good food," Lauryn said, her chin resting in her hand. She sat across from him at the round table, with her children between them. Her fretting over Bricene's betrayal and disappearance had faded already until she seemed to carry nothing more than a dull ache in her heart. The episode had added more gray strands to her hair anyway, and a few more wrinkles on her forehead. Lately, she seemed older than her forty-six years, though no less regal than the day he first saw her.

"I, on the other hand, don't." Warren picked at his biscuit, sulking because his mother had taken Robin's advice and cut him off from the treasury after the debacle with Bricene. The young man now had to beg for even a handful of coins. He deserved much worse for wasting so much of North Cascain's money on such idiocy as smuggling foreign art into the country.

Ambrye snorted, crinkling her sharp nose. "Maybe we should ask for a special meal of crap once. Just to see what happens." Harbor City's star investigator had long ago stopped treating Robin with true suspicion. She accepted his excuses for everything with a peculiar determination to see her mother happy, even if her suitor had appeared out of nowhere and happened to be ten years the Queen's junior.

Robin chuckled. "You'd all have to suffer with me, so I don't consider that much of a threat."

"Ambrye, Warren." Lauryn covered their hands with her own. "I want to tell you how much I appreciate your support during this trying time. You've both been more help than you'll ever know. Which is why I want to make sure neither of you objects too much if I ask Robin to become the Prince Consort."

Though he'd expected such an offer, Robin froze in mid-bite. He'd thought it would come in another few weeks, and he'd expected her to make the offer privately first. The subject hadn't come up, not even once. Broaching it himself had seemed crass after he killed her daughter and hid the body. She'd never know, but that didn't change his opinion of propriety on the matter. Besides, she had the power and title. She needed to be the one who asked.

"He's been a great comfort to me in all this. If he's not going to fail under the tests we've weathered lately, I can't see him failing in the future either."

Warren's mouth twitched down. He knew who'd directed the cutting of the purse strings. His mouth stayed shut, a sure sign he'd find some willing coquette later and rant to her breasts. After all, his mother ought to pine for his father forever. How dare she move on and find love again?

Ambrye flicked her gaze over Robin, assessing him for the five-thousandth time since they'd met. Her sharp eyes missed nothing. Except his original purpose here. "I like you, Robin, so please don't take this poorly. Mom, are you sure you're not just latching onto him now because of Bricene? This could wait another few months. No one is looking askance at him yet. You're allowed to have an unofficial bed-partner for as long as you want."

"Jealous?" Warren spat the word with enough bitterness to suggest he suffered from that affliction.

"Don't be a child," Ambrye said with a roll of her eyes.

Courting Ambrye had been the best investment of time and effort Robin had ever made. "I'm not offended," he said. If he played this right, he'd be the Prince Consort within a few months. The position held little power, but it would complicate the relationship with his handlers. Acarian and his flunkies needed more complications in their machinations.

"As it happens," Robin said, "I agree with you. Lauryn, don't feel you have to rush this. I know how hard Bricene's betrayal has been on you. If there's one thing I don't want, it's for you to try to fill that hole with me. Let it heal first."

His answer kept Ambrye happy. He could see it in the softening of her expression. Warren, on the other hand, seemed disgusted. Stepping between a man and his mother rubbed the prince in all kinds of wrong ways. And, of course, Lauryn melted. He'd charmed her so thoroughly and completely that the petty objections of her son made no difference.

"So that's settled," Lauryn said. "I'll have someone start planning a wedding."

"I'm at your disposal, Majesty," Robin said. He smiled at her, pleased he'd found someone he could both adore and hide things from, all without using or revealing his powers.

Warren huffed and dropped his fork with a clatter. Before he could say anything, a servant slipped to Robin's elbow.

"Message for you, Sir." The servant carried a silver tray with a small envelope. He thought he recognized the tidy handwriting with his full name and enough location information to get it to him, but the scribe it pointed to made no sense. Karina was dead. She could have sent a message before her death, but in that case, it had taken months to reach him.

Picking it up and puzzling over it, he nodded to the servant, who withdrew.

"What's wrong, Warren?" Lauryn asked. All three of them ignored both the servant and the envelope. They understood the concept of privacy. No matter what the envelope contained, he'd come up with some story about his false businesses in other countries. "He hasn't tried to replace your father, and he's not going to start now."

Robin turned the envelope over in his hands, wondering if he should open it in private. He couldn't imagine anything Karina would put in a letter that anyone else present should see.

"Mom, he's just—" Warren grunted and flicked a hand in annoyance far too petulant for his twenty years.

Seeing his chance to escape with his message, Robin set his napkin over his plate. A few bites of the delicious lunch remained, but he'd survive. "I can tell you need to discuss this as a family. I'll let you do that and see you all at dinner." He stood and gave the table a polite bow of his head, then left the room.

His boots clacked on the marble floor as he fled for a sitting room far enough to evade quick discovery. Green and gold dominated the room he chose. He shut the door and leaned against it, determined to avoid unwanted interruption. His heart raced as he pondered the possibilities. One deep breath in and out did little to help.

He pried open the envelope and slid out the contents. The piece of yellow-brown paper inside had been folded four times. When he held the sheet up, he found only four words in the same neat lettering.

She's alive

Shappa

Eldrack

Rubbing the ink, he couldn't tell how long ago it had been written. He re-read the message fifteen times, not sure what it meant. What woman did it refer to? Had Karina survived? No, of course not. He'd seen her body. Though her face had been ravaged, he'd noted the markings elsewhere on her body. To keep any Shappan authorities from asking too many questions, he'd had her body burned.

Likewise, his sister couldn't be alive. He'd watched his niece kill her and made sure of it. Bricene certainly hadn't survived. Dealing with her corpse had been a chore. One other woman had occupied his mind a great deal for the past year, but she, too, was dead. Chavali had died in his arms by her own hand. Had Karina mistaken Chastity for Chavali? And why had this note taken so long to reach him?

He needed to visit Shappa and find this Eldrack, whatever it was. It didn't sound like a town or guild. At least Karina had given him a country, but that only narrowed the search so much.

Folding the note and returning it to its envelope, his mind whirled on what excuse he could use to visit Todan. North Cascain had business with Shappa, but he had no official capacity yet. He could claim the note had called him to attend to urgent matters with his business. Lauryn would understand. She'd hate it, but she'd understand.

With the note tucked in his pocket and an enigma to occupy his mind, he left the sitting room. Servants and guards in the hallway behaved normally, so no one had come looking for him yet. Thinking he had until dinner to occupy himself, he headed for the nearest stairwell.

"My Lord Robin?" He turned to see a servant approaching, holding another envelope. "Another message for you, Sir."

Unnerved by the possibility of a second message from a dead woman in one day, he forced himself to smile. "Seems I'm popular today."

"Seems so." The servant handed over his second envelope and walked away.

This one had different handwriting, and he knew without a doubt who'd sent it. Acarian needed to leave him alone. Doing the Creator's work took time. Nuance. Subtlety. Creativity. With an annoyed huff, he ripped the envelope open and scowled at the message inside. An order to meet Acarian's favorite errand boy face-to-face rankled. As if he needed supervision or close handling. He knew his job and how to do it.

At least the meeting had been set nearby. He stuffed the second message into his pocket and considered the costs of leaving without a word for this meeting. Lauryn needed pampering to prepare her for his absence, not abandonment. Above all, he didn't want to make her feel that she'd spooked him with her offer to marry him.

He could send someone to arrest Acarian's toady and drag him here for Robin's convenience. Of course, then he'd have to explain why Kirk deserved arrest. Wishing he had another option, Robin hurried to a hidden entrance into the Palace's emergency exit tunnels. He asked a servant to inform the Queen he needed to step out for a little while to handle the contents of his message.

As he rushed through the tunnels in a cloak left at the entry for clandestine purposes, he vowed to dote on Lauryn from the moment he returned until he left again. His curiosity about the mysterious "she" could wait a few days, unlike Kirk.

His chosen escape brought him to the wrong side of town, but he needed to avoid getting messy. The other three options for escape all carried the likelihood of encountering garbage, sewage, or liquids of questionable virtue. A few blocks away, he hired a carriage to take him partway. If he took a carriage to his final destination, Ambrye could discover it, and he needed to avoid that possibility. The shop his carriage stopped in front of did business with the Crown, giving him every reason to be there. He hopped out and plunged through the streets to reach the slums.

Smoke filled a forgettable bar in a forgettable part of Harbor City. Robin didn't care about the ambiance, other than the satisfactory amount of noise made by its lunch patrons. He cared about the idiot sitting in the back corner booth. In his head, he grabbed the slim man by the tail of dark hair at the nape of his neck and hauled him into the back alley.

He slid into the booth opposite Kirk. "What do you want?"

Kirk scowled. "Nice to see you too."

Robin didn't have time for this crap. He glared at Kirk and shoved his way past the younger man's worthless shields. His thoughts revealed he'd been sent to accompany Robin on an urgent mission to South Cascain.

"Get out," Kirk snarled. He clenched his fists until his knuckles turned white, flailing at Robin's mental intrusion.

Acarian should've known better than to send someone Robin could overpower so easily. He also should've known better than to explain as much as he did about the mission. Kirk knew the mission intended to get Robin out of North Cascain so Acarian could send someone else to do Robin's job.

As if he'd let that happen. No one would get past him to kill Lauryn. Not now.

"You're pathetic," Robin spat. He reached across the table and slapped Kirk hard enough to turn his head. With a flick of his mind as effortless as a wave of his hand, he crushed Kirk's consciousness. "Now you're a message."

Kirk's eyes popped and his liquefied brains flooded out, spattering on the table and bench. Robin reached with his power and tapped into the nearest bar wench as he slipped out the back door, convincing her he hadn't been there. If, by some chance, Ambrye wound up investigating Kirk's death, she'd find the victim of a telepathic battle with no trace of his opponent and no reason to finger Robin, who had no known telepathic abilities.

Before leaving the area, he set fire to both messages and watched them burn to ash on the concrete of a back alley. On his way home, he stopped in to speak to the employees at that Crown-serving shop. By the time he returned to the Palace, Lauryn had finished her afternoon audiences.

They met on the stairs. She took his arm.

"I trust your business wasn't too difficult to handle?"

"No." Robin guided her up the hallway to her suite. "Urgent and in need of hands-on attention, but not challenging." He opened the door for her. "I will need to travel and tend to some issues on the supply side, but it can wait a few days."

She nodded and let go to step inside. "I'm sorry I sprang that on you. I've been thinking about it for a week or two now. Every time I try to spend time alone with Ambrye, something comes up. She's so busy. There she was, and she seemed to be in a good mood."

Robin shut the door and took her in his arms. "I love you," he said, meaning it. He'd enjoyed Karina, but her blind, devotional worship had put her on par with a slave. She'd been a student, not an equal. Lauryn couldn't fend off his mind, but she commanded an entire nation. She deserved his respect, and he intended to defend her from whoever come calling.

"I love you too."

He kissed her and savored another of the finer pleasures of life.

ABOUT THE AUTHORS

Erik Kort abides in the glorious Pacific Northwest, otherwise known as Mirkwood-Without-The-Giant-Spiders, though the normal spiders often grow too numerous for his comfort. He is defended from all eight-legged threats by his brave and overly tolerant wife, and is mocked by his obligatory writer's cat. When not writing, Erik comforts the elderly, guides youths through vast wildernesses, and smuggles more books into his library of increasingly alarming size.

Lee French lives in Olympia, WA with two kids, two bicycles, and too much stuff. She is an avid gamer and member of the Myth-Weavers online RPG community. In addition to spending too much time there, she also trains year-round for the one-week of glorious madness that is RAGBRAI, has a nice flower garden with one dragon and absolutely no lawn gnomes, and tries in vain every year to grow vegetables that don't get devoured by neighborhood wildlife.

She is an active member of the Northwest Independent Writers Association and the Science Fiction and Fantasy Writers of America, as well as being one of two Municipal Liaisons for the NaNoWriMo Olympia region.

Thanks for reading! If you liked this book, please take a minute to post a review of it wherever you buy your books.

www.ingramcontent.com/pod-product-compliance
Lightning Source LLC
Chambersburg PA
CBHW070623260626
47161CB00007B/2564